I0763456

WINGLESS

Wingbound Series: Book Two

HEATHER TRIM

This is a work of fiction. All characters, places, and events portrayed in this novel are either products of the author's imagination or are used fictitiously.

WINGLESS

www.wingbound.com

ISBN: 978-1-7329090-2-1

Published by TrimVentures

www.trimventures.com

ALSO BY HEATHER TRIM

THE WINGBOUND SERIES

Wingbound

Wingless

Join the email list for new releases and more. Go to www.heatheraine.com

PRAISE FOR WINGBOUND

"Unexpected, funny, serious, wonderful,
and above all; magical."
-Fantasic Books & Why to Read Them

"Spellbound by Wingbound... I was swept away
by visions of the castle in the sky."
-Author A.C. Gaither

"Sprawling castles and desolate oceans
in a soft, simplistic fairy-tale writing style."
-Bookish Creature

"A new world, new cultures, adventure, danger, triumph,
true-to-life characters, humor, romance, and dragons."
-Author Melissa Keaster

DEDICATION

To my wingless sweetheart:
Though we are so very different, I can't fly without you.

PROLOGUE

TOLLIVER

"Father sent me for you, and Mother said you were out here." I pause at the sound of rustling in the bushes. Ledger grabs my arm. He's hiding something. "Wait. There's something in the—"

"It's nothing." Ledger tries to lead me away, but a muffled sneeze comes from the leafy mass.

I knew it! He is *doing something sneaky.* Knocking my little brother to the side, I crouch, peering beneath the branches. "Hello," I say.

"Hello," answers a female voice.

Ledger is sneaking off with a girl? I frown at her. "Who are you?"

She attempts to stand, but the branches are tangled around her. "I am Alouette."

Ledger introduces me. "This is my brother, Tolliver."

"Who is this?" I ask, confused by the foreign name. "I've never seen *her* before." I know every face in Balfour. She has beautiful brown eyes, smooth olive skin, and a white smile.

“She is a…visitor.” Ledger’s vague answer piques my curiosity. We never have visitors.

“From where?” I politely offer her my hand as she struggles to get out of the bushes. She accepts it, and I pull her free. Enormous white wings snap out of the shrubs and into the air behind her, vibrant and alarming. A gasp escapes my mouth and I yank my hand away from the enemy. My fists ball in an instant.

“Tolliver, I can explain.” Ledger’s voice squeaks with panic.

“She is Ellerian!” Anger spreads through my body like a brushfire. She is an intruder, a spy.

“It’s okay, she’s not a threat.”

“Not a threat? She is one of them!”

The trespasser leaps into the air above us and off our land.

“Wait, don’t go,” Ledger calls with one hand reaching out to her. “I know she is one of them, but…” He stretches the other hand out to me.

He has betrayed us all. Frustration flares into my tone. “Does Father know?”

Ledger shakes his head with the look he always has when he is in trouble: wide eyes and bottom teeth bared. It irritates me to the core how he is silent, stubborn, and refusing to face facts. I back away, disgusted with him.

“Please, don’t go!” he begs.

What does he think he is doing with the enemy? I square my shoulders and lower my brows at him. “This is unacceptable.”

He looks skyward. "Please stay."

"Goodbye, Ledger." The girl darts to the cloud layer. A blanket of navy and gray conceals her.

My muscles tense. Someone needs to knock some sense into him. I wouldn't mind doing it myself.

"Please calm down," Ledger says.

"How can you do this? Betraying your own people!" I almost call him a cruel name to get his attention and bring him into reality.

"It's not betrayal. She's my friend." His hands shake as he shoves them in his pockets and hunches his shoulders.

"Making friends with the enemy is exactly what betrayal is." I rub my head in irritation. He isn't making any sense.

"She was only a little girl when we met. She was curious about us," Ledger explains. "Mother knows, but no one else can."

Shocked Mother would tolerate this, my fists clench over and over. I bite my tongue to protect Ledger from the furious words threatening to fly out. He's lucky I sift through it all. He deserves a reprimand, but not ranting, so I groan and walk away.

"Please, Tolliver. No one can know." Ledger's voice echoes down the mountains side.

My feet grind pine needles against the rocky path as I stomp over the mountain pass to the Hundred Harvest Tree. By the time I reach the clearing, my jaw aches and my teeth are pulsating from the tension.

Blazing through the village, I burst through the door of our cottage, where Mother is darning a black sock. Ledger says Mother already knows, so her face will tell.

"Ledger is a traitor," I announce.

Without looking up from her chore, she takes a deep breath and lays the sock aside. There is no surprise in her eyes, no defiance of the truth, only sad eyes and downturned lips.

Panting from the trek, I want to yell again, but the way she silently walks to the back bedroom quenches the red-hot anger in my belly. I follow her. The window over the bed lights her movements to the dresser. She pulls open the bottom drawer all the way out and lays it on the floor. She reaches into the dark space and pulls out a leather book with a strap wrapped around it.

Facing me, she says, "Close the door."

Dread washes over every last ember of anger, throwing me into darkness. I don't like not knowing what she's going to say. It's as if I've fallen into a cavern and have to find my way out blind. I push the door shut and sit beside her on the large bed.

"There is something I've wanted to tell you for quite some time. I've thought of a hundred ways to say it, but nothing seemed good enough. I know you, son. You jump to conclusions and argue when you're wrong or unsure about something. So all I ask for the next few moments, Tolliver, is for you to remain silent until I can tell you everything."

She turns her brown eyes toward me, pleading and full of worry. They are wrinkled at the corners, and her brows pinch together with a question. *Will I remain silent?*

"Yes, Mother."

Her expression softens, and she purses her lips. I have no idea what she is going to say.

"You are Ellerian."

The words ignite me. My mouth drops open to argue. I want to reject it.

"Tolliver," she whispers, reminding me of my promise.

She knows me, my nature. Ashamed that I've dishonored her, I wait for her to continue. *I'm better than that.*

"Each year Ellery returns, and on the second day of battle, I journey to the lake. I meet an Ellerian guardian carrying a package. The midwives of Ellery must, by law, dispose of any child born without wings. The king commands them to throw them off the island wherever they are, but many mothers cannot bear the thought of their children being lost to the wind like criminals. So the midwives devised a plan to bring them to Balfour. On rare occasions, the delivered package is crying. Most often they are not. When they are not, I walk over the next ridge beyond the lake and bury them beside their kin."

She stops, wipes a tear, and continues. "But when they are crying, I feed them, swaddle them, and carry them back to Balfour. That is how you came to be in our family."

A torrent of emotions makes my head ache. I press two fingers to my temples. *How can this be?*

She glances at me again. "You were the tiniest child I ever held in my arms. You must have only been hours old or weeks too early. I loved you from the moment I saw you. I was able to hide you in that drawer." She points to the askew drawer on the floor. "After the Harvest Festival, your father went on a two-month hunt in the North Mountains. I tucked a small pillow in my skirts as if I were pregnant, then bigger and bigger pillows. When enough time passed, Balfour met you for the first time as the blacksmith's son."

A deep breath fills my lungs, drawing in everything she is saying. Doubting thoughts reel through my mind. My mouth clenches shut to keep from denying it aloud. *No. I am Tolliver, son of Fergus. I am Balfourian. I will be an elder one day and lead our army against—*

"I know you have questions, so you may ask them now." She wipes both of her eyes and lays her hands over the small book in her lap.

I ask the first thing that comes to my mind. "Does Father know?"

She abruptly looks at her hands. More tears flow as she says, "No, he does not."

I am taken aback. I want to yell at her for the lies, but I don't understand. "How can he not know? He is your husband. Wouldn't he have seen? Or heard?"

"I would have told him, had he seen. But he was not accustomed to living with a woman when we were first married. He didn't know how it all worked. Then the hunt was planned, and I had the perfect opportunity. I told him I was due the week after he was to return. He promised to be back in time. So I made sure to bring you forth before his return. When I presented you to him, he was so proud and full of love for you. It didn't matter to me that you came from another woman, another father, another land." Her voice trails off.

Another woman. This small woman at my side is not my real mother. Someone else is. Someone with wings.

"She is a midwife."

"Who?"

"Your mother." Grief shows on her face as the confession spills out. "She was one of the ones who would send the wingless children as the women birthed. I wasn't always the one who would receive them on the ground. There was another before me, who handed me the responsibility when she was unable to make the trip anymore. This was done years and years before me. We even buried winged children because families sometimes exceed the allotted number of children permitted by Ellery."

The more she shares, the more horror must be evident on my face. "It's okay, Tolliver. I give them a proper burial and honor them, when the Ellerian king thinks it's right to throw them out like spoiled vegetables."

"What am I supposed to say to all this? It seems too crazy, too unbelievable. I cannot possibly be Ellerian." My head won't stop shaking back and forth. It can't be true.

Mother opens the leather book in her lap. She turns to the middle. It appears that each page is dedicated to one child. A small sketch with a baby's face, rounded cheeks, closed eyes, and a tuft of hair fills half the page. A name is at the top: Lilstar. A date, probably birth date. A list of attributes: girl, wingless, pale skinned, blonde, blue eyes. Another date: deceased. My chest constricts at the thought of the dead child. She was only a month old when she died.

She turns the page slowly, and my name appears on the next sheet: Tolliver. With a completely different name below it.

Tylanu?

The weight of it all presses down on me until my neck aches, so I rub and stretch the tight muscle.

"You were so small." She strokes the sketch. Eyes open, hairless, wingless, and alive.

She gives me the book with shaking hands. "I need you to know, you can tell your father if you choose. I will not stop you from being who you truly are."

"And who is that?" I don't mean to sound angry, but the pain shoots out of my mouth like a poison dart from my soul.

"Whoever you choose."

My pointer finger touches the birth date. "This isn't right."

"It is the real one."

I shake my head, realizing how long she had to wait to bring me out of the drawer. Four months. *Can this be true?* My head throbs against the only reality I've ever known, raging against this new truth. My throat constricts as fear and anger choke the air from me.

A tear drips onto the page.

I am a wingless Ellerian.

1

FROM DUST TO LIFE

LEDGER

"They will sentence me to death, and this conversation will be wasted breath," Alouette whispers, barely audible over the many voices in the dank prison. Seated on the stone floor, she pulls her knees to her chest. The waning torchlight from the hallway reveals weeks of grime and despair smeared across her face. Her wings, which used to be brilliant white, are dull and gray with ash from when I pulled her from the fire.

"They wouldn't kill you for being related to him," I say.

Beside me, Hollis puts a hand on my arm. I connect with her pale blue eyes. Her brows pinch together. *I must tread lightly.*

"They've killed for much less." Alouette sighs and rests her forehead on her knees, shutting down another conversation. Her golden dress is now faded and dirty. In a fit of rage, she ripped several layers from her billowing skirts on the day we arrived. The fabrics lay in the corner near a mess of feathers, discarded and trampled. She has barely spoken a word to anyone since.

The longer we sit in this dim cell, the more it seems I should never have boarded Ellery in the first place. They were our sworn enemy, and when their island drifted by Balfour last harvest, it was empty. We didn't have to fight to keep our crops. But I *had* to find Alouette—my friend—and her people. When we found them and helped them back to the island, they weren't grateful. They pounced on us one after the other and threw us in this dank prison.

Hollis leans into me. Her blonde hair tickles my cheek. I'm tired, leaning my head on hers. I can't wait to get home, back to the way it used to be.

Tolliver, my brother, fair-haired and strong, hunches next to Kava. The black of his tunic and pants blends into the darkness of the cell. I thought he, of all people, would never feel this low. His head bobs as he fades in and out of sleep. There's nothing to do but wait. With his arm around Kava, it appears as if she is holding *him* up. That's a first. Her dark hair is knotted and pulled tight on the top of her head. Her face is streaked with dried tears. She cried every day for the first couple days. Seems she's all out of tears. She traces patterns into the fine layer of dust covering everything in this place—including her brown overdress. Her white underdress is nearly the same color where it peeks through at her elbows and tears in the skirt.

After all we sacrificed to help Alouette and her winged people, none of it mattered at all.

The guardian makes his rounds with our daily water. Voices rise throughout the prison and jumble in my ears. Then something rings above the din. The jingle of keys. Hollis sits up abruptly. She must have heard it too. They are taking another prisoner to stand before the advisors.

Alouette doesn't move. Her dark hair spills down over her arms and legs, nearly touching the floor.

The jingling nears. Voices cloud my ears as the prisoners all yell, begging to be freed. I never join their cries because they never come to our cell door.

"Balfourians!" A low voice cuts through the clamor.

Tolliver and Kava jolt to attention.

Dread sinks to the bottom of my stomach. Everyone in our cell leaps to their feet, including the other two Ellerian prisoners who keep to themselves in the corner.

The prison guardian approaches our door, dressed in black leather, muscles tense. His gray wings stand at attention behind him. "You're not going to give me any trouble," he states gruffly. "Guardian Belamy will enter, place your hands and feet in shackles, and then we will escort you to the advisors."

Hope brings Balfour to my mind: wood cottages, fields of ripe grain, and our sacred Hundred Harvest Tree.

The glorious jingle begins again, and the shouts of the prisoners crescendo. We back away from the door to give the guardian room to enter with an armload of chains. He slams them on the ground at Alouette's feet, and the clang reverberates throughout the prison. She startles but never lifts her head.

The prison falls quiet at the deafening crash.

Guardian Belamy is a tall, dark man with hair like black sheep's wool. His wings are an inky black, folded neatly behind him in this tight space. Black leather is stretched across his chest like a breastplate. He is wearing black pants and a belt around his waist with an empty scabbard and other loops where his many weapons should be.

He kneels before Tolliver first and clamps an iron around each ankle with a chain in between. Rising, he shackles my brother's wrists together in front of him. Tolliver's eyes are full of fire. I catch his gaze and shake my head at him. *Calm down,* I warn with the stern look, hoping he gets the message. The guardian nearly knocks Kava down as he locks her legs together beneath her dress. Tolliver catches her. He lifts a hand to punch the guardian, but metal hinders the swing. Guardian Belamy jerks at him with a fist raised.

"Please," I interrupt. "Please, we just want to get out of here." I put my wrists together, offering to be shackled next.

The guardian studies me with lowered brows. He fastens Kava's wrists into the irons and turns to me. Tolliver takes Kava's hand, his lips tense and head shaking. He needs to keep it together so we can get out of this horrible cell.

Guardian Belamy binds my wrists first, then ankles. The iron is cold and heavy. I'm worried I won't be able to make it up the stairs with the added weight. He shackles Hollis last. She glances at me, eyes wide with fear. What's going on inside her head? My hand reaches for hers as the guardian outside the door bellows, "Line up."

We snap into a line facing the door.

Another guardian enters. He's not as tall as the first, but his wings are white and jagged where they were recently singed. He must have been in that burning cottage along with Alouette. He herds the other Ellerian men to the back corner and says to Alouette, "Hey, move to the back." She doesn't stir. The keys jingle impatiently at the door, and

Belamy reaches for her. I step out of line and touch her arm. "Alouette."

"Step back," Guardian Belamy shouts in my face and pushes me aside. The other guardian lifts Alouette to her feet and shoves her to the back of the cell. Something hits the stone wall with a meaty smack. Guardian Belamy's dense body blocks my view.

The man at the door yells for us to get in line again, but I'm trying to catch a glimpse of Alouette when Belamy throws an elbow and hits me in the neck. My throat makes a choking sound as I reel back in pain. I bounce off Tolliver's chest and quickly regain my balance but not my breath.

"Prisoners secured," Guardian Belamy says with an intense scowl.

The door clinks open. We shuffle out the door and down the hall. Wiping away tears, I worry we will never see her again. Anything could happen at the top of those stairs. We may die, but I refuse to give up hope. We must get home to Balfour.

***

The brilliant light of day stings my eyes as we are escorted center of the castle. The innermost part of the inner tower is a rounded courtyard. Level after level of carved-stone balconies overlook our death march. There are tall windows and doors off each level all the way up sixteen stories, with Ellerian people flying all around: men, women, and children. They flit from floor to floor with the ease of dragonflies going about their business inside the circular tower. Some carry pails, mounds of leathers, or burlap sacks.

Our chains clink against the stone floor. By the time we reach the middle of the courtyard, near the fountain with the statue of a winged man, every person within view stops what they are doing to watch us, the wingless ones, being escorted to the throne room. Quiet descends upon the busy hub of Ellery.

Hundreds of eyes are on us. More Ellerians emerge from their homes and approach the railing to get a look at us. Even the statue gazes upon us with judgment.

When we reach the open doors of the throne room, I feel too tall and awkward with everyone watching us in eerie silence. I hunch a little, trying not to stand out too much behind Hollis's short frame. Her animal-skin leggings are matted and dirty, and her tunic hangs stiffly. It is so full of sweat and dirt, it has its own form. My clothes are in a similar state. I resist the urge to adjust the crusty tunic hanging from my lanky body.

The prison guardian escorts us down the line of gold tiles in the middle of the throne room, past where Tolliver and Kava said their vows months ago. The smooth, beige stone walls still bear the faded tapestries of the generations of Ellerian royal families. The room is lit with a candelabra between each tapestry and four hanging from the arched ceiling. I've never seen so much light or so many faces in this enormous room. Almost every available space in the room is taken up by bodies and large feathery wings of varying shades of white, black, and gray. A wing brushes the side of my face and I swat it away.

The throne is on a raised platform of three steps, but

the tapestry from the back wall has been torn down and draped over the throne. Maybe it's a sign of mourning or just acknowledging the obvious absence of their king. We are led to the foot of the throne, where a tall table is set up with seven men seated behind it, all wearing black robes.

"Balfourians," is whispered among the people all around as we stop before the table. The room fills with muttering, and my nerves vibrate my whole body. We are a flock of chickens in a circle of hawks.

"Children, come," a man speaks from the center seat behind the table. His curly, gray-and-white hair stands up on the top of his head, making him seem wild and intimidating. He strokes his short beard absentmindedly.

I grind my teeth and frown. *I'm not a child. I'm eighteen harvests old.*

We stop five paces before the wood table, and the guardians prod us to stand side by side before what appears to be the elders of their people. Hollis, to my left, leans into me so our arms are touching. Her blue eyes are pinched in worry. Tolliver and Kava on the other side of me are stoic and emotionless, which worries me even more than Hollis.

"These four Balfourian children are guilty of trespassing on our land," he declares without looking at us, as if addressing the other people in the room. "The sentence is death."

Each man at the table votes, "Aye."

He grabs a tall staff leaning against the table and slams it on the floor with finality.

I yell without thinking, "What? No!" The room erupts in shouts and scuffling.

Hollis starts to cry. I reach with chained wrists and hold her hands.

"I refute!" a voice booms over the ruckus from the right side of the room. We all turn, even the men at the table, toward Dayson, the man to whom Alouette was betrothed. I remember his eyes—bold, blue, and fierce. He steps forward, adjusting the black strap across his white tunic. "I refute," he says again. He looks much better than the last time I saw him when he and Alouette escaped the fire, covered in soot. Now he is cleanly shaved, his black hair slicked back out of his face, and he is wearing neatly tailored black trousers.

The man in the middle of the table scowls. "There will be no refutes on this case. They are guilty. There is no other punishment listed for trespassing. It is the law."

"Yes, Advisor Caedus, but they saved some of our people from a fire," Dayson replies. The muscles in his arms tighten, and his jaw clenches. "They should be considered refugees, because they too were involved in the war between Ellery and Lianmin. Our own Tristeh escorted them to safety. She doesn't know any different but to return to her cave."

"I see," Advisor Caedus says. He strokes his beard again.

"I agree," the man beside him says. His gaze is locked on the group of us. I've seen him before. Maybe at the fire or in Ciel's court? I'm not sure. His eyes are familiar—deep gray and kind. "The dragon was simply returning home. They had no other choice."

A smaller man on the far right of the table, speaks up, "What about the amount of time they spent on our island, pillaging our homes and using our supplies over the last year?" He peers down his small nose at us, furrowing his brow.

Dayson responds before any of the men can agree, "Advisor Cabot, we cannot be sure it was them." A hint of a smirk plays at the edge of his mouth. "We had reports of the Lianminese boarding Ellery near Heping, which was at least a week from our location."

Is he really vouching for us? Why?

"Besides," he continues, "they are heroes. They saved me and over twenty others from that fire. You yourself would not be here had this boy not intervened." He points at me, sending a shiver down my spine. The man in the middle bobs his head and looks away.

"Advisor Caedus, I make a motion to modify the sentence for these…" The familiar man pauses and chooses his words carefully. "Refugees."

"Aye," the two men beside him say, and another on the other end agrees.

Advisor Caedus declares, "These refugees will be taken into protective custody and put under house arrest, until such time their departure will guarantee them safety upon reaching the ground in exchange for their services to our people." Again, he grabs the staff and pounds it on the ground once. It echoes around the room.

"Confine them to three-eight. The Coetzee family did not return to Ellery." He turns to the man next to him and says, "General Talon, assign guardians to their door."

General Talon doesn't speak. He merely acknowledges Advisor Caedus with a sneer and stares at us with lowered brows, lips tight beneath his black-and-gray striped beard. His graying hair is cut short, making him seem even more severe, and a throbbing vein stands out on his forehead. He nods again at the prison guardians.

The people shout an uncomfortable mixture of cheers and aggression as we are directed toward the exit. I catch a glimpse of Dayson as the crowd presses closer. He smirks at me and winks.

I silently mouth, "Thank you," before we are shoved out the door.

The guardians hurry us to the stairs across the courtyard. Still in chains, we ascend. Hollis has trouble reaching each step with her ankles cinched together. Irritated at our slow ascent, Guardian Belamy groans and tells us to hurry up. Then he grabs Hollis's arm, pulling her up several stairs. She cries out and trips. Just as I am about to tell him to let her go, he grabs her in his arms and dives from the stairwell into the open air.

His enormous black wings flap and lift them both. I stop and gape at them. Hollis's blonde hair swishes as she beams at me with a big stupid grin. He darts up to the next floor as we continue one more flight of stairs, prodded by the other guardian.

At the top, the guardian and Hollis stand eight doors down, waiting for us. I shake my head and shuffle over to them, followed by Tolliver, and Kava.

Hollis is smiling and ogling Guardian Belamy with his tanned, muscular arms and powerful wings. "Inside," he says, pushing Hollis in the door.

Level three, eighth home on the right. *At least we don't have to climb to thirteen.*

Inside, Guardian Belamy pulls a key from his belt and unlocks our wrists and ankles from the irons. He drags them out the door and says, "Good luck."

2 LAY LOW

TOLLIVER

Kava whispers my name, and I pull her close. Inspecting her face to gauge her level of trauma, I brush her dark hair from her cheek and tuck it behind her ear. She used to obsessively keep her clothes clean, but now she adjusts the grungy brown dress like the dirt isn't even there. With a raise of my brows, I ask, *Are you okay?*

She presses her lips in a sad smile.

I hug her, relieved and able to breathe deeply.

Hollis is laughing and babbling, "Did you see me fly? It was even better than my swing. I think he was trying to scare me, so I pretended to be scared." The sound of her voice grates on my nerves.

Ledger appears as if he rolled around in a cold furnace full of ashes. It's hard to tell the difference in color between his white tunic and brown trousers. Even his brown hair is matted down like a dingy black hat. We haven't talked since our yelling match in the prison cell, where I blamed him for everything that's happened. I called him a "blunder-headed fool." I was fired up about being imprisoned, stuck. *I should apologize.* His brown eyes connect with mine. Guilt scalds me.

Ledger glances away—avoiding conflict as usual. He traipses down the hall and digs through the supply closet. I shouldn't have shouted at him. I unloaded all of my frustrations on him, afraid we'd never get out of there and I'd never accomplish what I came to do.

I guide Kava to the padded bench along the wall. She leans against me, and I hold her tight. Her touch keeps the anger at bay, like a blanket over a flame. Our new home sits before us: stone floors, a fireplace, and a bedroom down the hall. Away from that prison, the walls of hopelessness begin to crumble—I can find my family now. Though with all I've done, I don't really deserve to get what I want.

Hollis continues chattering about how happy she is to be alive and how it smells better in here than it did in lock-up.

I wish I had a pillow over my head to block her out, along with the punishing thoughts echoing through my head. This really isn't Ledger's fault. It's my fault we left our home in Balfour.

Last harvest, when the island arrived empty, I couldn't believe Ledger had the audacity to fly to Ellery. I knew he was friends with an Ellerian girl. I just didn't know he built something to make him fly.

If I didn't help Ledger retrieve his confiscated flying balloon and lead our little group of misfits to the enemy island in the sky, we'd all be safe at home. *But, no. I had to find my birth family. My Ellerian family. What was I thinking?*

Kava might have a child growing in her belly by now,

and if anything happens to her, I will never forgive myself. I should have stayed in Balfour and followed the path laid neatly before me. But when my mother told me I am Ellerian, it consumed me. It became all I could think about as I trained to be an elder of Balfour, or brought in the hay, or proposed to Kava.

Hollis dances around the room, dirty feet scraping on the stone. Ledger sits and watches her with a goofy grin on his face. "I'm just glad we're all together and out of that horrid prison," she says.

Her words send a shock through me.

"We're not *all* together, Hollis," I growl.

She stops mid twirl and meets my eyes. Beads of sweat form on my brow and sadness spills from my soul. I hold my tongue to keep from berating her. She didn't mean to forget Angus, even though she never thinks of anyone but herself.

"I'm sorry, Toll. Poor Angus," she says pressing her hands to her heart.

Tears gather in her eyes, and Ledger soothes her. "It's okay, Hollis. We'll find him."

It's my fault too that Angus is gone. Aching to see my cousin, I wish there was a door to slam. But it's locked. The weight of responsibility is enough to break me. But I refuse. Our situation has finally improved after weeks of confinement.

By evening, we are eating together in the kitchen. My eyes stare blankly. I'm a bit rattled by the events of the morning. The door creaks open and voices drift in. A familiar face enters. I scowl. *Why he is here?*

Dayson's intrusive gray wings seem poised and ready as

he walks into the room. His crisp white tunic glows brighter than the torches on the walls. He shuts the door and, looking us each in the face, he introduces himself. "I'm Dayson. Maybe Ledger has told you about me?" He clasps his hands together tightly.

Ledger's eyes are bright and accepting. The boy trusts too quickly. I squint at Dayson and analyze what he could possibly want from us.

"I wasn't sure they were going to go for changing your sentence to refugee status," he says, wringing his hands. There it is. Is he planning to do something to us?

Hollis smiles at him and says, "I don't really understand why you did that for us. But thank you."

Ledger leans close to her. "Remember, we saved him from the burning building?"

"Oh, I guess I wasn't there for that," she says. "Sorry. Hope you weren't singed too badly. I'm Hollis." She waves awkwardly at him.

"Nice to meet you, Hollis," he replies, bowing slightly. His wings swish with the movement.

"This is my brother Tolliver, and this is Kava," Ledger says, pointing at us.

"I'm his wife." Kava puts her hand on mine.

Dayson greets us with a wry grin. Every tiny expression on the Ellerian's face throws me into more and more distrust.

"Thank you," Ledger says.

"You're welcome. I owed you a debt for pulling us out of the fire, and I always repay my debts." His arms tense and wings twitch. "In about six weeks, when we pass over Balfour, it may take some negotiation, but I will get you home."

My pulse quickens as joy bubbles up. I shove the feeling away. I can't afford to trust this man. I can't let the promise of returning home safely overshadow the idea of finding my Ellerian family.

Hollis thanks him again. "Why would you do that? You don't owe us anything else."

"I know, but Alouette would want me to."

Ledger trembles at the sound of her name and stammers over his words. "Is sh-sh-she okay?" I am embarrassed by how easy he is to read.

"For now," Dayson says, shifting from one foot to the other. His posture is stiff and formal. "They haven't scheduled her trial yet. Which means they haven't decided what to do with her. I'm hoping it will stay that way for a while."

Ledger bobs his head in agreement.

"They will surely sentence her to death." Dayson glances down at his hands. He is wringing them again. I can hear their roughness from across the room. That's what his worries are about. Alouette.

"Can you speak to the advisors for her, the way you did for us?" I ask. "They listened to you."

"I have been forbidden to attend." His stubbly jaw tightens, and his blue eyes intensify. Ledger opens his mouth, probably to protest, but stops when Dayson says, "I'm afraid I have used up all my influence with you."

Everyone looks away in shame. *Oh, great,* I think. *He is manipulating us.* I cross my arms to keep from lashing out at him. He's trying to make us feel guilty for what he did. I refuse to owe him. We are even.

"I've requested they give you time to bathe," Dayson interrupts the awkward silence. "They are still arranging your guardian rotation, so it may take a little while to put into action."

"Thank you." Kava's tension eases and her eyes connect with mine. I smile briefly.

Perfect. More debt to Dayson.

"If you need anything, pass me a message through the guardian at your door. I know all of them," Dayson says. "Anything." He yanks the heavy door open with ease.

"Sure, yes, okay," Ledger agrees. He is too eager to trust Dayson. Then an idea hits me. Maybe this will prove whether he has our best interest at heart.

I calculate the risk of asking and decide it's a worthy test. "Can you do one thing, right now?"

With one foot out the door, Dayson faces me. "Yes?"

"Can you find out what happened to Angus?" Saying his name makes anger blaze through my veins.

"Who is that?"

"He is our cousin," I explain. "He was with us when we landed on Ellery. We were separated before getting locked up, and I never saw him again. No one would talk to us in prison." I examine every expression for malicious intent. He seems glad to do it. *Could I trust him to help me find my family?* Claws of doubt clamp my mouth shut.

"Maybe." Dayson pauses for a moment like he's going to say something else, but dismisses it and leaves, pulling the solid wood door closed behind him. He didn't seem fazed by the exchange. I blink away angry tears and hope Dayson is true to his word. Something about him makes me uneasy.

I'm sure they didn't tell us about Angus because he is dead. From what I can figure, we will be home in a little less than two months, when we can mourn Angus properly.

Kava slides her chair back, interrupting my thoughts. "I think it's best if we just lay low until we get to Balfour. They will return us home, and we will never have to see the top side of this cursed island ever again."

Ledger and Hollis both agree. She pats Kava's hand.

They gaze at me. While my head nods in agreement, my insides rage against laying low. It's for their own good that I don't tell them my plan to sneak out and find my family. The less they know, the better.

3

ELLERIAN LIFE

LEDGER

Loud voices violently shake me awake. I jolt straight up in the cot and accidentally kick Hollis, who is curled up at my feet like a house cat. *When did she crawl up here?* She fell asleep on a mat on the floor. Tolliver and Kava are still asleep on the big bed.

I meander to the kitchen following the sound, my neck still aching from sleeping on a stone floor for twenty-one nights in a prison cell. Oddly the door is ajar, and my tired hands pull it all the way open. Ellerian men fly upward with large buckets in their hands. I'm startled every time one soars past me, one after the other. Water sloshes from one of their large pails. Then they zoom down again with an empty one.

"Is there a fire?" I wonder out loud.

The guardian outside the door suddenly notices me and yanks out his sword. It happens so fast. My entire body is shoved through the door and against the wall at sword point. I'm barely able to catch my breath when I hit the hard stone.

"You are not permitted to leave the premises," Guardian

Belamy yells in my face. His lips are curled in a snarl. Loosening his grip, he blinks as though he's shocked. He lets me go and straightens his leather breastplate.

I'm surprised at how awkward he acts, as though it was a thoughtless impulse.

He blinks, clears his throat, and says, "There's no fire. Water delivery. I will, um, bring in your basin. Stand away from the door."

I get as far from him as possible and sit at the table, trying to appear non-threatening.

His dark wings turn the corner for a moment. When he returns with a large pail of water, he sets it beside the fireplace. "Morning meal will be up shortly," he says, returning to his post outside the door without closing it.

"Shouldn't you shut that?" I ask from across the room, doubting he'd hear me over the noisy courtyard. He doesn't react.

Hollis joins me at the table, rubbing her drooping eyelids.

"Hi, Ledger," she says yawning. Her blonde hair is jagged on one side and flat on the other. The guardian glances into the room, and I swear he flexes his muscles as he brushes the side of his head. He straightens with a jerk, abruptly steps into the room, and bows his head as another Ellerian enters. The woman is tall and slender with wings that are even longer. They match her shimmery gray hair and long, silver-blue dress. She carries a tray of food. "Eat up little ones," she says with precise diction. "I'm sure they were terrible to you in that nasty prison."

"It was miserable down there," Hollis agrees.

Hollis gasps as the lady sets the tray on the table. It's not mush, but a colorful assortment of berries, greens, and even meat. My stomach growls as I grab a piece of meat.

"Oh, darlin', there's no need to be uncivilized." She hands me a fork and unloads four metal plates. She sets them gently around the table. Her long, slender fingers lay more forks at each setting and give one to Hollis. "That is wildebear meat. We don't normally eat wildebear. But when you're low on supplies, you take what you can get."

"Yum," Hollis jabs three times and shoves it all into her mouth.

Guardian Belamy eyes our tray.

"You hunt?" I cram a few bits of meat in my mouth.

"Oh, no, no, no. I gather," she says with a smile. She peers down her long nose and says, "I know where the good spots are."

Belamy reaches for a piece of meat and pops it into his mouth. She swats his hand. "Bel, that is not yours," she scolds him like a child.

Hollis giggles.

He winks at her and says, "Oh, Becarah, I couldn't resist your beautiful array of delicacies."

Her brown eyes sparkle as she straightens the tray proudly. "This is the best time of year for sweet peas," she says pointing to the raw green seeds. "Harvest has begun, yes, sir."

Hollis and I glance at each other. The words make my heart swell. *Home*, I think to myself, *we're almost home.* With one simple word, I know we're going to make it. I touch Hollis's small hand across the table. She scoops a few peas on her plate.

"Oh, they are sweet," Hollis says.

"It's a good thing it's harvest time. If we'd have gotten back home to Ellery in the dead of winter, there would have been no chance of survival." She continues with stories of where and when they find the best fruits and vegetables. Her shimmery, floor-length dress swishes back and forth as she uses her hands expressively. "And when we reach Balfour, they will pay tribute and we will be all set for the winter—" She stops and peers around at us as if she said something wrong. Wiping her hands on her dress, she awkwardly shifts from one foot to the other.

Hollis smiles, softening the moment. "Why don't you plant stuff up here?"

She forces a laugh, recovering her lighthearted composure. "Nothing grows up here. Our ground is either hard rock or fine dust."

Becarah turns her back and heads for the door as Belamy snatches another piece of meat. Hollis giggles at his stealthy move. I scowl at her reactions to him.

As Becarah leaves, Tolliver and Kava join us in the kitchen, and two Ellerians step through the open door. They definitely aren't guardians. They must be from the working class. Each wear simple brown clothes, and the woman has a gray linen headwrap covering her hair.

"Ah, yes," Belamy says when he sees the Ellerian couple, as though he just remembered something. "It's time to bathe. One female follow Calista, and one male follow Elijah."

Hollis's eyes light up and she pleads with Kava. "Can I go first? Please, pretty, pretty please?"

Kava gives a slight nod and Hollis squeals, darting out

the door after the Ellerian woman.

"Go on," Tolliver says.

Excitement fills my body, and I try not to bounce out the door like Hollis.

***

After a good, long bath, I patter back to the confines of our room and muse about the how the washmaids filled the large recess in the floor with hot steaming water. I wanted to swim in there all day. The smell of rosemary in the air made it seem as though they were cooking me for dinner, but I didn't care.

All the months we were on this island alone, I never once used that room as a bath. I used the privy on nearly every floor. But I bathed outside in a pool of water on the backside of the castle. Never with soap and never in warm water.

When I return to the room, the washmaids escort Tolliver and Kava to the baths in separate directions. Kava will go below to the next floor. Tolliver will go to the men's bathing room, four doors down.

The guardian outside pulls the door shut, and I am alone with Hollis.

Her blonde hair is wet but combed neatly. She sets down a pile of wet clothes on the table and approaches me. "They let me keep my old clothes. I want to be able to change every so often." She gives a smile, and I feel as fresh as she looks in her white dress. Her face is free of the grime from three weeks in lock-up. Her hair is washed of oils and sweat.

She approaches me, bare feet padding across the stone

floor. She puts her hand on the arm of my clean white tunic. I study her eyes, her white, wispy dress, her smile.

"You okay?" Her eyes sparkle.

My mind won't focus. We are alone for the first time since, well, since ages ago. My head bobs and she runs her hand up my arm, my shoulder, to my cleanly shaved face. "You're so handsome," she says with a giggle.

I slowly reach for her. My hands touch the curve of her waist. My pulse races. I can't think about anything else. Just her.

"You shaved those weird hairs off your face," she says.

I smile.

"Are you going to say words?" Her cheeks push back.

Remembering the kiss in the dragon's cave, my hands slide around her and I pull her close.

"Hello? What's going on inside there?" She runs her hands through my curly, wet hair, sending a strange sensation to my gut. Her voice fades into the background as my heart beats louder than her questions and giggles.

Leaning into her, I brush my cheek along hers. She is so smooth. I inhale her scent. She wraps her arms around my body, squeezing me to her. I duck my head to her other cheek and brush it gently with mine.

"Ledger," she whispers, and chills tingle up my back.

"Hollis," I say, as she pushes away from me. I am dizzy with her smell and her body against mine. I can't understand anything except how I feel, pulling her tighter against me.

"Ledger," she says leaning away. "Ledger, we can't."

Her words reach my ears, but they confuse me. My mind is dizzy, intoxicated with her. I need her lips against mine.

She pulls away a little and she rests her forehead on mine. Her vibrant blue eyes are so close they're blurry.

"Ledger," she says. "I love you."

"I love you, too, Hollis." It's as if I've opened a door that won't close. I ache for the closeness her, but her tone reminds me of a promise. It emerges from the fog in my mind. A promise to our people. I sigh deeply and loosen my grip. Her hands are still draped around my neck. "I just—"

"You just need to know I'm still yours," she completes my thoughts better than I would have. "We are in this together, Ledger, till the end."

"Till the end," I agree, feeling foolish as I come to my senses.

Suddenly, the door bursts open, ripping us from our intimate moment. Hollis jerks in my arms, but I don't let her go far. Tolliver is dragged in with his hands tied behind his back. He is clean, shaved, and wearing new clothes. But his dark green tunic is torn on one arm and his face is red hot with anger.

A guardian takes him to the bench and slams him down.

"What happened?" My eyes bulge in confusion.

The guardian chuckles and leaves.

Tolliver stands and says, "Untie me."

I dig at the frayed rope and yank at the knots. Someone very strong tied this.

"What happened?" I ask again.

Tolliver groans and fights against his bindings, yanking them from my hands.

"Hold still," I say, and pull at the rope. "Talk to me, Tolliver."

"What?" Tolliver snaps. "What do you want me to say? I tried to escape. I saw a moment, and I took it."

"Why would you try to escape?" I'm shocked as I pull the last loop from around his wrists, releasing my beast-of-a-brother. "You can't go anywhere."

Tolliver whirls around and throws the rope down.

"What were you going to do? Jump off the island?" I cross my arms.

"No!" He scowls at me, rubbing his wrists.

"Then what?" I've not raised my voice at him since our argument in the prison cell, and I promised myself I wouldn't do it again. But he's spiraling into a dark place, and he's going to get us all in trouble.

"I need to find my family!" he yells. The words echo down the hall and bounce back, hitting me in the heart.

Of course. The memory of his whispered confession makes me feel even more alone. *He is not my real brother.*

He steps toward me. "You think this is all about you," Tolliver says, spit hitting me in the face. "It's never been about you. Get your selfish head out of the clouds!"

My nostrils flare in disgust. I'm too shocked to say anything. I never thought any of this was about me. It was about Alouette and finding her. My body is frozen in place for a moment, unable to move or breathe as he rages at me.

"I've been waiting for two harvests to find them! Now we are here on this island, and we are stuck in this ghastly room. Waiting. Doing nothing. I can't take it!" He paces back and forth, out of my space. He groans again and stomps off to the bedroom.

My head swirls and the room tilts. I wish I had something

to say to comfort him. But I don't.

Hollis's eyes are wide, and her mouth is hanging open. I wrap my arms around her and press my face in her clean hair as one tear streaks down my cheek.

4

CIVIL UNREST

LEDGER

After three days of routine visits from Becarah and her delicious trays of treats, with a guardian at our door every moment of every day, a blaring shofar startles me awake. At first I think we are in Balfour and Ellery has been spotted in the sky, because that is the Balfourian alarm. Opening my eyes, I realize I'm actually on Ellery, and something out of the ordinary is happening in the courtyard.

Feet scuffle nearby. Tolliver leaps from the bed and runs shirtless down the hall. I follow him to the front door, and he yanks it open. We both dash out, the morning light glaring in our eyes. As mine adjust to the brightness, we reach the low stone balcony railing and peer over the edge. Several Ellerian men fight below. Swords clash and shouting echoes all around us. Many emerge from their homes all the way up the inside of the tower. Even Guardian Belamy is overlooking the skirmish below, paying no attention to us, his prisoners.

The statue on top of the fountain in the middle of the courtyard, with wings outstretched and arms reaching skyward, is covered in red liquid. Over its eyes hangs a black strip of cloth with a haphazard metal crown poised on its head. Hollis and Kava fumble out the door in their sleeping-clothes and crash into me. I direct their eyes to the vandalized statue. Belamy catches all of us peering over the railing.

"Hey!" he yells, "Get back inside!" When he makes eye contact with Hollis, he doesn't get violent with us. He simply points at the door, and we do as we are told. Hollis takes one last gander over the edge and scurries to catch up with me. I grab her hand and pull her into the room. Belamy steps in and closes the door. He rests his forehead and hands on the wooden door. He seems quite rattled, hidden behind tense black wings.

"What was that about?" Tolliver stands in front of the fireplace with his hands on his hips. He hasn't looked me in the face since he screamed at me in prison.

Belamy turns around, wide eyed and speechless.

Kava twirls her hair around her finger. Hollis squirms awkwardly. I fiddle with the hem of my shirt, feeling uncomfortable. My mouth opens to ask if he is okay, but Belamy finally speaks. "I didn't think they would take it so far."

"What? Who?" Tolliver's intensity cools as he realizes Belamy is muttering to himself and not us.

Hollis grabs a chair from the table and drags it to Belamy. The bronze, muscular guardian seems weakened, with his head hanging low and hands trembling. He plops into the chair with a thud. His inky black wings flap and hang limply behind him. With his hands on his knees, he breathes for a moment.

Hollis sits on the bench near him. "Are you okay?" It irritates me that she is being so nice to him.

Belamy clears his throat and looks around the room at us. We are staring shamelessly, but I don't care. He's making a fool of himself. "I'm sorry," he says. "There has been a lot going on."

"Since you got back to Ellery?" Hollis asks.

"No, since King Halcyon was murdered." He wipes his face with his large calloused hand. "It seems my people are divided. Right down the middle."

"Half the people want to continue the monarchy, with the traditions of our ancestors. The other half want to rebuild and create a republic," Belamy explains.

"What's with the blood on the statue?" Tolliver sits on the hearth before a barely lit fire, leaving me the only one standing. My entire body is tense with distrust, and I can't help but keep my fists clenched.

I didn't realize it was blood, and my stomach churns at the thought. I hope it is animal blood.

"Yeah, it was blindfolded with a crown, too. Did you see that?" He shakes his head and scrunches his nose in disgust. "Someone was yelling, 'Kings are blind to the people.'"

I cross my arms over my chest, growing impatient. *How long is he going to sit here panicking? He isn't very guardian-like.*

Hollis's brows press together. "What's a republic?"

"There are several civilizations around the world who run successfully as republics. It means we would be equal. There would be no king, but we would choose a group of men to lead our people."

"That sounds like Balfour," Hollis says. She reaches out and touches his hand. I dart to her side protectively. As soon as I sit next to her on the bench, I feel like an idiot, because Belamy is startled by my sudden movement. Hollis pulls her hand back and glances at me.

"Balfour is a republic?" he asks.

Tolliver chimes in, "Sort of. Our village is run by the elders. There is always an odd number so there will never be a tie. But we don't exactly choose as a group who becomes an elder. We actually train for it and compete for a seat, but only when an elder is ready to retire."

"Sounds better than having one flawed man in charge of everything." Belamy stands and carries the chair back to the table. "Sorry to get you wrapped up in my troubles."

"It's not like we have anything better to do," Hollis says with a chuckle.

"Yeah." Belamy composes himself and walks to the door holding his head high. "Maybe I can help you with that." He steps out the door and shuts it behind him. We sit and wait for a long while for him to return. I expect him to walk in at any moment, but he doesn't. Becarah brings our meals, and there's a different guardian at our door. We go about our day as though he said nothing at all. Hollis doesn't ask where he went, probably because she doesn't want to talk about how she touched his hand. I cringe at the memory.

***

The morning is gray and dreary. The sound of gushing rain

fills the room. I roll over on my cot, pulling my blankets to my chin. I don't need to get out of bed yet, or ever, really.

"What were you thinking?" a man's voice says out in the kitchen. "I thought you were smarter than that." He chuckles.

I'm not sure who it is, but Tolliver answers him as if he knows him. "Where were you?"

"I had—" He pauses. "Things I needed to do."

They descend to a whisper and my ears strain to hear. "Really? What?" Hollis asks.

I shift abruptly on my pillow and gaze around the room. All the beds are empty. I'm missing something. I scramble off my cot, yank my yellowing tunic over my head, and tighten my brown trousers around my waist with a drawstring.

"I had heard something and needed to find out if it's true," the voice says as my bare feet patter down the hall.

"What?" Hollis presses. "What did you hear?"

I enter the kitchen and they all pause.

Hollis gasps as though I am an intruder to their private conversation. She, Tolliver, and Kava are huddled around the table with Guardian Belamy as if having a secret meeting. And I'm not invited.

"Belamy heard something and was about to tell us about it," Hollis explains and pulls out the chair next to her. My foggy brain guides me into the seat.

Across the table, Kava is cleanly dressed in a blue overdress next to Tolliver. The sleeves of his black tunic are shoved up, and they are all eating breakfast. Almost all the food is gone. Belamy puts something in his mouth and I scowl at him. *He's eating our food—my food.*

He rubs his dark, woolly hair and starts talking, "I heard

one person from the royal family is still alive."

No one says anything for a moment. I'm not sure why we care. Or I'm not quite awake yet.

"Isn't this good news?" Hollis is still in her long, white sleeping-clothes. I wish she would cover herself around him.

"It's more like shocking news." Belamy pulls his belt to the side and leans forward in his chair. His brown hands fold on the table top as he continues, "Ciel killed the entire royal family, including his brother's family, so King Halcyon's royal line would end."

"Oh, so now the people who want a king will have one," Tolliver explains.

"Yes," Belamy whispers and looks around warily. "But that is not really a good thing. I heard someone say an assassin might be sent to get rid of him."

"The people who want a republic?" Hollis eats another grape from the plump purple bunch in her hands.

"I thought you wanted a republic," Tolliver asks. Finally, someone is suspicious of him along with me.

"I do, but not like this." Belamy looks down. His eyebrow twitches and it seems as though he's not withholding information.

Wanting to catch him at his game, I ask, "What are you not saying?"

He avoids eye contact, as if he is answering against his will, "The royal is hiding in Balfour."

The air goes out of my lungs when I realize what it could mean. They are sending an assassin to my village. Someone I know could die.

"Oh my lands," Tolliver exclaims. "Who is it? Who's the

royal?"

"That, I don't know." Belamy puts his hand to his brow as though he has a headache. His black wings droop behind him. "I'm sorry. I tried. But the person who shared the information is in and out of consciousness in the medical ward. She was in the fire back in Lianmin. She is not healing well and may die very soon. They may never know who it is. I tried to explain to her that I didn't want to kill the royal. But she refused. She refused to talk to anyone. Anyone but you."

His dark brown eyes connect with mine.

It takes me a second to realize he's talking about me.

"Me?" I raise my brows.

How does anyone know me from anyone else on this stupid island?

"You saved her from the fire," Belamy says.

I remember the night the Lianminese attacked. They descended on Ellery's new castle, and Alouette refused to leave with me. She went back for her father, the man who ruined everything: Ciel. He killed off the royal family to become king and get the entire Ellerian race on the ground. When I finally got there, her father was dead, and the Lianminese barricaded her and many other people in a cottage, setting it on fire. The flames blaze in my memory and burn in my gut.

Studying my hands, I pick at a hangnail and resist the urge to chew on it.

"Can he go talk to her?" Hollis asks.

"She sent me for him." Belamy slides his hand across the table and taps his finger. My eyes connect with his. "Will you do this?"

"What in the wild world do you expect me to do?" I blurt.

"Talk to her," Belamy says.

"Skies, no!" I lean back and cross my arms, but the curiosity is killing me. My mind races to each man in my home village. "There isn't anyone with wings in Balfour."

"Don't be a fool, Ledger," Tolliver says. "You obviously don't need wings to be Ellerian."

My face flushes and my ears start ringing. I want to throw a fist across the table at his smug face. I hate when he makes me feel like an idiot.

My mind churns for a moment. *Tolliver is a wingless Ellerian.* In my irritation, it takes me a moment to realize the royal could be anyone.

Belamy pulls his hand away and whispers, "The advisors are deliberating the validity of her claims and what finding a royal could mean. Meanwhile, we have an opportunity right here, right now." He stands up and pulls an empty grain sack from inside his long black pants.

A laugh bursts from Hollis's lips.

My brows lower. "What's that for?"

Hollis explains with a chuckle. "He's going to carry you like a sack of grain to the medical ward." She can't contain her laughter until Belamy shushes her. "Sorry," she whispers and crosses her arms.

I stare wide-eyed at the thought. *This is dangerous.*

"Ledger," he says my name for the first time. "I can sneak you out and back in, no problem." Belamy fluffs the bag.

An awkward silence falls. It feels like a heavy hand on my throat while everyone watches me deliberate. *If this goes wrong, I could be thrown back in prison. I could be tortured for the information. I could be killed.* My teeth grind under the pressure.

And I'm supposed to trust *this guy* to keep me safe?

"No way." I shake my head, slow at first, then faster as I solidify the decision in my mind.

"When the advisors stop the analyzing and debating nonsense, they will come get you and force you to talk to her. They will listen to what she says. The information will go everywhere."

My arms cross in resistance to his logic. The pressure of the decision compounds in my skull. My head aches. I don't know who to trust, and Belamy hasn't shown any reason for me to trust him. I could get caught, and I'm not willing to take that risk for *him*.

I swallow hard and answer with finality, "No."

5 DROP OF BLOOD

TOLLIVER

"Tolliver, I thought we were waiting this thing out?" Kava puts hands on her hips. My eyes blink slowly. I want to tell her to calm down and sit. But it will only make her louder.

"We are," I say softly. "We are waiting for me to make a rope." Sitting on the floor of the back bedroom, I continue to tear a gray sheet into wide strips.

Another rip echoes through the bedroom, and Kava gets angrier each time. Her lips tighten and nostrils flare. "I don't want to take a risk of climbing out that stupid window and not have any way to get off this island. What is your plan?"

My head swims with frustration. "I don't have one," I say, returning the intensity. I'm approaching a line I don't want to cross. She's the only one I haven't hurt yet. But nothing in me wants to stop what I'm doing.

Sitting on the floor in the corner, scratching the wall with a piece of metal, Ledger sighs loudly at the rising tension. Kava turns her wrath on him. "What is your problem, Ledger?"

His eyes widen and he shrinks back from her like an animal at the end of her arrow. He should run. Ledger gazes at Hollis, who is equally horrified at Kava's outburst, and she shrugs.

Taking the sheet in my hands, I pull the edge downward with a vibrating rip.

As she whirls around to face me, her voice peals through the air. "I can't take this! We are not doing any more dangerous things. I mean it!"

The front door slams open and a guardian rushes into the bedroom, no doubt because of Kava's screaming. He isn't as big as Belamy and is paler than Ledger. His white wings swish into the room. His sword flashes in the afternoon light and nearly slices into me. He swings, whipping the strips of fabric out of my hand and onto the floor. We are all frozen with shock as he stops with a dagger to my throat. I throw my hands up, ready for his next move. I remember my first time on the battlefield against the Ellerian army. They are swift and nimble, but I too am fast. They are deadly with swords, but if you disarm them, their wings and distance are the only things that can save them.

"Stop what you are doing," he commands. He slides his sword back into its sheath and grabs my tunic. Defenseless, I let him yank me to my feet. Rage pounds in my head. I consider spinning and thrusting his dagger away from me. My neck stings at the edge of his blade as he pushes me against the wall. "You, girl." He points at Kava. "Pick it all up and hand it to me."

Kava, with tears spilling down her cheeks, gathers every strip, including the finished rope, and holds it out for the guardian.

His muscles relax as he slowly lowers his blade. I consider making my move, knocking him out, and climbing out the window. But the rope is too short, time is too short, and Kava is crying.

She hands over the fabric and backs away. He accepts it without a word. He steps to our open window and peers out, obviously assessing whether we could make the climb.

"This will not go well for you," he says, marches toward the door. "I hope they end you for it." His heavy footsteps echo down the hall and the door crashes shut.

Crying Kava, shocked Ledger, and little Hollis glower at me for an uncomfortable second.

"I'm so bored. I needed something to do." I touch my neck and find a drop of blood.

Kava is stunned, staring at the floor. Big tears tumble down her cheeks.

"What do you think they'll do to us?" Ledger asks.

"I just want to go home," Kava cries. She walks to the bed, lies down facing the wall, and wraps her blue dress tightly around her legs. I've traumatized her. I am ashamed of myself for causing her pain.

Hollis goes to her and puts a hand on her shoulder. Ledger shakes his head and walks to the window.

I can't help thinking if Kava didn't scream, the guardian would not have come rushing in. On the way out of the room, I punch the stone wall. It pales in comparison to the pain of how stuck I feel. *I can't get away with anything around here with all their eyes on me. I need a better plan.*

6 BEST JERKY

LEDGER

By evening, a guardian flies to the outside of our back bedroom window with a mallet and a large gate. The nails being hammered into the stone sounds like sitting inside a bell. Bong, bong, bong. Over and over as they seal us inside. I imagine Tolliver's head inside that bell getting hit with the sound.

At least we can still see between the bars. They raised the security to two guardians, one outside the door, one inside because Tolliver couldn't wait this out. Frustration bubbles in my stomach, and I swallow back the desire to yell at him.

In the front room, the new guardian stands in front of the closed door with his hands behind his back and chest puffed up. I've not seen him before. His dark hair is parted in the middle and wedged behind his ears. His white wings stand at attention, covering most of the door. He is bearing a sword at his side and several knives along the front of his leather belt. His black clothes might be hiding other deadly weapons.

"Do you think we can breathe around him?" Hollis

whispers. I know she wants me to laugh, but I pretend not to hear. "No sudden movements." She gets up and tiptoes awkwardly across the room while gawking at him. She's wearing a white linen tunic and small black pants again today and I sneak a glimpse at her curves, then roll my eyes at her nonsense.

Arms crossed, sitting on the bench, I stay as far from Tolliver as possible. Hollis joins him at the kitchen table. Kava shows her a hole in the side of her blue overdress. I don't know why it matters; she is covered by a white underdress.

The door opens again, and Dayson enters with his head held high. His hearty laugh fills the room. "Making trouble again, are we?" The tension in my shoulders eases, relieved it is Dayson and not an executioner.

He nods to the guardian who steps out the door, shutting it behind him. He is covered collar to foot in several layers of gray and black. I wonder where he's been and where he's going.

"I brought you something," Dayson says, still chuckling to himself. He pulls a small canvas bag from inside his black cloak. He tosses it to Tolliver, and I join them at the table. We watch him open it. Hollis tries to rush him and pulls back a section of fabric. Tolliver swats her hand away.

"It's the best jerky in the world," Dayson says with a smile. We all take a piece. "We learned how to make it from this tribe in the High Plains. Gruffalo meat. We smoke it for a long time with this special wood." He makes a grunting noise.

Hollis's eyes brighten as her jaw works the dried meat.

He is right. It is delicious and tender, with a different flavor than I've ever had.

"Oh, that's good," Hollis exclaims, taking a larger piece.

"So I need to warn you, the more trouble you make, the harder it will be for me to convince the advisors to let you go when the time comes," Dayson says.

My heart sinks. I should have known this jerky was a bribe. Dayson pulls a stool up to the table and sits with his foot propped on my chair's crosspiece.

He leans in and talks a little quieter, "It's not impossible to escape this place with eyes everywhere. But it is a last resort."

I scowl, not understanding his meaning.

"I made you a promise to get you home safely. And I will, but please make it easy for me. Agreed?" Dayson crosses his arms.

Tolliver says, "Agreed." He better be the one to agree. He is the one making the trouble. I understand he wants to find his family. But how does he do that without risking all of our lives? There's no one we can trust. Except for maybe Dayson.

"How are the trials going?" Kava asks.

I come back to reality and listen to Dayson's reply. "They've executed several people over the past couple of days, but something has come up, putting it all on hold."

"What's come up?" Tolliver asks the exact question on my mind.

Dayson frowns and looks thoughtfully at the table. "I'm not sure yet. But it was on the heels of the preposterous thing that happened three days ago."

"We saw that," Hollis blurts.

"What do you mean, you saw?" Dayson unfolds his arms.

"Oh, we heard the ruckus. The guardian was distracted. We wandered out on the balconyand saw some Ellerians going crazy in the courtyard."

I am embarrassed at the way she says it. But she's right. It was crazy.

Dayson explains, unfazed by her bluntness. "Everything is a mess right now. The advisors are keeping everything running while many want a new king and others are fighting to form a republic. Can you believe they want to erase our traditions like that?" His question hangs in the air. *So he wants a king.*

Dayson switches subjects abruptly as he looks away. "I'm worried Alouette won't make it out of prison. With all the stalling and nonsense, she might die down there. I know they aren't good to prisoners."

He is visibly upset about Alouette, adjusting his collar and clearing his throat. *Does he love her?* I wonder. "Can't you get a message to her to find out how she is?"

He shakes his head, and a strand of black hair falls on his brow. "I told you, I'm forbidden to have any contact with her. My family wants her executed. The advisors are all too willing to agree. And I don't know what state she's in."

"She wasn't doing well," I say. His thick shoulders slump. "I mean, she was alive, but—" I stop myself, wondering why in the skies I'm saying anything. This isn't encouraging.

"What?" he sits up straighter, bracing himself. "Tell me. I can handle it."

"She was beaten," I explain, avoiding his intense blue

eyes.

"Who did it?" His face contorts in anger.

"I—I don't remember,"

"It was the other prison guardian—not Belamy—who brought us to the throne room," Hollis says. I flash her a stern look, hoping to shut her up. "What?" she asks innocently.

"She's lost hope. She doesn't eat. She knows they're going to execute her."

Dayson adjusts his drooping, gray wings. He wipes the emotions from his face. "I'm sorry this is a day full of bad news. I asked around about your friend."

Kava reaches for Tolliver's hand, anticipating Dayson's news.

"Cousin," Hollis interrupts. "He's their cousin." She closes her mouth and leans back in her seat.

"Your cousin," Dayson corrects himself. "When you arrived, he fought the guardians and was hit in the head so they could subdue him enough to put him in chains. The healer I talked to said he arrived at the medical ward unconscious. He laid in the bed for weeks without waking. She said he eventually stopped breathing."

Hollis shrieks and grabs onto me.

"Oh my lands!" Tolliver yells and slams a fist on the table. Everything on the table bounces in the air. The candle in the middle lands and I grab it before it topples over. At the edge of my vision, Dayson's wings snap to attention.

In shock, I watch Tolliver roll through his emotions—anger, frustration, and sadness. He finally puts his head in his hands. Kava leans over him in an awkward embrace.

Hollis sniffles on my shoulder.

Breathing again, I realize what Dayson just said.

Angus is dead.

7
NO TIME

TOLLIVER

Pacing the bedroom several times, I debate my next move toward finding my Ellerian family. I head down the hall where Belamy lounges on a chair in front of the door. Though it is mid-afternoon, he blends into the dark room in his black shirt and floor-length trousers. I want to blurt a question but consider my words carefully.

His feet are resting on another chair, and his hands are propped behind his head. I need to find someone trustworthy to help me find my family. *Is Belamy that someone?* He seems nice enough. But I'm not sure he will be loyal to me above his own people.

"Hey," I say, acknowledging him. Out of any guardian at our door, he seems to be the most personable. I strike the flint several times, light the smallest candle on the table, and sit. But I need someone who is willing to take risks, and just because he is friendly doesn't mean he's willing to help me. Dismissing the thoughts, I stare into the tiny flame.

The scent of the burning wick reaches my nose as I face

the fact that I'm running out of time, and Belamy is all I've got.

"Mind if I ask you something?" I break the silence.

Belamy yawns and rubs his head. His wings come to life as he stands, stretching and flexing. They are like black ghosts following him as he walks toward me.

He joins me at the table.

Pushing the sleeves of my black tunic out of my way, I lean toward him. I keep my voice down so everyone else stays in the back room. "What are your thoughts about population control?"

He laughs quietly, blowing air through his nose. "You want to talk politics? I think the population laws are ridiculous. People should have a choice to have bigger families."

"And the fact they kill second-born children…" I trail off, hoping to get a rise out of him.

"What? No." He shakes his head vehemently at first and slowing as I stare him straight in the eye. "Really?"

I nod.

"I thought they had a way of preventing—"

I shake my head *no*.

"That's inhumane," he says. "Maybe it shouldn't surprise me. I realized there were a lot of things I didn't know when Ciel got us off the island." He leans back in his chair, lips pursed in disappointment.

"You agreed with Ciel?" My jaw drops with surprise.

Belamy speaks a little too loud, anger heightening his tone. "I did not agree with his methods, killing people and tying up the ones who didn't follow his orders." He clears his throat and quiets his voice. "I found out we were never allowed to leave the island. It was one of those unspoken laws. If anyone tried to leave without the king's permission, they were punished or executed."

I listen to what he is saying—and what he is not saying. I'm curious if he is defiant toward the laws because he is a criminal or if he desires freedom. *Can I trust him?*

Belamy continues, "On the ground, I was on sentry duty around the castle as it was being built. It felt odd to actually be alone. On Ellery, no one's ever alone. Someone's always there breathing down my neck. When Lianmin attacked, I was in the training arena. They were good fighters, really good. After they killed over half the men in the arena, the Lianminese gave us the choice to live and return to Ellery or die in the dirt. I'm not one for running away from a fight, but as they cut through our numbers, the only *real* choice was to return to this pitiful island. I was highly disappointed our time on the ground was up." He leans forward, with his elbows on the table. "That little taste of freedom got me thinking about our ridiculous laws, which is why I'm all for a republic."

He is as open-minded as I could've hoped, and I run a hand through my dirty-blonde hair. "What about the wingless?"

"Is that what you call yourselves?" Belamy raises one brow at me.

"No, when a child is born on Ellery without wings, they too are… discarded."

His nose flares in disgust. "Are you bloody kidding me?"

Gazing deep into his horrified eyes, I trust him with my

secret. “I am one of those wingless children.”

His brows lower. “You are Ellerian? I’ve never seen an Ellerian without wings. Well, except for those who lost their wings in war or as punishment.”

A momentary silence hangs between us. My sleeve falls down and I push it back up. I wish I could just rip them off. I whisper, “They smuggled me out when I was only a few days old.” I wait for him to speak, but his mouth hangs open as he grasps what I’m saying and what I’m about to ask. “Can you help me find my family?”

Belamy leans back in his chair. Someone stirs in the bedroom and we both pause. He rubs his hands together, and I instantly regret telling him. I should have waited, asked more questions, built up to it more. But there’s no time. I need to find them, or this whole year—this whole mess I got us into—will be for nothing.

After a few moments, when no one emerges from the bedroom, Belamy replies, “I don’t know how, but I’ll try.”

I must have been holding my breath because when I exhale the pain in my chest dissipates. I resolve to watch him closely over the next few days. I’ll be ready if he turns against me.

Furrowing my brow, I say, “Start with the midwives. If most of Ellery doesn’t know second-born children were smuggled off Ellery, the midwives will be the only ones who know wingless children were smuggled off, too.”

8

CROWLESS ROOSTER

LEDGER

Snuggled under a blanket in the front room, Hollis and I watch dancing tendrils of fire in the hearth. They are so happy and bright, the way I feel with Hollis. I periodically catch a glimpse of a smile on her face and touch the little dimple in her right cheek. Candles light Tolliver and Kava's card game at the table. They converse softly back and forth about what their life will be like back home in Balfour. It almost feels like we are home again. Except for the guardian blocking the door, fading in and out of sleep on his feet.

Belamy bursts through the door. "It's happened." Belamy enters, fists clenched. "The worst has finally happened."

The sleepy guardian jolts to attention.

"What?" Hollis's eyes are wide and her fingers tighten between mine.

After enjoying the warmth of the fire on my face and the closeness of Hollis, I'm irritated at Belamy's rude interruption.

Belamy pats the guardian on the shoulder. He yawns

and takes the cue to leave. White wings brush through the doorway and disappear into the evening.

Belamy pushes the door shut and says, "The informant is dead."

Hollis gasps, and I jerk upright. *Oh no.* I declined seeing the informant and figured I could change my mind later, when I felt better about it. Shame washes over me and the blood drains from my face.

"That's not the worst of it," Belamy continues. "They are sending an assassin to Balfour to kill the last living Ellerian royal," he nearly shouts. His cheeks redden, and his eyes bulge in anger.

I fall back against the cushion with Hollis like I've been punched in the chest. Now I can't change my mind and go talk to the informant. Looking down, I fiddle with the sleeve of my tunic, ashamed that I am so gutless. We may never know who the royal is, until it's too late.

Belamy rubs his head. "It's only rumor at this point, but this source is usually forthright. I knew this was going to happen." He looms over me, dark wings poised angrily. "You idiot, we should have been ahead of this."

"I'm not an idiot," I defend, feeling very small and ridiculous for saying anything.

Tolliver interrupts, "Of course they want to assassinate him. Why would they allow a monarch to take the throne?"

"No." Belamy turns his anger toward Tolliver. "My people would never…" He trails off, eyes blazing.

"It doesn't matter who is sending the assassin," I say, realizing it as it comes out of my mouth. "What matters is what we're going to do about it."

"*We* can't do anything," Kava says.

A sudden weight presses on my soul. I am responsible for letting this information slip out of our hands. I'm ashamed of myself for being such a crow-less rooster. "Angus is dead. There is nothing we can do about that, so we need to get back to Balfour before the assassin does. Before someone else we love dies."

"Do you have any ideas who the royal could be?" Belamy asks.

I shut my mouth, because several people come to mind. "It could be anyone."

I glance at Tolliver—a wingless Ellerian. He is standing in front of me now, tense with concern. His eyes are deep gray and gazing at me thoughtfully. It feels like I haven't made eye contact with him in weeks. Especially not after he raged at me. I look away quickly.

I search the faces of Balfour in my mind, one after the other: suntanned faces from plowing, planting, and harvesting. *Who could it be?* Someone tall or short; brown or blonde hair, red or gray hair?

"It has to be someone old." To Tolliver, I say, "It could be Thelonious's father, our grandfather, or even old man Dudley."

"Whoever it is, whether Balfourian or Ellerian, they don't deserve to die," Tolliver says. I'm shocked we agree on something.

"Then we've got to get out of here," I say boldly.

Tolliver nods and we both turn to Belamy.

"All right," he says.

Tolliver asks the girls, "You in?"

Kava's face turns a bright pink and she huffs.

"Let's get out of here," Hollis says. She brushes the top of my hand, sending tingles up my arm.

"We're going to need some help," Belamy says. "There aren't many we can trust who will be willing to take the risk."

Blue eyes flash in my mind. "I know someone who will… Dayson."

"No," Belamy cuts me off. "His father is…*no*. He isn't on the right side of this war."

"No one is on *our* side," Tolliver says. "Your revolutionaries could be the ones sending the assassin. How do we know we can trust *you*?"

Belamy cracks his knuckles and straightens his shoulders. "Go ahead and ask him. If that is a risk you're willing to take. Just don't mention my involvement. If Dayson turns you in, at least I won't be executed."

"So how do we get off a flying island without wings?" I ask.

"Oh, I have an idea about that," Belamy says. A toothy grin spreads across his bronze face.

***

It takes Dayson seven days to respond to our summons. Every time the door opens, my heart trips into an uneasy rhythm. What used to be a relaxing room has filled with anxiety and fear that we will miss the opportunity to get home first. I find myself doing menial tasks to keep busy: wiping off the table, straightening the chairs, and even making my bed this morning. Hollis laughed at me, and we ended up in a punch-for-punch match that lasted too long. One of my punches really hurt her and I gave in first. Skies know that she would never concede.

"Look at this bruise!" Hollis squeals with delight. Her smile is too big for showing off a wound—especially one that I gave her. Her upper arm is already turning purple and black.

I flare my nostrils in disgust. "Don't show Kava." I quickly pull her sleeve of her white dress over the bruise.

"Why? This is the champion of all bruises," she says.

I'm tempted to check my arm for injury, but Kava startles me. "Show me what?" She and Tolliver join us in the front room.

The front door swings inward and Dayson enters. He gestures for the guardian to step outside the door with a flick of his wrist. As soon as the guardian is gone, he relaxes. "How are the Balfourians this fine morning?" he asks.

Tolliver quietly scoffs but covers it up with a laugh as if Kava said something funny. I can tell he doesn't trust Dayson. Not one bit. Tolliver puts his arm around Kava as they sit together on the padded bench.

"We are well," I answer, trying not to frown at Tolliver. "We have a request."

Dayson sits on a stool near the hearth, eyebrows poised expectantly.

I've analyzed how to say this without implicating Belamy. I wish I could have rehearsed it, but I would have felt ridiculous doing it in front of Tolliver. He speaks so concisely, and I am barely better than a blithering two-year-old in comparison. I take a deep breath and speak my best.

"We hear the whispers outside our door. Is it true there is a member of the Ellerian royal family still living?"

"Oh, that," Dayson says. "Then I'm sure you've heard the rest?"

I shrug. "They are in Balfour?"

"Yes." Dayson purses his lips. "I was going to ask if you knew who it might be."

"No. I don't, but it worries me."

"Because there's a traitor in your village?" he asks.

Ignoring my racing heart, I say, "No. Because there is an assassin being sent to kill whoever it is."

Dayson's wings jerk to attention, and I don't miss the brief startled expression on his face. He smiles and says, "I'm sure it's just a rumor." But his jaw muscles tighten, and I'm not sure if we can trust him. "What was it you wanted to ask?"

"If it isn't rumor…" I gulp hard. "If they…" I can't seem to finish a sentence, feeling so indecisive about whether we can trust him. Half of me says yes because he saved us from execution. But the other half doesn't know if he would betray his people for us.

Hollis groans in the corner. "Ledger, just say it."

I sigh and stretch my neck. Bones crunch together under the weight of this decision.

Tolliver speaks for me, "If it isn't a rumor, we need to get back to Balfour before the assassin."

I frown at him as if he's stepped on my chest. I find my voice. "We have to find out who it is so that assassin doesn't go around killing everyone until they find who it is."

Dayson sucks his teeth and says, "So you need me to

help you get off Ellery."

"You're the only one who can help us," Tolliver says. I'm annoyed he keeps hijacking the conversation, but Dayson can't know about Belamy until we are sure he will help us.

"I think I can arrange that. Let me see who I can get to help out." Dayson stands, brushes dust from his smooth black trousers, and straightens the collar of his crisp white shirt.

"Do you think you would smuggle us out one by one?" I ask.

Tolliver clears his throat. Everything he does feels like a reprimand. "Or some other way to get out of this room?"

"I guess that is the question," Dayson says. "How to get out of here and off the island with four wingless Balfourians."

"How far are we from home?" Kava is poised on the edge of the bench near Tolliver, hands folded neatly in her lap.

"Hmm, I'd say about three weeks."

"We need to go as soon as possible," I say.

"Give me a couple days," Dayson says, heading for the door. "I'll figure something out."

After he's gone, I grind my teeth at the thought of waiting any amount of time for him to figure out whether he should help us. *If* we can even get out of here.

I slam my fist in my hand and think of Angus. A sharp pain radiates in my gut at the loss of my cousin. I miss him. When the masked men held us in the prison, he exercised his body. I joined him, and it made me feel so much better. I need that feeling now. I scuffle to the back bedroom and whip off my shirt. Getting down on the floor, I imagine Angus, his red hair and dark red beard. I break a sweat pushing myself off the floor using only my arms. I hate that we have to escape. I would much rather wait this out and go home in the good graces of Ellery.

I stand and lunge forward on each leg back and forth until they ache. Nothing has worked the way I thought it would. I thought the Ellerian people would be grateful we intervened and welcome us on the island.

I lie on my back and sit up over and over. I thought finding Alouette would bring us closer together. I punch at the air as my body starts to give out. Sweat and tears spill down my face. I fear everything I have done—boarding Ellery when Father told me not to, surviving almost a year on this island, and saving Alouette from the fire—was all for nothing. I lie back on the cold floor and cover my bleary head with my sweaty arm. I want to go home, back to the way it used to be. Simple. Calm. And worriless.

***

I gaze out the bedroom window into the cold autumn wind. We have waited eight full days for Dayson to come up with a plan to help us escape. I'm sick of waiting. My body aches, partly because of the exercise and partly because of the anxiety running through my veins. This must mean he is rejecting our idea of escaping.

I wake to whispers in the front room this morning and bolt to Tolliver's side only to find him exchanging jokes with Belamy. I thought it was going to be Dayson laying out the escape plan. But it isn't.

Belamy swigs from a wooden cup on the table and opens the door, switching spots with the guardian on the outside. "This is Estefano. He's one of the good ones," Belamy says with a wink, leaving us alone with this hulking man-bird. He has long brown hair, big pale ears, brown wings, and an awkward grin.

"Ledger," Tolliver says my name and I resist his eyes for a full five seconds. I don't want to talk to him, or look at him, or be near him. I'm sick of waiting. I'm sick of him being angry. "I'm sorry," Tolliver says out of nowhere.

My mouth drops open. His usual routine is holding a grudge until he dies.

"I'm sorry for treating you badly and calling you…well, you know." Remorse fills his eyes.

My insides sink. It's not fair. If he's not going to keep up the usual brotherly customs, then I will. He should be punished for treating me horribly. He doesn't deserve my forgiveness. If he won't punish himself, then I will. So I stomp back to the bedroom and ignore him completely.

I slip into a clean gray tunic and a pair of black winter trousers the washmaids delivered yesterday. They are soft on my skin and smell like lavender. They've sewn the wing holes closed for us. That was nice. I feel bad that I like these clothes better than my Balfourian ones. Ellerian fabrics have the smallest weave, making them lighter and more comfortable. My tunics back home were thick and bulky and my trousers were wool, which made me sweat all year long.

I step to the back window and pull the shutters open. Gazing into the pink morning sky, I inhale the crisp autumn air. Hollis and Kava eventually wake up and join Tolliver in the front room eating breakfast. Leaning my head on my hands, I watch the darkness dissipate from the landscape beyond the floating island. The leaves are beginning to change, and the air is getting cooler.

Below, a strange silhouette flies up over the rocky edge of Ellery. There are wings and limbs jutting out oddly, and as it comes near, I recognize Dayson's gray wings. In his arms is a person. White wings hang limply. Who is it? When her head lolls and hair spills to the side, Alouette's face is revealed.

My throat constricts and I can't breathe. *Is she dead?*

Dayson's eyes dart around as his wings lift them slowly toward my window. His face is red and when he speaks, his voice is strained. "Ledger, let us in." He sticks a hand between the bars and offers me a metal key.

I scramble into the deep window opening and take the key. I feel around for the lock on the outside of the barred window, trying not to focus on Alouette's lifeless body. I fumble with the key, then finally insert it. The lock clinks and the gate pushes open. I leap backward out of the way.

At the sound of my feet hitting the floor, Tolliver yells from the front room, "You okay in there?"

I don't answer, and they all come running. Guardian Estefano is one step behind them as Dayson flies through the open window with Alouette in his arms. I wait for some sort of clash between them, but it doesn't happen.

"What the blazes!" Hollis blurts as she sneaks around the guardian's obtrusive wings.

"Help me," Dayson says, panting. I assist in laying Alouette on the bed. She is soaking wet in her golden dress.

Her chest rises and falls. She is unconscious, but alive.

My head spins with relief. *She is alive.* "What happened?" I pull a blanket over her and accidentally graze her hand. I lift it into mine, so small, pale, and cold. I try not to cry in front of them all.

"Execution day." Dayson's voice wavers. His eyes glisten with tears and hands shake. I've never seen him so raw with emotion. I steel myself against his sadness.

Kava hurries to the bed and sits on the other side of Alouette. Kava is the daughter of our village healer, trained to care for the sick and injured. Her eyes are focused, and her actions are methodical, feeling Alouette's head and checking over her body.

"She's not ill. She's in shock," Dayson explains.

"What did they do to her?" Kava asks.

"The usual Ellerian execution: immobilized descent."

The formal term cuts like a sword to my heart. I pull away from her frigid hand. "They tied her up and threw her off the island?" I don't mean to shriek, but everything in me panics at the thought of Alouette falling to her death.

"Yes." Dayson hunches in defeat.

A warm hand touches my back, and I turn to meet Hollis's sad eyes. I rise from Alouette's side and wrap an arm around Hollis. I'm afraid to say what I'm thinking, but it comes trickling out anyway. "I thought we were getting out of here?"

Dayson kneels beside Alouette and lays his hand on her arm. His black tunic and trousers are soaking wet too. "When her trial was scheduled, I couldn't go…" His voice is strained as he blinks back tears. With a deep breath, he regains his composure. "I was going to take you all through the window, but I can only carry one at a time." He peers around the room at each of us. "The more time it takes to carry you off, the higher the chance of us getting caught. Your window is in full view of the southwest tower."

One word brings my hope back to life: *us*. He is on our side, fighting for us, helping us escape.

"In six days, it will be a new moon," he continues. "That will be the best time. When the sky is the darkest. The only way out is to climb down the privy."

"Wait, what?" Hollis's face contorts in disgust.

Dayson guides a strand of hair out of Alouette's face and gently strokes her cheek. His chin quivers and he visibly shakes a thought away. "It's the only way. It's a long tube on the outside of the castle with a clean-out door at the bottom. I'll have you escorted to the bathing rooms, you'll climb down, and I will fetch you when night falls." The strength in his voice returns as his plan solidifies. "We will travel to the dragon's cavern, where I will fly each of you straight down to the ground one by one from there."

"What about Tristeh?" Hollis blurts.

I scowl at her interruption and Dayson doesn't blink. "Tristeh is not an option." He glances from Tolliver to me and says, "I will pack supplies. What do you need for the hike through the mountains?"

"We don't need to hike," Hollis says louder. "We can fly."

Dayson shoots a dark look at her. "I am not experienced with dragons. I cannot be responsible for you people and that unpredictable beast."

Hollis shakes off my touch and puts her hands on her hips. “There’s no way we hike home faster than Ellery.” I am not surprised she’s fighting to fly Tristeh, but I’m annoyed at her persistence.

“There’s also no way we hike home faster than a flying Ellerian assassin,” Tolliver says.

Dayson looks around at each of us. “I don’t know if I can arrange that.” He mumbles something and heads for the window. “Please care for Alouette. I’ll be back in six days.”

He eyes Estefano and dives from the window ledge. Estefano pulls the gate shut with a clang. Pulling the key out of the hole, he locks us inside.

9

VEILED GOODBYE

TOLLIVER

Knowing what comes next, I do my best to enjoy the little moments. Kava smiles at me. Her brown eyes sparkle with joy in anticipation of going home. My chest swells. I am proud to be in her sights and the one she gives *that* look.

"He will be so happy," Kava says of her father as I wrap my arms around her. "First thing I will do is give him a big hug. I'm sure he won't be mad anymore because I'll be back snug and secure."

I smile and kiss her cheek. "He will be very happy to see you."

She continues talking about where we will live together and whether we will do a second ceremony, since our first wedding was on Ellery away from family.

One of the drawstrings on her blue overdress sleeve is hanging untied. I gently wrap it around itself and make a bow. The white of her underdress is bright and clean. It peeks out at her neckline, each elbow, and the front of her skirt. Her little feet stick out from beneath several layers of fabric. They are wrapped in brown leather with crisscrossed leather straps halfway up her calf. I'm glad Belamy provided her with extra clothing.

Ledger is pacing in front of the fire, chewing a fingernail, and sighing. I want to tell him to calm down, but that's the thing about Ledger: telling him to do something, I might as well be talking to a doorpost. He almost always does the opposite. I grind my teeth, hiding my anger at him. All I want is to clear the messy field between us. But he shoveled more frustration at me when he rejected my apology. He doesn't know I'm *not* coming with him. Will he will ever trust me again after this?

Hollis hasn't left Alouette's bedside since she arrived. Poor Alouette curled up on the bed and slept day and night for the first few days. Now she is eating and drinking a little bit here and there. She still hasn't said a word to anyone. Not even Hollis has broken through her traumatized state.

I hope they make it home, because Angus won't. My heart aches because he is gone. I would give anything to bring him back. I would thwart this mission of finding my family if I knew it would bring him back. *What am I going to tell Uncle Roan? He'll be furious.*

"Right?" Kava yanks me from my faraway thoughts.

At this point, I'll agree with anything she wants.

The front door clangs and swings open. Belamy's black wings graze the top of the doorway. "It's time for a bath, stinky Balfourians. Who's first?" He points at Ledger and Hollis. They step forward. "Ledger with me. Hollis with her." A woman with white wings and matching headwrap walks through the door.

"What about—?" Hollis almost says Alouette's name in front of the woman.

Belamy whispers, "Dayson will handle the extra details. Come on."

Alouette is cleanly dressed and hiding in the storeroom in the hallway. No one else can know she's here—or alive for that matter. Hollis braided her dark hair and chattered about its color and softness for a good twenty minutes before the washmaid arrived. Why she is so confused about the plan?

I try to catch Ledger's eye, but he pulls the door closed behind them without glancing my way. I sigh with regret. I know what I need to do. I'm just sad it will hurt everyone I love.

We wait in silence for a long while as Kava's left leg nervously bounces on the stone floor. I have a thought and stand. I bow slightly with my hand extended. "May I have this dance?"

She takes my hand. I hum a song and sway to the tune. I love the feel of her against me. She is my north star, my constant.

She sings the song as I hum along. "I love you more than the sun; I love you more than the moon…"

Her smile almost allows me to forget what I'm about to do. This moment in her arms feels like a lie. I keep lying and swaying to the sound of her voice, spinning her and making her laugh. It's almost a carefree laugh. Close enough. I smile and reassure her with my touch that I love her and only her.

I pull her close as she sings the last line of the song, "I love you more than the sky; And the beautiful stars too."

"One day our life will be normal," I promise.

She is startled by the scrape of the key in the door.

We follow the washmaid and Belamy. The wind is whipping up the center of the tower. I let go of Kava as she heads left, toward the stairs, and I follow Belamy to the right. We must appear to be doing what we are supposed to be doing. Bathing.

I have no idea how we will go down the same privy when we are headed to two separate washrooms. Dismissing the thought, I follow Belamy, keeping my hands behind my back and head down. We enter the washroom; the ceiling is swirling with steam. He leads me past the pool of water, which appears as though it was used too many times.

There are dark blue velvet curtains at the back of the room. They don't cover the two large windows over the men's privy. Belamy draws back the curtain. A passageway leads downward.

He puts his finger to his mouth as we descend the steps. At the bottom, he peeks through the curtains, pulling them fully open into another steamy washroom. Kava stands before the women's privy making a face: gaping mouth and horrified eyes. The board covering the poop-chute is up, and a single rope hangs over the edge. It's wide enough for two people to climb down side by side, which is what she will have to do. Ledger and Hollis have already gone down.

When Kava sees me, she says, "I don't know if I can do this."

The washmaid holds up a handkerchief. "To cover your mouth and nose."

Kava sighs. "Thank you." As she lifts the fabric, I race it to her lips and win. Kissing her, I inhale. Tears threaten to come. I put all my passion into this moment. I draw her up into a hug, lifting her off the ground. My veiled goodbye.

"All right, you're making me uncomfortable," Belamy says.

When I set her down, Kava is blushing. She wraps the kerchief over her nose and mouth. The washmaid helps tie it around her head. Kava's skirts are all tied up, the same way they were when we first flew up to this island on Ledger's hot air flying contraption. She steps onto the edge of the privy, turns, and climbs down the rocks on the inside.

"We poured water down the privy to wash off the front wall, so your descent shouldn't be too…" Belamy smiles, searching for a word, then says, "slimy." He grabs the rope and loops it around his forearm, preparing for her weight.

"Not too slimy. Great," Kava says, eyes narrowed and sarcasm dripping from her tone.

I must tell her now or never. I don't want to have to shout to her at the bottom. Putting my hands on hers, I hold her still. "Kava, I'm not going with you." Her mouth opens, but I interrupt whatever she was going to say. The less she says, the less guilty I'll feel. "I'm sorry. I need you to get to safety. Go to your father. Stay with him. I need to find my family."

"But *I'm* your family." Tears well in her eyes.

I purse my lips, angry at myself for doing this to her. "I know, and we will be together soon. I just need to do this."

"How will you find them? You can't go back to that room with us gone. You'll be thrown in prison—or worse." She scowls at me.

"Belamy has agreed to help me. I'll hide until he tracks them down."

"He's had no success finding them up to now. What is a few more days? Won't Ellery be in Balfour in less than a week?"

Belamy nods.

I thought the same thing, but I can't leave the possibility hanging wide open. "If there's a chance of finding them in the next few days, I need to take it. Whether I find them or not, when Ellery arrives at Balfour, I will come home. I promise."

"You promise?" she insists, turning her hand over and grasping mine.

"Yes. I swear it." I can't hold back the tears, and one falls on her cheek. Leaning down, I kiss where it landed. "I'll meet you in Balfour. Find us a cottage, Kava. Find a home for us to be together."

She gazes deep into my eyes for a long moment. I prepare to plead with her to go, but as more tears fall, she takes the rope and descends into the pit of excrement. Her weeping chokes me. I hang my head and watch her disappear into the darkness.

The rope in Belamy's hands jerks and Kava screams.

"Kava!" I call into the dark hole. "Are you okay?"

Silence blankets the moment until her sobs begin again, angrier than before.

The rope is taut. I wait a few minutes more and it goes limp.

"Kava made it," Ledger's voice travels up the pit. "Come on, Toll."

"I'm not coming."

"What?" Ledger's voice is laced with panic.

Kava's cries rip me to shreds.

I steady my trembling voice to conceal my guilt and say, "I'll meet you in Balfour. Take care of Kava for me."

"No," Ledger's whisper echoes from the blackness. "No, you get down here right now!"

I bite my lower lip trying to think of something he will accept. "I'm sorry, Ledger. I have to do this. I'm sorry I was so cruel to you. Please. Take care of her and do what you do best."

"And what is that?"

"You're inventive. Don't just follow the rules—follow your gut."

DOWN AND OUT 10

LEDGER

I can't believe he would do this to me! Tolliver left me with Kava, who hates me more than the dung we're standing in. Tolliver isn't coming with us. Father will never forgive me. It's bad enough Angus isn't coming home. Now Tolliver?

My mind swirls round and round with all the things Father and Mother will say. *What will the elders say?* They were mad enough I flew to Ellery in the first place. Now I'm going to be exiled. My body sways with the weight of this failure. I can't breathe through the stench of the privy, and my head tingles as if I'm about to pass out. *I can't fall into this muck. I must stay standing.*

Kava's hiccupy cries echo around the small space. In the pitch black of the privy, the girls stand huddled together. Hollis comforts her. I have my back against Hollis, holding me up, giving me something solid to lean against. The dizziness subsides as I inhale tentatively through the kerchief and bottle up the shame of being abandoned by my brother—well, my fake brother—who doesn't give two heads of corn about what happens to me. He's so wrapped up in his own obsession with finding the people who threw him away. I clamp my fists, pressing my fingernails into my palms.

There is no way to know what time it is or how long we've been at the bottom of this sewer. I'm guessing more than several hours because I can no longer smell Kava's vomit. Hollis has stopped whispering, "It's just mud, it's just mud," over and over. Also, whatever I touched on the way down has dried. I rub my crusty hands together and it flakes off.

When we hear several people relieve themselves one after the other, I hope it is the sign of evening falling along with the urine. They are preparing for bed.

With every lungful, I choke down the stench. Even with a handkerchief over my mouth and nose, there's no avoiding that stench.

When more excrement splatters down the stone walls, Kava whimpers.

"Shh," Hollis quiets her. "We can't be found out, or this will all be for nothing."

Kava whispers something I can't hear, then comes a sound I don't recognize. *Thud, thud, thud.* The wall beside me clangs and swings open. Fresh air wafts in, and I follow my nose into the night.

The girls rush out behind me and we pry the fabric from our faces, breathing deeply. Kava cries again, but this time, she sounds relieved. My chest loosens, and each gasp of fresh air brings new resilience.

"Where's your brother?" Dayson's words are sharp and bitter.

"He ditched us," I say.

Dayson cuts me off with a groan. "Why?"

"He had…" I'm unsure what to say. I keep it vague, so I don't get emotional. "Unfinished business."

"Ledger! We cannot have any deviations from the plan." Dayson runs a hand through his dark hair, probably considering how to fetch Tolliver.

"I agree. I would drag him out here if I could, but I climbed down first. There was nothing I could do." I would also punch him in the gut if I could. But he's not here to punish. Tolliver's words flood back to my mind, battling for forgiveness: *You're inventive. Don't just follow the rules—follow your gut.*

"Come on." Dayson stays several paces back and waves the smell away. "You smell horrible."

Even though it is a dark night, I make out spiky black trees across the horizon. Cloudless and moonless, the stars twinkle bright. I am thankful for those stars.

We follow Dayson along the stone wall on the right. I gaze straight up. The lookout tower is only about halfway up the sixteen levels of the main castle. Belamy told us they station two guardians on each lookout. As we sneak around the base of the southwest tower, thankfully no one sees or hears us. We reach a pool of water on the western side. It's the water supply leading to the kitchen. Tolliver and I had to stop it from overfilling during a rain storm before the Ellerian people came back to the island. Thinking about Tolliver makes my head ache.

Dayson points at the pool and says, "Clean yourselves. I'll meet you on the other side."

"Dayson, this is drinking water." I don't know why I care if they drink dirty water. After all, they imprisoned us after we helped them.

"It is filtered on the way down there," he whispers. "Get on with it." He shifts from one foot to another. "Try not to make a sound, or someone will discover us."

Dipping my toe first, I get in slowly, wheezing at every inch submerging in the icy water. All the hairs on my body stand up as I rub the muck off my feet and legs.

Hollis slips in up to her neck, washing her gray linen dress, which had a brown streak up her right side. She unties her skirts after rubbing off her calves and bare feet. I gag at the thought of the muck getting between her toes. I kept my leather shoes on. I considered wrapping a burlap sack around each one but didn't want to look like a complete pansy.

Kava takes a bit longer scrubbing her entire body of the putrid smell. Her nostrils flare in disgust as she agitates the water. Dayson lowers his brow at her. She doesn't acknowledge him as she scours the bottom hem of her skirts.

Hollis finishes and checks Kava for anything she may have missed. She brushes the back of Kava's right arm. "Did you bring any soap?" Hollis asks.

Dayson scowls. "Let's go."

I get out, checking my clothing for any last bits. Wringing out her stained blue dress, Kava swipes a water droplet—or a tear—from her cheek. Hollis gives her skirts a once over and squeezes the frigid water from her blonde hair. Kava shudders and Hollis wraps an arm around her. They follow Dayson and me toward the front entrance of the castle. It seems crazy to go back in when Dayson could easily fly us off the edge one by one, right now.

Before entering the grand doorway, Dayson puts a finger to his mouth. I shiver violently, waiting for the go signal. He steps from our hiding place and tells us to stay. Hollis peeks around the doorway and watches him pass under the beige stone that arcs over the wide entrance. I have always found it odd that there are no doors, just a long hall with an ornately carved ceiling. I lean around Hollis to see the stone carvings of Ellerian men and women in knee-length tunics. Their muscular bodies are well defined, posed menacingly with bows and arrows. Their enormous, intricate wings reach from wall to wall in some places.

"Go," Hollis whispers, and we leave wet footprints across the smooth stone floor. Dayson directs us to the entrance of a stairwell. He leans casually in the opening to the courtyard, pretending he's simply loitering.

We don't wait for Dayson's directions to run down the steps, and then I hear him approach from behind. I can only see his silhouette as we pass a few lit torches on the way down the circular staircase. My heart races as we patter past the prison hall and spiral to the dragon's cave. As we approach the silhouetted doorway, Dayson says, "Stop here." He passes us, entering the cavern first, and stops short.

"Dayson," a man's voice says. "What brings you here this late?" He sounds older, authoritative.

Hollis, Kava, and I dart to either side of the doorway to hide.

"I am running the stairs, sir," Dayson says. His voice is calm, though he is breathing hard from the descent. "I like to run as many stairs as I can before I retire for the night."

“I see,” the man says. “I was visiting Hellwig and his dragons.”

“Yes, sir.”

With nowhere to hide, we’ll be spotted if the man climbs up the stairs toward us. We must run back up and hide. I startle them when I grab Hollis’s and Kava’s shoulders. I silently signal for us to go upstairs. We tiptoe up the first few, then we take the steps two at a time, round and round. The man’s voice stops and heavy footsteps begin. When we reach the prison hall, we duck through the doorway and hide on either side. Out of view of the stairs, we heave loud breaths and glance at each other wide eyed.

***

We are all gasping for air. I shush them with a finger to my lips as footsteps grow nearer. They are slow and heavy. Finally, the man passes by, continuing up the stairs to the main floor of Ellery.

Scanning the empty stairwell up and down, I find only the stretch of stone stairs in either direction with torches dotting the walls. We head back down again. By the time we reach the bottom, I can hardly breathe.

“Where’d you go?” Dayson waits for us on the last step. “I thought for sure he’d see you.”

“Prison hall,” I manage to say, lungs aching for air. “Who was that?”

“Advisor Tiberius. He’s probably the one who sent the assassin in the first place.” Dayson leads us into the large cavern at the bottom of the stairs. We step through the doorway onto the wide, rounded balcony overlooking the dragon's cave.

Hollis gasps. "I can't believe we were so close to him." With her hand to her temple, the blush drains from her face.

"Running while wet is not comfortable," Kava comments.

"Nothing you do for the next couple days will be comfortable," Dayson says. "I hope you're prepared for that."

Kava tightens her lips and narrows her eyes at him.

"But I have brought you each a change of clothes." Dayson forces a smile.

Hollis says, "Oh blessed skies, I'm glad. This wet dress is giving me a rash." She flaps her skirts against her legs, flicking water droplets on all of us.

Dayson rolls his eyes and walks to the stairs descending along the right side of the cavern. Iron bars protrude from the balcony in an arc, up over our heads, connecting with the wall. Half of the enclosure is lit by torches along the right side of the pit below.

Approaching the edge of the balcony overlooking the expanse of the cavern, Hollis whispers, "Tristeh."

A loud shriek peals through the air.

My insides flipflop. I'll never get used to that terrifying sound.

Across the wide space below are two dragons. Their eyes are trained on us. The smaller one bounds into the air in an instant. Her red scales shimmer as she flies up the side of the cage rails to the jagged ceiling.

The other dragon holds its head high, on alert. Dull green scales fade into black down to its claws. Watching Tristeh swoop around the cavern on crimson leather wings, it barely moves a muscle. It shows awareness of us with the slight flare of its nostril and twitch of its eye.

Hollis drags her hand along the bars toward the stairs. Tristeh circles back toward us as we descend the bar-covered stairs. It's only been a month or so since we saw her last, but she seems bigger. When she lands, it appears as if I can walk beneath her legs and Hollis would have to stand on my shoulders to reach her withers, where the saddle lies.

"Look at you, girl. So lovely." Hollis leads us around the cage, cooing at the dragon.

"Stop that." Dayson pushes Hollis away from the enclosure. "Hellwig, good sir."

"Well, Tristeh is happy tonight," The little man says. He has a friendly face with snow white hair, which matches his wings. He shakes Dayson's forearm. "Tiberius didn't come all the way down. He kept to himself. Seemed distracted until you showed up."

They chuckle together. I don't get what's funny.

Dayson introduces us, and Hellwig gives a toothy smile. I'm anxious to get out of here, but with Dayson leading the way, it has really put me at ease. He knows everyone.

"Alouette is in here." Hellwig waddles to the small storage room where they keep the saddles. We find her lying on a pile of backpacks and blankets. When we enter, her wings twitch. Her sad eyes meet mine, and a small smile peeks at the corners of her mouth. It's the most coherent she's been in a while. She is dressed snugly in trousers with knee-high, brown leather boots. She is wearing several layers of tunics of varying lengths and a heavy black cloak that is open in the front. I'm concerned she won't be able to fly with so much extra weight.

Dayson shoulders past me, helps her to her feet, and latches her cloak shut. He gives her a brief hug and I look away, feeling a strange gnawing in my gut. I want to reach to Hollis for comfort, but she is with her dragon, making it dance and caw.

"Ledger, help me with these," Dayson says, picking up several backpacks.

I grab a few and follow him out of the storeroom.

"I packed food, water, flint, a sleeping mat for each of us. Plus there's a change of clothes for everyone." Dayson digs through one of the packs.

"Us?" I ask. *He's going with us?*

"Yes," Dayson replies. "I can't get you off this island and expect you to walk there all by yourself."

"We aren't walking," Hollis says. She puts one hand on her hip and pushes her blonde hair out of her face. One eyebrow up and pouty lips. I know that look.

Dayson ignores her and thinks aloud, "But now there are only three of you. If I could get one more Ellerian, we *could* fly."

"We will fly," Hollis says. "Tristeh will take us."

Hellwig interjects, "I will get in serious trouble if Tristeh goes missing on my watch."

"Tristeh will not go missing." Dayson eyes him intently. Hollis's nagging is getting on his nerves.

"Hollis," I whisper trying to get her to stop it.

"Don't *Hollis* me," she says, moving into Level One anger. Her fists ball up and her body stiffens. "We are flying home on Tristeh. It will take half the time, or even less."

"Hmm, it is true," Hellwig agrees, changing his mind. "She is your best bet of getting there in a hurry."

I am shocked the little man is agreeing with her.

Dayson is obviously surprised and argues with Hellwig. "She may be fast, but I don't want you getting in trouble."

"You know, there may be ways for me to avoid suspicion." He squints and wiggles his white eyebrows. "Will you return her when Ellery reaches Balfour?"

"Yes, yes, yes," Hollis says, with a pleading smile.

"Then I will continue my duties as usual, and if anyone comes looking for her, I will tell them Gabriel is out for a ride on her."

She bounces on her toes and claps.

"What if Gabriel actually wants a ride?" Dayson asks.

"Don't you worry about that." Hellwig pauses abruptly, gazing up at the stairwell. "Hide," he says.

We all dash into the storeroom. I drag my pack along with Hollis.

"Good evening, sir." Hellwig's voice echoes through the cavern and into our hiding place. Hollis, Kava and I sit along the wall and pile the backpacks in front of us. Dayson and Alouette stand in front of us, completely shielding us with their wings, gray and white.

"Hellwig, I thought Dayson came this way," Advisor Tiberius replies.

Dayson darts for the door. "I'm here," he says.

"Dayson, I was so rude earlier. I was just surprised to see you. I know you were betrothed to Alouette. So I wanted to extend my sympathies."

A strange silence fills the moment.

Dayson replies, making it sound like a question, "Thank you."

"I want you to know, I was adamantly against Alouette's execution. There was nothing I could say to sway the others," Tiberius pauses. "Even your father."

Dayson barks. "My father would never—"

"Oh. You didn't know. I'm sorry, son."

Trying to remember which advisor is which, I can't recall any of their names.

"Again," Tiberius says, "I am sorry for your loss."

Footsteps fade into the distance, and Hellwig fetches us.

We exit the storeroom. Tiberius is gone and Dayson has his hands around the bars of the cage. His gray wings droop, touching the dusty floor. Alouette puts a hand on his shoulder.

"Let's just get out of here," he growls. His knuckles whiten.

"I'll get her saddled up," Hellwig says.

"The rest of you, if you're going to change out of your wet clothes, do it now." Dayson stomps off toward the stairs, with Alouette one step behind him.

Hellwig shuffles into the storeroom and comes out with that dreaded saddle. White leather with embossed red flowers. The only time Hollis used it, she broke her leg. Bile rises in my throat. I'm not happy about getting close to the blazing red dragon again.

But Hollis is. She squeals and gathers the straps dangling from the saddle. She follows Hellwig as if he needs her help.

The small man enters the cage, telling Hollis to stay

by the door. He says something in a low voice to the green dragon. It strides to the darkness of the back of the cave but doesn't sit, remaining watchful. Then he approaches Tristeh. Her red talons wiggle and tap on the stone with excitement. He whistles once, and the trained beast kneels before him, bowing her head. I can't tell if she's showing reverence for him or what. But it's quite surprising.

Hellwig pulls a strappy leather cone from the pile and slides it over the dragon's mouth.

"You don't have to do that," Hollis says.

Hellwig rumples his brow in confusion.

"She doesn't need a muzzle," she says.

"You obviously have never met Tristeh's mother." Hellwig chuckles. "I'm following protocol. What you do after you leave this cave is up to you."

He finishes tying it and whistles again. Tristeh lowers to the floor, leaning her back toward him. He heaves the leather over her back and gives a double whistle. She gets up on her feet, except one of her front legs stays on her knee. Hellwig can barely reach the straps as he hooks them all neatly together and cinches the saddle tight.

A triple whistle and she rises, prancing on her toes.

"She's excited," Hollis says, smiling wildly. "So am I." She claps her hands as the dragon bounds into the air.

Hellwig triple whistles again, and Tristeh dives for the door. "Hey!" Hellwig shouts, sounding like a reprimand a father would give to an overexcited child. The way Hollis's father did many times. I laugh as the dragon lands and extends a wing before Hollis.

"She's all yours," Hellwig says with a wink. "Might want

to walk her down the hall before getting on her. Sometimes she gets a little too excited and might crush you against the ceiling." He points to the tunnel leading outside.

Hollis laughs. I gape at him, feeling nauseous. Across from the enclosure door is a long, roughly hewn hallway. It's probably only as high as Tristeh's head, or three of me, one on top of the other.

"How are you going to fit three of you on there?" Dayson asks.

"Oh, Mister Hellwig, sir?" Hollis says. "I need two more straps for Ledger and Kava. And is there a way we can hook the backpacks to her too?"

He musses his white hair, exits the dragon's cage, and heads for the storeroom. He returns with a handful of straps and latches. "Will this do?"

11
FICKLE THING

TOLLIVER

Belamy unfolds the burlap sack and holds it open. Shoving away my guilt, I climb into it and make myself into a ball. He cinches the top of the bag closed with a string. I can almost see through the weave of the fabric. I breathe deeply, trying to separate the panic of leaving Kava from the worry of being enclosed in this bag.

He lifts me over his shoulder with a grunt. "What are they feeding you?" Belamy chuckles.

I think of several rude things to say about him being weak, but I am choked with sadness. I can't believe I'm doing this to Kava, but she can't stay here. Her best chance is to go home.

Belamy heads up the back stairs. Daylight penetrates the bag as he exits the bathing room and steps over the railing into the open air. My stomach lurches as he flies downward three whole floors in an instant, landing with a thud in the courtyard. He carries me through the south hall and down a dark stairwell.

The flowery scent of soapwort seeps through the burlap as we enter the laundry area of Ellery. The sound of swishing water echoes around the large room as we enter. I remember finding this room months after arriving on Ellery. Several women are speaking to each other near the carved-out pools for washing. One greets Belamy as he heads into the darkest part of the cavern.

"Just some old sheets," he says.

We whisk around a corner and stop. Pushing me off his shoulder, he sets me on the cold floor.

His whisper doesn't travel over the stirring water. "I'm sorry it doesn't have a door."

I carefully climb from the laundry sack to find we are in a small cove off the large room. The floor is roughly hewn, as well as the walls, and the ceiling is craggy and dark. There are piles and piles of cloth all around the room, some stacked over my head.

"It's a storeroom. They rarely come in here."

Disappointed by the cramped space, I consider the comfortable home I just left. "Why can't you hide me in one of the homes on the top level or something?"

He rolls his eyes and says, "I never go higher than the eighth floor. Someone would notice me up that high."

"Are you sure?" I ask.

"Yeah, I'm sure." He rubs his brow. "You can trust me, you know?"

I meet his eyes. They are dark and thoughtful. He has already helped me more than I ever imagined he would. I don't have much choice but to trust him.

I accept his statement with a nod.

Trust.

It is a fickle thing.

"This is fine," I say, dusting myself off and pulling at the neck of my black tunic. "I guess I'll hide back there if anyone comes."

Along the left wall, Belamy pulls back a swath of fabric to reveal a table with room enough for me to lay stretched out underneath. A sleeping mat with a candle, a small box, and a water pouch lie in a heap.

I laugh. "Oh my lands, I'm your stray mutt."

Belamy chuckles with a goofy grin. "Let me know what else you need. I'll get you more food when I can. You'll find some in that box."

"Thanks, brute!" I say without thinking. It's what I would have said to Angus. My heart constricts at the loss of my best friend. My eyes widen as I blink back tears.

Belamy sees my face change and leaves me alone.

IN THE WIND 12

LEDGER

The wind is fierce at the end of the tunnel that opens at the base of Ellery. Standing beside quiet Alouette, we overlook dark, craggy mountains with swaths of even darker evergreens between them. The sky is black and moonless. Even the stars seem to have dimmed as I stare beyond their flicker, hoping Alouette will someday return to her delightful self.

I'm glad to be in dry clothes with a coat that buttons all the way up. The night air feels good on my face now that I'm warm.

Tristeh rests on her belly with her wings splayed out on the ground as Dayson and Hellwig attach the last pack to the straps across her chest. They secure them tightly, and the dragon rises with Hollis already atop, nestled into the white saddle. The red scales glisten in the torchlight, and her blazing orange eyes are on the horizon. Nothing holds her back from leaping off the ledge of the cavern. To my surprise, she doesn't even lean in that direction.

"Come on, Kava," Hollis argues with her about who

should be next to board the dragon.

"Why do I have to be near *him*?" Kava doesn't want to touch me. At all. "I should be in the front, then you, then Ledger."

It hurts my feelings when she eye-rolls while saying my name. I don't understand why she has to act like I'm a disease to be avoided.

"Are you going to direct Tristeh?" Hollis asks.

They eye each other in a battle of wills until one of them looks away.

"Fine, I'll be in the back," Kava yells, startling the large beast with sharp teeth and talons. Tristeh's head flicks in Kava's direction, and a vertical pupil follows her as she crosses her arms in a huff.

"Ledger," Hollis calls with a winning smile. "You're up."

I blink and pretend the man-eating beast doesn't make my insides twist. The dragon's glassy eye watches me place a shaky hand on her extended wing and climb. The feel of it—warm and leathery, sends a chill up my spine. I crawl like a toddler across the crimson scales of Tristeh's enormous back. She is about four times the size of a regular horse. The scales feel like snail shells—cold and hard. I detach my mind from the reality of climbing on a living, fire-breathing beast.

Showing my teeth in an awkward smile to Hollis, I settle in behind her on the saddle. I am relieved Tristeh doesn't eat me or scorch me for touching her. *I am okay.* Blood rushes back to my head.

Hollis hooks a strap around me. Her eyes twinkle with anticipation. She wiggles her little eyebrows and snaps the end of the strap to the saddle. My backside hangs off the saddle a little, which means Kava will be fully on the hard scales. I have an idea.

"Kava, bring a blanket from one of the packs," I say.

She scowls at me and asks Dayson to retrieve one. After much coaxing, the ornery girl in the damp dress is on the dragon, hugging me from behind, and strapped in snugly. She refused to change into the clothes Dayson provided: a long sleeve tunic and winter trousers. She called it *shameful man-clothing*. At least she accepted the cloak.

Hollis doesn't seem to care that Kava called her shameful for wearing men's clothing. But it is odd that there is a hole in the back of Hollis's shirt and coat—for wings.

I feel Hollis urge the dragon to the edge with the shift of her bodyweight. "I hope you don't have to pee," Hollis shouts and leans forward. "Fly, Tristeh."

Enormous wings spread in one moment and we dive in the next, from the cave in the bottom side of Ellery. My stomach lurches into my throat as we drop straight down. I'm glad it's empty. Tristeh gains speed until the skin on my face is flapping. My eyes water and Hollis sits up. Thankfully, the dragon levels out at each shift in the saddle.

Under the cover of night, we soar across the treetops and head northeast toward the mountain range, part of the North Mountains behind our village. I think of Tolliver and the fact that I am leaving him on Ellery. I knew he wanted to find his Ellerian family, but I didn't think he would abandon us to do it. Pain pierces me. Betrayal or fear, I can't tell them apart.

The forest thins until it meets a wide lake. Tristeh dips low and skims across the surface. My heart races with exhilaration. I forgot how much I loved flying with Alouette. I search my left and right flanks to find her. Alouette is up at treetop height flying alongside Dayson. I can see her white wings, even on this moonless night. Dayson's gray wings blend into the dark. He flies slightly ahead of her. Sadness pools at the edge of my vision as tears gather. She almost died. I guess I didn't realize how horrible it would be to lose her until now. After losing one dear friend, I can't lose another. Silent tears dry in the wind.

The mountains jut up in front of us, and Tristeh follows Dayson and Alouette to the right around the rocky surface. Dayson said we were getting out of sight of Ellery as quickly as possible and flying until Alouette is tired. Her wings slow and she dips. It seems she doesn't have the strength to go much further. We reach the lowest crest of the mountain and descend behind it into the trees. Alouette's wings fold and her body crumples. Dayson catches her before she hits the ground.

***

We land a dragon's wingspan away and unlatch ourselves from the saddle. Kava climbs down first. I hug Hollis and say, "Thank you." Flying Tristeh was the best idea. Kava hurries to Alouette, kneeling in the dirt and leaves. She pushes Alouette's hair out of her face and touches her forehead.

Dayson asks sharply, "What are you doing—" and catches himself.

Kava squints at him, her chin jutting forward. It would make my insides shrivel if she glowered at me like that.

He shakes his head and changes his tenor. “Thank you. Will she be okay?”

Kava puts two fingers to Alouette’s wrist for a few moments looks into her eyes. “She will be fine. She’s just exhausted.” She helps the limp Ellerian to the sleeping mat Dayson laid out for her. Kava mutters a few questions and Alouette dips her head.

Dayson spouts orders at us as though we are his little army: set up a perimeter, clear those bushes back, build the tents, gather firewood, make a fire, tie the dragon between those trees. His tone bothers me more than the tasks themselves.

It’s probably best to keep my mouth shut, but it seems we are going through a lot of trouble to fix up a place we are only using for one night.

“Ease up, military man,” Hollis says.

Kava lays out several sleeping mats under the tent and lies down on one of them in a heap of wet and dirty skirts.

Hollis finishes stacking wood in the pit I scraped out for a fire. She saunters to the dragon. *We already unloaded the packs and took off the saddle…what is she doing?*

She unties the straps from between the trees and walks Tristeh over to the fire pit. She removes the muzzle and says, “Enflammer.”

Tristeh lowers her head and whimpers.

Hollis points to the wood and says again. “Enflammer.”

The dragon’s jaws unclench, and a long flame shoots from her mouth. It stretches across the camp, nearly reaching my tent. All the grass and dried leaves light on fire.

The blast startles Dayson as he hammers the last stake

for his tent. “What the bloody skies are you doing?”

Tristeh stops and Hollis dances her back between the trees, tying the straps around the tree trunks. Dayson insisted she be tied up at night, but he hasn't seen her rip a tree out of the ground like I have. I stifle a laugh as the pile of wood crackles and stays lit.

“See, she's useful after all.” Hollis strokes her giant, scaly pet.

Dayson stands with his hands on his hips and growls. I'm sure he is cursing at her inside his head. He tightens his lips and finishes pounding the stake with extreme force, and then drops the mallet on a metal pan near the fire with a loud clang. I cannot believe the amount of stuff he packed. I've never camped with so much…junk. Just give me a mat to sleep on and I'm good.

It will take several days to get to Balfour, but setting up camp like this every night will make it take longer. I hope we can get home in time. Maybe the assassin wasn't planning on leaving until the day before Ellery arrives at Balfour? Will the assassin will wait until the day of arrival? So many questions hammer through my head. *Who cares, as long as we beat him there.*

“Come and eeeeeeeeat!” Hollis shatters the tense silence. A startled Dayson pulls a dagger from his belt in a split second. I freeze, unsure of what to do. Then Hollis starts laughing. “Take it easy, Dayson. We are alone out here. No one followed us.” She gets louder and louder. “And no one can hear us.” Her voice echoes off the cliff face in the darkness.

“Shut your yippy mouth,” Dayson whispers with his

eyes as sharp as an arrowhead.

I cannot let him talk to her like that. "Come on, Dayson," I say. "She's right. No one followed us. We are clear of Ellery. We can relax."

"We can *not* relax." Dayson stomps closer with his dagger still poised in the air. "They aren't the only ones who could find us. There is a tribe of savages in these mountains who could find us at any moment."

My mouth goes slack. A tribe of people in our mountains? I didn't know that.

Dayson pulls a second dagger from his belt and darts into the dark woods, no doubt to check the perimeter. I run circles in my memory. Was there always a tribe in this mountain range stretching to Balfour? I shake off a startled feeling.

HOMELESS 13

LEDGER

The sun beats down on us, when a cloud isn't hiding it from view. It's been a long morning of flying over the most beautiful fall colors I've seen. I peer from side to side, soaking in their brilliance. I am tucked between Hollis and Kava on Tristeh's back. The wind makes me tired, constantly streaming across my ears. Eventually my eyes dry and I close them.

A voice startles me. "Time for a rest," Dayson shouts from below us.

Hollis doesn't move. I shake her shoulder and she jerks. Was she sleeping while flying a dragon?

"They need a break," I say, pointing to our two winged friends descending toward a hillside with a clear stream trickling between boulders.

Hollis leans forward. Tristeh takes the cue and nose dives for a few terrifying moments. She leans to the right, and Tristeh swirls round and round until we reach the ground where Dayson and Alouette landed.

I unclip Kava and myself from the saddle. After Kava

climbs down, I make my stiff body slide off the dragon's back, down the wing, until my boots hit the dirt with a thud. Stretching my arms to the sky, I hear a giggle behind me. Before I have time to move, Hollis slides down and knocks my feet out from under me, sending my head flying backward and onto the hard ground. Stars flash in my vision for a moment. When I catch my breath, I yell, "Hollis! That hurt."

Her hand is over her mouth, trying to hide a mischievous smile.

"I'm so sorry, Ledge." She stifles a laugh. "I thought you heard me coming. I imagined you jumping up, and then I would slide right underneath you."

"Why would you ever think I would do that?" I stare at her blank-faced and wait for the inevitable giggling-walk-away.

"Oh, yeah, I forgot you're not fun," Hollis laughs. "I guess I must have enough fun for the both of us." She offers me a hand, and I don't accept it. I stand up on my own and ruffle the dirt and leaves from my hair, flinging them on her as she squeals in delight.

The dirt hits her in the face and some gets in her mouth. She spits it out with a giggle. I brush off her cheek and pull her to my side to escort her to the stream. "You're a crazy twillerbird."

"Thank you," she says, sliding an arm around my torso.

Walking by her side, I ask, "Did you fall asleep on Tristeh?"

"Maybe." She peeks up at me with a shrug and a grin.

I'm pretty sure I don't feel safe riding on the back of

a dragon while Hollis is awake, let alone asleep. But I'm unsure how to tell her without sounding like a complete wimp, so I chuckle instead.

Dayson stands knee deep in the stream, and Alouette dips her toes in the cool waters from a nearby boulder.

Hollis and I kick our shoes off and join them. She wades in, gasping at the cold. She wobbles and grabs my arm for support. I take a few steps in, which is as far as I'm willing to go.

Kava sits on a low boulder upstream filling an armful of water pouches. One after the other, she dips them in. I can hear the *glug, glug, glug* from here. Her eyebrows are low, and her stare is far off. No doubt thinking about Tolliver. She hasn't said much since we left. Normally, she finds plenty of reasons to boss me around.

"At this speed, we will be in Balfour in no time," Dayson says. His bold voice echoes down the watercourse.

"How soon do you think?" Hollis leaves me behind and wades out near Dayson.

"Two days."

"Wow! Ledger," Hollis flashes me a bright smile, making my whole body tingle. "We will be home in two days! Woohoooo!" Her cheers echo all around us.

Her joy is infectious. *Home.* The thought makes excitement flow from my heart, to my head, to my toes, and back again. "Woohooooo," I join in her cheers. Our voices increase in chaos and volume with every echo and every shout.

We hoot together until Kava screams over our voices, "Enough!" She throws the water pouches on the bank and stomps off into the woods.

I bite my lips closed. Hollis has the same expression on her face, wide eyed and mouth clamped shut. A giggle sneaks out.

"You should go see if she is okay," Hollis says.

"What? Why me?" I'm incredulous she would suggest it. "She hates me. You're a girl, you should talk to her."

She scoffs with a weird throaty sound. "Fine," she says, shoulders drooping. "In a minute. Let's give her time to cool off. No sense getting yelled at twice."

I laugh because it sounds like something I would say.

I take a seat on the edge of the flat boulder next to Alouette. "Hi."

"Hi," she says. It's the first time she's spoken to me since Dayson carried her to our room. The first time since her… execution.

"How are you feeling?" I gaze up at her. The sun bounces through the ends of her brown hair, making it shimmer a dark golden color. Her heart-shaped face almost forms a smile.

"I'll be okay," she says, playing with a handful of fallen yellow leaves. She bends them and folds them between her small fingers. Her fiddling reminds me of the harvests we spent together as kids.

"I'm glad you're alive," I say, trying not to choke on my words when the sadness sneaks up on me.

Her chin quivers. "I'm glad to say, me too."

I sit in silence, unsure of what to say next.

Alouette continues, "I gave up. I didn't fight what was coming—at the trial, or even when they finally pushed me off Ellery." Her voice wavers at the last word.

Kava saunters out of the woods. She joins us next to the trickling water but doesn't look at any of us, still angry and red-faced. She places the water pouches on the boulder.

"They tied my wings so tight. And when I started to fall I couldn't move, even if I wanted to." She pauses and her throat bobs. "But I didn't even try to fly."

I felt a presence beside me as Hollis leans against me, enraptured by Alouette's words.

"Suddenly I wasn't falling anymore. When I opened my eyes—" Alouette connects with Dayson. "I was disappointed." She shakes her head, tears streaming down her face. "I'm sorry."

I reach out a hand, placing it on her knee.

Hollis mirrors my actions and places her hand next to mine on Alouette's warm leg.

Alouette gazes across the water at Dayson, "I almost told you to let me go." She lets out the saddest cry and admits, "I wanted to die." She puts her face in her hands.

Dayson weaves his way across the stream to her. "I wouldn't have let you go, even if you begged me."

She peers up at him, squinting against the bright sky, and says, "When you took me into the water, it washed it all away. It was so cold and painful, it drowned all those thoughts. When I came out of the water, I was relieved to be alive. And sad for having wished for death. And terrified it almost happened."

Dayson reaches for her. He slides his hands down her shoulders to her arms and lifts her hands gently in both of his.

For a few quiet moments, they gaze at each other. I grow

uncomfortable, as if Hollis and I are invading an intimate moment.

Alouette sighs, “And now I’m homeless.” Her eyes flit toward me. “We are taking you home, and I realized I don’t have a home anymore. What am I going to do once we’ve brought you back to Balfour?”

I raise my eyebrows. She can’t return to Ellery—she’s supposed to be dead. “You can stay in Balfour,” I offer.

She gives a sad smile and blinks slowly. “Your people would never receive me.”

My mind starts reeling with the idea of Alouette living in Balfour. Would they accept her? Would they send her away? Would they execute her?

She shakes her head and peers off downstream.

“All we can do is try.” I smile at the idea.

14

RELIEF

TOLLIVER

Morning brings the echo of the washmaids scrubbing and stirring. My knees ache and my shoulder has a sharp pain that could use a good stretch. I push back the fabrics hanging over the table and peer into the darkness. A small amount of light spills through the doorway from the adjoining washroom. Several voices echo off the stone walls. A woman sings to the rhythm of swishing water.

I sneak out from underneath the table and stand slowly, stretching my hands high in the air. Rising up on my tiptoes, I feel several bones pop, and my entire body is relieved to move again. Suddenly, the urge to use the privy hits me. I look around. *What can I go in?* I breathe through the growing pain. With nothing but heaps of cloth all around, I pull back the curtain of my small bunk. *Where is that box with food in it?*

I search around for the candle I had last night. A sharp pain shoots through my bladder. I stop and bounce for a moment. I sweep the bunk for the candle with an outstretched hand. Down by the foot of the sleeping mat, I hit something metal, round, with a lid.

Did he really sneak a chamber pot down here? I pull it out and hold it in the small bit of light drifting in through the door. *Yes, he did! Thank you, glorious Belamy, old pal!*

I relieve myself into the chamber pot. I've never had to go so bad in all my days. Covering the pot with the lid, I slide it beneath a rumpled heap of woven blankets.

Someone scuffles by the doorway of the storeroom, and I dive beneath the table, glad I'm dressed in all black. Pulling the dangling fabrics tightly closed, I lie back on a rumple of sheets and listen to the unfamiliar sounds of this place. I'm relieved no one enters this dark, dank room.

Kava must be so angry with me this morning. She'll wake without me, in some foreign place in the mountains. The thought of her sad face makes my chest ache. I punch the wall with a thud. The pain in my knuckles relieves the one in my soul.

"Kava, I'm so sorry," I whisper. Her eyes haunt me as I eat some of the wrapped meat and a few bites of the cheese lump in the box. I ration it. Who knows when Belamy will return?

It is difficult to gauge time down here because sunlight doesn't reach this place, just the glow from the torches. Staying hidden this long reminds me of playing a game of Seekers with Angus. No Ellerians to avoid, no threat of death. Just fun. He almost always won. He was great at finding me but even better at hiding.

I started making rules to make sure I didn't lose as badly: stay inside the castle, no closing doors, nothing above level two, and the seeker must touch the hider. He was great at finding the best spots, like the smithy shop, underwater in the kitchen trough, and one time, he climbed one of the chandeliers in the throne room. I silently chuckle at the thought of finding him hanging upside down from a chandelier with his curly red hair dangling wildly.

But he is gone now.

My shaky breath echoes inside the small space. Leaning my head on the wall, I mourn Angus, my cousin, my best friend. The sadness wraps around me tighter than the darkness of my hiding place.

ONCOMING JAWS 15

LEDGER

When we descend to the ground for the night, tired to the bone, Tristeh walks away, wings sagging in exhaustion. I'm grateful for her wings. I wish I had my own. I imagine mine would be as white as Alouette's but as large as Dayson's—feathery and expanding side to side, twice my height. I wonder if they are heavy and daunting. But then again, it's normal for the Sky People. I guess it would be like wondering if my own legs are heavy and daunting.

Tristeh circles a leafy spot among the trees and plops to the ground.

Dayson starts in again with shouting orders. "Set up yours here. Alouette and I will set up over there." He paces to a flat spot on the ground in a mess of fallen orange leaves. The tree above him swishes in the wind and dying leaves fall helplessly around him. Alouette rolls out a mat. Her wings hang lifelessly. She crumples into a pile on the ground almost the same way Tristeh did.

"It isn't going to rain, so I don't see a need for a roof,"

Hollis says, trying to get out of work.

"Just do it," Dayson commands. He grabs the metal pan and starts scraping the ground for a place to start a fire. "Gather some wood, Ledger."

I walk past Hollis standing with her arms crossed, not unrolling the tent. Wishing I were invisible, I duck my head and slip into the woods.

I kick clumps of wet leaves and pine needles, glad to be clear of all the demands of Dayson and conflict with Hollis. The night air is cool on my skin, and I marvel at the last few fireflies blinking above the dying grass. Bushes rustle up ahead and I halt. *Something's out here.* Wild stories fill my head. A beast, a mountain lion, a jaycoon? Or is it the savages Dayson was talking about?

Kava steps out from behind a tall bush, brushing her hands down the front of her rumpled dress. The sleeves are ratty, and the bottom hem is frayed. "Ledger," she says, startled.

"Kava."

We halt in place. I refuse to be the first to say anything of substance. I'm sure she blames me for Tolliver staying behind, and there's no need to poke a rabid jaycoon. Her face softens as she walks away. I may have just caught her doing her business. My cheeks warm and I grit my teeth against the need to apologize. She traipses off toward the campsite, and I take a good long while to gather wood.

By the time I emerge from between the colorful trees, the sun has dropped below the horizon and cast us all in graying light. I dump the logs in the center of the dirt circle.

"Hollis?" She peers up from her resting place on her

mat next to Kava, under nothing but overhanging branches. She didn't put up our tent after all. Tension pulls me in two directions. Dayson will probably tell me do it. Will Hollis be mad at me if I comply?

I arrange the firewood, ignoring the buzz of stress in my head.

"Can you light this?" I ask Hollis. Tristeh is tied between two trees again, still wearing a saddle. Hollis is being lazy. Scanning the camp, I can't find Dayson. His tent is up. Alouette is sleeping beyond the open flap. "Where's Dayson?"

Then I hear it.

Skittering.

I dismiss the shiver clawing up my back.

Hollis makes her way over to Tristeh, our live flint and stone.

Another scamper, closer this time. My stomach leaps into my throat

"Dayson?" I call. *Is he messing with us?*

I am poised and waiting for the next sound. Maybe I confused the sound with my fears. Maybe it was Dayson running a circle around us. Maybe—

Rustling leaves.

The snap of a twig.

A howl from above us on the mountain.

A long, pregnant silence waiting to slice through the night.

A low growl emerges from Hollis's dragon.

Then a large ball of gray fur slams into the clearing on top of Dayson. They roll around in the dirt and leaves, then a knife flashes as he stabs the wolf over and over.

Stunned by the ferocity, I am frozen, except my racing heart.

Hollis reaches the dragon as the leather straps snap from around the trees. Tristeh darts in front of Hollis to protect her from sharp teeth and claws. The sound of Tristeh's loud caw yanks me out of my panic.

Stop freezing, Ledger! I shake myself free of the fear holding me hostage. *Do something!*

Screaming comes from the other side of camp where Alouette was resting. I scramble from the surrounding wolves to the brown tent on the other side of the bonfire. I pull back the flap to find a black wolf approaching Alouette through the other side of the tent. She shrinks away from the bared teeth. One of Dayson's bags is lying open and a blade peeks out. I grab it as Alouette scrambles toward me. Yanking her from the tent, I yell "Fly!" Her terror-filled face turns skyward as she leaps. Her tired wings carry her wearily to the trees.

"Kava!" I call. "Where's Kava?"

"Over there," Alouette says as she lands on a high branch.

Dayson is off the ground, covered in blood, and grabbing Kava around the waist. He bounds into the air and soars to Alouette. I'm relieved they are safe.

Growling comes from several directions. I whirl around to find two—no, three wolves surrounding me. The first wolf leaps at me as I hear, "Enflammer."

The beast hits me full force, and sharp claws dig into my thigh. Slashing at it with the small blade in my hand, I fall to the ground. The weight of the animal knocks the air from my lungs. For a brief moment, I can't breathe. The wolf rolls to the side and snaps at my neck. I put an arm up to protect myself from the oncoming jaws, and it grabs hold of the back of my upper arm. Sharp teeth pierce my thick coat, digging into my skin.

The heat of the dragon's breath keeps me from blacking out. The light from its flame keeps my eyes open, and I catch a glimmer of the pearl-handled knife in my other hand. I jab the wolf over and over until the pressure on my arm eases. I keep stabbing and stabbing as tears spill from my eyes and rage growls from my mouth. *No! You will not kill my friends!* I think the words so loudly they gradually come out of my mouth.

"No! *Nooooo!"*

I push the lifeless beast off my body and leap up. *Hollis, where is my dear Hollis?* Fire almost consumes the camp. The dragon blows another flame across the nearest wolf. It doesn't move, but its fur curls and melts. Hollis is on Tristeh's back cooing at her. Another flame. I swallow a metallic taste as I realize there are four dead, scorched wolves all around the area. Tristeh paces from one corpse to the other and back, blowing flames onto their singed fur. The tent and sleeping mats are ablaze, the grass and fallen leaves all around are sending up tiny sparks floating into the sky past the three people hiding in the trees.

"Stop!" Dayson says as he flies down from the trees. "Stop that beast right now!"

Hollis frowns and shrugs. Another flame leaps from the dragon's mouth. The fire scorches a dead wolf and ignites a group of bushes on the edge of the woods.

"Stupid, bloody dragon!" Dayson lands near his burning tent, cutting the rope holding it up. Flinging it to the side, he digs through the scorched cloth which used to be his packs. He grumbles and growls, anger echoing around the small camp. "Why, why, why?" He gasps and picks up a bow, shaking off bits of ash and burning burlap. Digging further, he pulls out a quiver of arrows. A yellow flame snakes down the side of the quiver. He dumps out the arrows and stomps on the quiver, extinguishing it.

I'm not sure approaching a panicked dragon is the best idea. It's only been a few heartbeats since the flames stopped. I take a few steps in Tristeh and Hollis's direction. "Are you okay?" I ask.

She leaps from the dragon's back, to the wing, and onto the dirt. The expression on her face makes me shake. Her eyes are as round as a full moon and mouth agape in horror.

She runs toward me across the charred ground. "Ledger, you're bleeding!"

I feel nauseous and dizzy. Blood drips from my blurry right hand. I drop the knife and attempt to lift my left hand to search for the source of blood, but pain slashes through my upper arm. I fall to my knees as Hollis reaches me.

"Breathe, Ledger, breathe through it." She coos at me the way she speaks to her dragon. Inhaling the smell of smoke and ash, I remember the day on the island when we went over the volcano. All of the ash everywhere. We survived.

Dayson shouts something in the distance and Alouette replies from the trees.

"Kava, help me," Hollis shouts. She squeezes my arm, pressing hard on my hands. "He's bleeding… a lot." I hear the stress in her voice.

"Dayson, help me. I can't carry Kava by myself." Alouette's distant voice calls.

He groans and the sound of his wings fill my ears. Blackness claws at the edge of my vision. I try to stay conscious, focusing on Dayson and Alouette carrying Kava down from a tall pine tree. The smoke curls around them as they descend.

Kava too digs through the flames. She grabs a handful of things and rushes to kneel in the dirt with me.

"I'm sorry, Kava," I say as her face fills my view. Straight brown hair down to her elbows. Light brown eyes, like acorns. They are sad. Sad eyes.

She shushes me.

Dayson dashes back and forth. I hear water sloshing and sizzling flames. He's trying to salvage as much of his junk as he can. "You idiot dragon!" he screams.

Hollis removes her hands from my bleeding arm.

Kava says, "Let me see," as she pries my fingers from my wounds.

"Tolliver shouldn't have left you," I say. My tongue feels fat and my words sound weird.

She shakes her head. "Quiet, Ledger." She unbuttons my coat and slides it off my arm.

"I'll get you home. I'll make sure." My throat closes on its own and I hold my breath to keep from throwing up.

Her brows are pinched together and serious. She rips my sleeve off and presses it tightly on my arm. "Hollis, find some sap. Pine sap." she says.

Hollis races off. I watch her golden hair bounce into the

tree line. My vision blurs.

Cold water pours over the puncture wounds. The coolness refreshes me. Breathing through the pain, I gape at the red all over my arm, and my body swerves to the side.

“Don’t look, Ledger,” Kava whispers. “It’s better if you don’t look.” The sound of her voice calms me. She rips at the bottom of her dress, all the way around, making it several hands shorter. Flicking the blood-soaked sleeve to the ground, she presses the new cloth to my skin and squeezes hard.

I moan at the sharp pain.

“I’m trying to stop the bleeding,” Kava says.

Dayson grabs a long branch and swats Tristeh. “Stupid dragon!” He hits her again and again, pushing her back, out of his way.

“Stop it, Dayson, you slack bucket of cabbage!” Hollis yells from somewhere in the woods.

He scours the ground, kicking ashes back and forth, ignoring her commands.

She returns with a handful of hard sap globs. “Is this enough? They are like rocks.”

“Heat them,” Kava says.

Hollis dodges for the metal pan. The sap rocks jingle as she holds them over a random flame consuming our campsite.

“Where is it?” Dayson shouts. “What did you do with it?”

Alouette mumbles something I can’t hear.

“You were the last one in there!” he says.

Again, inaudible words from Alouette.

Kava checks my arm. “Good, the bleeding has slowed.”

Hollis brings the warm pan, and Kava smears the melted sap onto my arm. The yellow-brown substance seals the half circle of puncture wounds on the back of my upper arm. It's warm and soothing. I'm breathing again and seeing straight.

Dayson blows air from between his tight lips and runs a hand through his hair. He collects everything that hasn't burned and is holding only one pack. He hits Tristeh one more time, tosses the stick, and stomps off into the woods. Of the six packs we brought, we are down to one pack of supplies. All the sleeping mats and tents are gone.

Alouette stands with her hands open and peers into the flames.

We need to get home. And soon.

GONE 16

LEDGER

I wake in the leaves, alone and cold. The sun peeks through the treetops but isn't strong enough to warm me.

"Where'd they go?" Hollis's voice makes my ears hurt. *Why is she talking so loud?*

Irritated, I roll over to find Kava and Hollis sitting beside the fire eating something. I inhale the smell of grilled meat. The pain from my arm wakes me faster than usual. I wish I could fall back asleep. I close my eyes in protest of the morning.

Kava swallows her bite and says, "They found a stream and are filling our water pouches." I open my eyes enough to see her point at the peak to the south and take another bite off a bone in her hand.

My stomach growls. The stupid thing.

Against my better judgment, I pry myself off the ground. I must have slept with my mouth wide open because my tongue is dry. I move it around and lick the roof of my mouth.

"What are you eating?" I don't really care what it is—I'll eat anything.

"Wolf," Hollis says.

I half gasp and half laugh. "Really?" I have never eaten wolf.

"Tristeh is a pretty good cook." Kava smiles and I'm a bit wary of why. She is being pleasant. Almost nice. I look around, waiting for something odd to happen. Back in Balfour it would have been a moment where Tolliver or Angus would throw something at me and expect me to catch it. Of course, my arms never obey at moment's notice, and whatever they threw would hit me in the chest, or the crotch, or flat in the face. I miss those awkward moments. Angus will never do that again. I choke back the grief surfacing as I take a seat on the log next to Hollis.

I grab a piece of meat out of the pan on the ground as Dayson and Alouette land on the other side of the fire. I bolt upright, flailing my arms, and my body immediately starts buzzing.

Hollis howls with laughter and Kava chuckles.

My face feels hot enough to cook an egg. I hate being startled.

"Good morning," Alouette says with a polite smile. She takes a seat beside me on the log and touches my back. "How are you feeling?"

Confused, I say, "I'm fine. How are you feeling?"

"I'm feeling better." She takes a deep breath as though she has a new vigor for life. "I think the more I fly, the better I feel. You know me, I need to fly, Ledger."

I know her? I scowl. It seems I haven't known her for two harvests. But it doesn't seem to matter to her. It is the first time she's said my name since before we were locked in prison. I used to hang on the chance she would smile at me, talk to me, or say my name. I lived for any moment with her. And now, she's just another person I know. It feels weird to let her go from my heart, even though I still want her to be safe and alive.

Deep in thought, I stare at her until Alouette says, "Where'd you go? You were off in crazyland again, weren't you?"

"No," I deny. "I'm not quite awake, yet."

"What's crazyland?" Hollis asks.

"You know, that daydreaming world he goes to when his face goes blank with thought." Alouette and Hollis giggle together, then turn and scrutinize me as if they're waiting for me to do it again.

I turn my eyes away and clear my throat. "What's Dayson doing?"

Alouette chuckles under her breath. It is a wonderful sound. She explains, "He can't find all the weapons he brought."

"He has more weapons?" Two daggers and a medium length sword in a black leather sheath hang from his belt as he rummages through the ashes and refuse. He has a bow and arrows, too. *What more does he need?* "Did he bring extra weapons for us or something?"

"I don't know," she says, rubbing her neck and making a pained face. "He's a little intense about his weapons."

"What did he lose?" I ask.

She shrugs.

I shout to Dayson. "What are you looking for?"

"My…" He scrapes through the ash around the remains

of his burned tent. “My knife.”

I remember the blade I used to protect myself. I kept it near me as I slept last night, and I pull it from the back of my trousers. “Oh, you mean this?” I hold it up, revealing the pearl handle with a beautiful inlay of a silver bird with a twig in its mouth. He stomps over and snatches it out of my hands.

“That’s mine,” he says as he wipes it with his long black sleeve.

I am startled by his abruptness and don’t know what to say. He is definitely intense about his weapons.

“I…umm…thank you,” I say. “It saved my life. I found it when I was waking Alouette. And then the wolf jumped on me.” I peer at my empty hands, swallow hard, and say, “I would really like to hold on to it, if you don’t mind.”

Dayson stops and assesses me. His raging face relaxes. “Oh, I didn’t realize.”

“It all happened so fast,” I say feeling awkward and vulnerable, letting him see how much it bothered me to fight for my life. Dayson doesn’t seemed bothered at all that a wolf tried to kill him last night. There is barely a scratch on him. Jealousy presses on my skull, and I put a hand to my temple.

“You can have one of these,” he says pulling a dagger from his belt.

He hands it to me, a small, double blade with a black handle. *Where can I put it?*

He tries to insert the knife into the dagger holster, but it doesn’t fit right. He tries again and puts it in his pack instead. I don’t understand why he doesn’t let me keep that one and he can have this dagger, which fits perfectly in his belt.

"Where's Tristeh?" Hollis rises from beside me and walks to where I remember Tristeh curled up last night, several paces into the trees and beside a bush. Hollis reaches the spot and shakes the bush. "Tristeh!" she yells into the sky.

"Good riddance," Dayson mutters.

"Don't say that," Kava says, standing up, hands on her hips. "Without her, you'll have to carry us."

I gasp. We can't do this without Tristeh. My pulse races and I scramble to Hollis's side.

"Tristeh!" she calls.

"Tristeh!" I mimic.

We race through the woods, scanning the skies in search of her. But she is nowhere to be found. Tristeh is gone.

***

"If he didn't beat on Tristeh, we would be soaring over Balfour right now. He ran her off!" Hollis says, throwing another rock as we walk across a cliffside path. "Uh, he's such a jerk!"

By mid-afternoon, Dayson and Alouette take to the skies and leave us to get our feet dirty. I understand they don't walk a lot, but refusing to fly us to the next summit and ditching us? Not helpful.

Hollis throws the last stone up the cliff face on our left. "Tristeh!" she yells into the sky. Her voice echoes down the mountain, seeking out her dragon.

It would have been easier if we lost our dragon while

traveling over flat land. Now we have to hike up and down each mountain and every valley. I shove the frustration down into my gut and think about something else. My upper arm still hurts from the wolf bite. It pulsates with every step. But Kava's quick thinking with the sap, sealing it up, has made it bearable to keep moving.

"I don't mind that they're gone," Kava says. "I'm tired of that wretch anyway. I needed a break from him."

"You don't like him?" I ask.

"It's not about liking. He's just a bit…much."

I walk side-by-side between the girls. Hollis pauses to gather a handful of rocks, then scurries to catch up. We keep a good pace, not walking slow, but not jogging either.

Maybe Dayson's right. It could have taken the same amount of time to carry each person across each peak one by one. Not to mention it would exhaust him.

Kava holds bunches of her dress in her hands, making her skirts knee length so her long stride isn't hindered. "I've been meaning to ask if you know who the Ellerian royal is?"

Hollis tosses two stones before I answer, "I have three people in mind. But I have no idea who it really is."

"You're quite committed to saving someone who might already be murdered before we even get home." Kava's small boots crunch, crunch, crunch across the ground.

"I feel as though I set things in motion, and I have to right it before something bad happens," I say.

"You blame yourself for an assassin being sent to Balfour?" Kava swings her free hand. "That's ridiculous."

"I would blame myself after the fact. I keep getting stuck. I freeze. I don't act. And when I don't, bad stuff happens.

This time, I will act," I say.

"Well, that's not what I see at all." Kava's intense eyes meet mine. I'm confused when she says, "You are about the only one who does anything around here. I mean, you boarded Ellery, for skies' sake. You saved these people who keep rejecting you."

"It didn't seem to matter though," I say. "They didn't need *me* to get back to Ellery. They would have done it anyway."

"Not Alouette," Hollis interrupts. "She probably would have been killed alongside her tyrant king of a father."

"Not Dayson, his father and a handful of other Sky People," Kava says, holding her stomach.

I feel a rush of realization. *They really wouldn't be alive. They all would have died.* I take a big gulp of air as we crest the top of the mountain. We all stop at once. There are several drop-offs on the way down. Dayson is wrong. It would have been much better if he flew us.

"Holy hiccup, how are we going to do this?" Hollis asks.

Kava whimpers and clutches her stomach. She abruptly turns and throws up on the rocky ground.

"Oh goodness." Hollis reaches for her. "You afraid of heights?"

"No," Kava says. "I've been nauseous for a while. I just…" She wipes her mouth. "I hate puking. But I feel so much better now."

She heads down the other side. Hollis and I follow close behind. We have to reach the next peak by nightfall, where we will meet Dayson and Alouette.

"Tristeh!" Hollis calls. "Tristeh, come back!"

HOSTAGE 17

TOLLIVER

Enduring endless hours of stillness has never been more excruciating. It is hard to stay awake cramped in the smothering darkness and humidity of the laundry. Choking on the potent scents of lavender, lemon, and eucalyptus, I put a swath of fabric over my face for a while. The voices echoing through the cavernous laundry room all day irritate me, a constant reminder not to move from this scrunched space.

I drift in and out of consciousness to a familiar song. "I love you more than the sun; I love you more than the moon."

I dream of dancing with Kava. Her brown eyes so close to mine they are blurry. Her arms around me and her voice drifting through my ears. "I love you more than the sky; And the beautiful stars too."

I want to sing along but my head is heavy and my eyelids droop. I feel as if I am melting away from her as a loud crash startles me awake.

"Sorry," a washmaid shouts from the far end of the

laundry room. Laughter drifts in. Images of Kava are yanked away, leaving me feeling trapped.

A sharp pain radiates from my spine. I stretch to relieve the pinch and halt when a foot scuffs nearby. Rustling around. Someone digs through the fabric. Beyond the thin shield of gray linen overhanging my hiding place, a washmaid stands with white wings glowing in the light of a torch, and another picks through a stack against the opposite wall. Her dark wings blend with the hair hanging in her face.

"It doesn't have to be pretty, Hana. It's just for a few washrags," the woman with the torch says.

"I know, but some of this has mold on it."

The woman with the torch scoffs.

"Ah! Here you go, Ava. This will get you four or five decent rags." Hana hands her the cloth and says, "Hang the torch on the wall. I'm going to sort out some of this moldy stuff. Wash it. Or maybe burn it."

"Okay, I'll see you tomorrow."

"Tomorrow," she mutters. The other woman is long gone as Hana continues talking. "Tomorrow, when we have to do the same thing all over again."

She tosses piece after piece of moldy fabric in the middle of the room.

"Wash, wash, wash it."

Another piece flops onto the pile.

"Oh yuck!" she gasps and leaps back—landing against the table concealing me. It clangs against the wall and my curtains shudder. Her hand grips the gray linen panel covering half my hiding place. It comes loose and she pulls it up to cover her face as she gags.

Then I smell it and quickly cover my nose. Rotting carcass.

The worry of being found consumes my mind. She is too close.

"Whew! I love how no one takes care of anything down here. I have to do everything." Hana stomps her foot.

She rips the piece of linen the rest of the way off the table and heads to the dead thing in the corner. The bottom half of my hideaway is completely exposed. I scowl. *Of all the millions of rags in this room, she chooses that one!* While her back is turned, I slide my body behind the rest of the curtain and hold my breath—though my blood pounds loudly in my ears.

"Oh, ew!" She scoops up whatever dead thing she found and runs from the room.

What the heck could be rotting in here? It's not as if they have rats on this island in the sky.

I exhale, relieved she is gone. To keep all of my treasures out of sight, I quickly tuck them underneath a rumpled gray sheet: a small candle, my wooden food box that is almost empty, a water pouch with enough water in it to last another day, and flint that makes a *tink* sound against the box.

Pausing, I listen.

No one comes.

Pushing away my worries, I stick my body out just enough to grab something on the table above to shield me, in case she starts snatching more of my makeshift curtains. I can't be found here.

When I yank a green strip of cotton, part of the pile on the table comes tumbling down. Suppressing an angry groan,

I take a risk crawling all the way out of my hiding place, gather it all, and throw it back on top. I tuck a couple of yellowing panels over the opening and scramble undercover just as she saunters through the door.

I bite back the irritation that wants to come screaming out my throat. But she is beyond a thin veil, plopping a basket near her laundry pile. She scoops it all up and hefts the heavy basket off the floor, to her shoulder, and onto her head. As she nestles it on top of her brown hair, the pile topples from my table again.

Stupid precarious mess! Luckily my curtains stay intact.

She grunts, sets her basket on the floor, and shuffles over. I stay absolutely still. My lungs ache for air as I imagine worst. What will she do if she discovers me? Within arm's reach, she gathers the material from the dirty floor. It takes several armloads to get it all picked up. "Well, this is moldy too," she says.

My thoughts scream through my mind. *Please don't find me. I might have to do something terrible if I'm found. Even though I don't want to.*

"Oh!" Hana says, startling me. "There's a table under this mound." The curtains overhanging my bunk flutter as she sorts her way to the surface of the table. Then she lifts the gray curtain between us. I can't move. She might hear me.

I take shallow breaths as I stare at the front of her white apron over a ragged brown linen dress. She hums and tosses a few more pieces into the basket behind her. I bite my tongue, tasting blood. When a soft piece of feathery silk hits the ground at her feet, my fears become reality. She crouches to pick it up and her eyes meet mine. With a jolt, she gasps. Her wings span all the way out as if she is about to take flight. Before she can, I scramble out and push her into a mound. I grab her violently with sweaty hands, covering her mouth. She moans beneath my fingers digging into her face. Her brown eyes are wide with terror, making me feel evil. *She looks like Kava, and if anyone did this to Kava, I would...*

"Shhh! Please, please, please don't scream," I whisper, trying not to crush her.

Tears pool in her eyes.

"Aw, don't cry," I say under my breath. *This is wrong. Very wrong.*

She pants heavily through her nose, and I wait a moment for the agitation in my body to dissipate.

Feeling pity for the terrified washmaid, I say, "I'll remove my hand if you promise not to shout."

She nod-nod-nods.

I loosen my grip and lower my hands. Her white and brown speckled wings flap, and she shoves me away. When she bolts for the door, I regain my balance and dive for her. I muffle her scream before it emerges from her throat. I feel like such a monster. I don't want to grab her from behind, around her neck. But I do. I restrain the small woman and cover her mouth at the same time, until she stops struggling.

Heavy breaths funnel through her nose as big tears fall.

I've got to restrain her. Digging through a nearby pile with one hand, I search for a strip of cloth. I find one, tuck it in her mouth, and tie it behind her head. I lead her to the back corner of the storeroom and force her to sit on a pile of dark fabrics. Shame claws at my gut, and I remove my hands and back away.

Her wings splay out awkwardly on either side of her cowering body. Wrapping her arms around herself, she says something into the material in her mouth. It sounds like a question.

“I’m not going to hurt you,” I say, assuming she fears for her safety. I hide my clenched fists behind my back, trying to relax.

She blinks away a few tears. Another muffled question. Hoping to calm her, I say, “I’m just stowing away. For now.”

She shakes her head, as if it wasn’t her question. Her little brows push together in fear as she turns away from me. I feel like a horrible thug. Frustration digs at the back of my head. I can’t believe I took a hostage. *What am I doing? I’m better than this.*

“I can’t let you go unless I know you won’t tell anyone I’m here.” Rubbing my pant legs, I try to wipe the sweat and guilt from my hands. I groan. *Skies, Belamy, hurry up!*

She cries for a little while, as I arrange more curtains over my shelter. I must make sure she doesn’t leave. I’m not a harsh or cruel person, but this makes me feel like I am. A shiver runs up my back.

She mumbles something again—more angry than afraid this time. I pretend to ignore her as I extinguish the torch on the cold floor and crawl under the table. Belamy is going to have to find me a new hiding place.

PLUMMETING 18

LEDGER

I bolt upright, startled awake by Hollis's screams. Heart pounding at an alarming rate, I scan for her. An arm's length from a dying fire, one tendril of smoke snakes up to the pale morning sky.

I scramble to my feet, dizzy and confused. Kava is a few paces away, still sleeping. She turns her head away from the ruckus, covering her eyes with her arm.

Screams come again, with piercing laughter and unintelligible words. Dayson sits up abruptly and glances at me, confused. Alouette stirs. It's odd she isn't lying near him. She's on the far side of the campsite from where I saw her last night.

I run with wobbly legs into the trees, tripping over roots and a rotten log on the way up the incline.

"Where were you?" Hollis screeches. I make it over the crest of the hill and into a field where an enormous dragon stretches her wings and bobs her head in response to the little blonde girl with her hands on her hips.

"Hollis," I croak. She spins to meet my gaze.

"Ledger! Look!" she squeals. "It's Tristeh. She's back!"

I squint at them and rub my tired head. I should be excited, but the weight of morning drowns my senses. "Great," I say with a monotone voice and walk away, colliding with Dayson. His shoulder hits me in the neck.

"You—are not allowed anywhere near her!" Hollis shouts at him.

I stop my retreat.

"Fine by me," Dayson replies, rubbing his neck. "Keep it under control, and I will have no problem."

"She was protecting us. You can't blame her for that."

"You're right, I don't. I blame *you*!" Dayson punches the wind.

My gut tightens as I step between him and Hollis.

"Me?" Hollis screeches. "Without her, we'd be walking day after day."

"*You* would be walking—wingless girl!"

"Shut up, Dayson!" she yells.

He groans, throws up his hands, and walks away. I wrap my arms around Hollis's stiff frame.

"What is his problem?" She huffs and refuses my hug, pushing me away. "I thought he was here to help us. You should send him home now."

"Why would I send him away?" My mind sputters in an attempt to catch up to the reality that Dayson is being harsh.

"We don't need him to take us home," Hollis says. "We know which way to go. And Tristeh is back, saddle and all." She squints in anger, little fists bunching. Hollis anger levels scare me more than any man or dragon. The First Level is mixture of seething dirty looks and gnashing of teeth. Level Two brings blurting meanness so you know she's mad. Level Three involves high pitched screams and fists that feel like getting hit will tiny hammers. She may be well into Level Two anger, and I'm not awake enough to handle it if she reaches Level Three. My hands wrap around her cold fists, taming the wildcat.

"It's not about him. It's about Alouette. We must find a place for her to go," I say.

Hollis's fingers loosen as her intensity dissipates.

"If we stick together, Alouette will be able to come live with us in Balfour. Dayson wants the same thing. He wants to see her safe. We can put up with him to save someone's life, right?" I raise my eyebrows at her.

Her head bobs.

Wary blue eyes meet mine as I say, "Your baby is back. Don't let Dayson ruin it for you."

She smiles and bites her lip. I pull her in for a brief hug. Then she runs to her dragon and hugs her around the knee. "Let's go," Hollis says.

It doesn't take long for me to fetch Kava. Coming back from the edge of the trees, she is wiping her mouth.

"Did you throw up?" I ask. She groans and walks past me toward the field. "Maybe eating that wolf was a bad idea."

She moans as she swishes her mouth with water and spits. "If I have to heave again, we'll need to land pretty quickly."

"Ew," I mumble, imagining her vomiting all down my back.

We waste no time mounting the dragon and taking to

the skies. Feet aching from an entire day of walking, I'm so relieved to be soaring again. Hollis steers the red beast toward the east. The morning sun is warm and glaring in our eyes. Below, the mountains zoom by. I shake my head at the thought of walking all that terrain. Hollis jerks, encouraging Tristeh to fly faster. She relaxes into the saddle only after we are in the lead, ahead of Dayson and Alouette.

***

On a hilltop between several high peaks, I stand with my face to the oncoming winds. The growl of thunder breaks the silence between us. All afternoon we've been trying to outrun a line of dark clouds. It consumes the sky, mile by mile, gaining on the speed of Tristeh's powerful wings. We needed to stop, to eat, rest, and refill our water pouches.

"We aren't going to beat that storm," I say, pointing at the dark line in the sky. "It's coming too fast."

"We can outrun it," Dayson says.

Hollis stands with her face to the wind. "Can't we just fly above it?"

"It's a big storm. The clouds look really high," I say, shaking my head.

"I don't know, but surely they aren't higher than Ellery." Hollis asks Dayson, "Right?"

Alouette sleeps in a swath of brown grass tucked underneath a clump of underbrush, reminding me of when we first met as children. She was caught in a bunch of shrubs and vines, and I cut her loose. I remember my shock when she bolted in the air above me, white wings holding her high in the air. I don't know what made her stoop to the ground and trust me. But ever since then, nothing has been normal. We were fast friends, flying together, keeping secrets, and falling in love. Since boarding Ellery and taking part in her world full time, each tie from my heart to hers has been cut and retied in friendship.

"It has been catching up with us all day." Kava's voice rips through my daydream. She hands out water pouches and we all drink together, watching the dark rim of clouds in the distance.

"I say we search for a cave or somewhere to hide for the night." I scan our path to the east, to Balfour.

"I think we keep going and fly above this thing." Dayson crosses his arms and steps out of my peripheral vision.

Kava has a question in her eyes. Hollis glances at me too. My heart echoes the approaching thunder.

"Why are you looking at me?" I ask.

"You're our leader, Ledger," Hollis says.

She doesn't flinch. She isn't joking, but I laugh anyway.

"I— We don't have a leader," I say, trying to hide my fear.

"We're going to get above this thing," Dayson says.

Another roll of thunder peals through the air, and goose flesh rises on my arms. Tristeh shrieks. Her feet stomp, rumbling the earth beneath us.

"What do you want to do?" Hollis asks me.

Kava answers, "I want to keep going, but..." With her face to the sky, her words trail off. "We are almost home, I can feel it. But I'm not sure if it's safe. We can wait until the storm passes, if you want."

“No,” Dayson says.

“Ledger, what do you think?” Hollis turns her back on him.

“No!” Dayson yells.

“Shut up! We are voting,” Hollis shouts waving a hand in the air. “We heard you. You voted no. You don’t have to yell it.”

Dayson growls and walks away. He mutters, “…doesn’t know what’s good for her.”

“Ledger?” Hollis leans into me. She pulls my face in her direction with both hands. “Hello?”

“I don’t know. I can’t decide.” My insides are torn between not wanting to make waves with Dayson, needing to stay alive, and the desperation of wanting to just get home already. All the conflicting reasons swirl in my stomach.

She lets go of my face. “Let’s ask Alouette.”

A gust knocks me backward as she and Kava scurry down the hill. The trees bend and sway in the force of the rising winds. I don’t want to stop. I really don’t. I want to get home, make sure they aren’t in danger, and sleep until all this trouble is behind me. I also don’t think we can beat this storm. But I don’t want to go against Dayson. He’s brought us this far.

A bolt of lightning startles me, stinging my eyes. After several heartbeats, the thunder follows behind it.

Dayson’s low voice fills the air. “We should get a move on if we want to get above it and cover some ground. We have a lot to make up for, because of yesterday.”

“Fine,” I agree. “Let’s just fly.” Kava shakes her head at me. Hollis bounces and claps her fingers quietly. She seems excited to outrun a storm, which doesn't make it any better.

"Let's go, Ledger," Dayson says. He closes the lid on his water pouch and hooks it to his belt. "Storms that dark mean they are dense. Get above it as fast as you can. Don't look back, just move."

"Should Alouette ride with us?" I ask.

"She will be fine," he says. "No sense weighing down the dragon."

"Fine." I follow Kava and Hollis to Tristeh's side.

"Mind if I ride in the middle?" Kava asks.

I raise my brows at her. "All right."

Tristeh lowers a wing and we climb up one after the other, experts after so many days of travel.

"We have time to find a cave and wait it out," Kava says, strapping in behind Hollis.

Dayson grumbles and stomps away. I secure myself behind Kava.

"Fly, Tristeh!" Hollis says. The dragon's wings swipe at the air, and we bound into the sky in the vigorous wind.

Dayson jiggles Alouette's shoulder. She stretches and rises to her feet. Dayson's mouth is moving as he points at us in the sky. Their wings spread and lift them into the gray skies.

For a while it seems as if we are outrunning the storm clouds until I feel the little hairs on the back of my neck stand up and a loud crash rattles me. Tristeh thrusts downward and Hollis screeches, "No, Tristeh, up! Up!" Tristeh flies erratically against Hollis's prodding to keep flying. "Higher, old girl, higher." Hollis's voice is sucked back into the wind.

Behind us, beyond Tristeh's long tail, the afternoon sky

reaches for me like a dark hand. I cringe. *We're not going to make it.* It's taking too long to gain the height we need. Dread clenches my stomach tight.

"Come on, Hollis, get above it," I yell above the wind.

A crack of thunder drowns out Hollis's response. She is bending forward with her hands on Tristeh's scales, then leans back hard against Kava.

"Lean back," Kava says with her hair in my face.

I join them, and the dragon's wings dig into the air, propelling us upward. Hollis laughs in delight as we all bend forward again, holding on for dear life as we ascend higher than we've ever been.

Higher than Ellery.

Behind us, Alouette and Dayson's wings work the air, pushing them farther and farther into the sky. Darkness engulfs the place from where we launched.

Lightning flashes again, and thunder follows directly behind. Hollis doesn't let Tristeh level out. The air is so thin, it doesn't feel like there is enough.

The storm encroaches faster now that we're not running *from* it. It rolls and consumes. Just when I think we won't make it out of the dark wisps, Tristeh's wings propel us over the dark edge of the clouds. Below, I search for Alouette and Dayson. They are gone within the darkness.

The top of the storm isn't flat, like I imagined it would be. We climb through layer upon layer of charged and churning clouds. Above us are mushroom-shaped bursts, glowing orange and red. The lightning zaps between them and into the blackness below.

Moments later, Alouette and Dayson dart above the bulk

of the storm.

Static prickles my neck, and a bolt of lightning slashes at us as we try to outrun its skyward-reaching claws. The girls scream and Tristeh screeches.

Hollis prods her to fly higher. We lean together, and Tristeh's whimper whips past us.

We rise higher and higher, above the angry, blinking supercell.

"This isn't going to work," Kava yells. I feel her rib cage expand and contract over and over.

There has to be a top to this storm. The clouds are higher than I first thought, and a loud boom rattles me. Tristeh replies to the thunder with another shriek.

The storm is upon us and gaining speed. Hollis is fully focused on dodging agitating plumes. A lightning bolt claps right ahead of us and Tristeh jolts. All three of us lurch to the side. Thank the skies for our straps, or we'd all be falling to our death. We work our butts to the middle of Tristeh's back. The blanket underneath me is askew and pinches my inner thigh against the hard scales.

Hollis settles back into the saddle and I tap her shoulder. When she looks at me, I point to the fading blue sky above. If she can get us above this mess, we can level out and enjoy the rest of the flight into the evening hours. We all lean back again, signaling to Tristeh to ascend.

Several wing-beats below, Alouette's brow glistens with sweat. She's presses a hand to her chest as it gets harder to work her wings through the thin air.

I hold tighter to Kava in front of me, pressing into her as we ascend. I crane my neck to look down and behind.

Alouette's wings falter, then she catches herself.

"Alouette!" I yell and point, hoping Dayson notices. He is between us, flying higher and harder, face set in an angry scowl.

I reach for Hollis. *Tap, tap, tap.* She leans, and levels the dragon and turns toward me. I point below and say, "Alouette."

Without a second thought, Hollis leans to the side. Tristeh responds by flattening out her wings and soaring to the right. I lose sight of Alouette for a split second.

When Alouette comes into view again, both of her wings have collapsed and she plummets to the ground.

Hollis screams and leans forward. Tristeh dives to our falling friend.

TOGETHER 19

LEDGER

My stomach lurches into my throat as we slice through the air in a nauseating nose dive. Hollis presses forward, and Kava leans onto her back, face to the wind. I gasp for air as we pick up speed. Alouette tumbles through the air, and I fear we won't reach her before she penetrates the dark, roiling clouds.

Dayson joins our descent. As we speed past him, I avoid his eyes.

As Alouette's crumpled wings and unconscious body are consumed by the storm, Tristeh's wings flap harder and harder. Lightning crashes all around us as we careen into the darkness.

My eyes adjust poorly to the lack of light, and all I can see is the three of us on the dragon and half way down the wingspan. The rest is concealed by the storm cloud that rubs against my skin like a soft blanket, making my hair stand up and my clothes rise off me. A loud crack rattles my ears and zaps through every inch of my body.

With no time to consider we might have been struck by lightning, we dart from the first layer. Alouette is conscious and flailing about. She pushes her wings straight out, in an attempt to slow her descent, but she's gaining too much speed.

"Alouette!" I yell, even though she can't hear me. I barely hear myself over the loud ringing in my ears.

Lightning crackles from cloud to cloud as we fall through another that feels damp and heavy. We've almost reached her when she vanishes into another dark mass. The consuming sound of rain gets louder as we follow her downward. Moments later, we burst through the bottom of a rain cloud. Alouette's wings light up in the blink of lightning.

Tristeh pumps her wings once more, and Alouette is within reach. The dragon dives underneath her as Kava and I reach through the pouring rain to catch her flailing body. Alouette's eyes are wide with terror and I grab her hand. Kava pulls a leg close, and I wrap my arms around Alouette's shoulders. Her wings go limp as she gasps for breath in my arms.

Tristeh spreads her wings, and my stomach lurches as she slows our descent. Hollis directs Tristeh to the ground. I don't know where we are or what direction we are facing. She dives for the nearest mountain, toward a grouping of trees.

Another bolt cracks through the sky, and a hair-raising zap makes my teeth chatter together. Tristeh can't slow down fast enough and plows between spindly pine trees. Branches whack me all over as the ground comes up to meet us, and we skid to a stop in the mud and underbrush. A loud whine emerges from the dragon.

I hurry to unlatch my belt as Alouette sits up. Her wings are drenched, and her face is contorted. Eyebrows low and jaw jutting forward. Her breathing is fast and shallow.

Dayson lands beside us and reaches to help her off the dragon's back. "No!" she screams above the thunder and splattering of rain.

I stand and offer her a hand to get down too.

"No," she says abruptly. She flexes her wings out to the side, seeming very perturbed. Wings nearly hit me in the face as she leaps from the dragon's back with the help of her own wings.

Dayson says something to her, and she yells back, "I am sick of this!"

I crawl down the dragon's wing, followed by Kava and Hollis. Hollis darts to Tristeh's head and tends to her.

Alouette swipes her soaking hair away from her face. "I am done following along with your stupid decisions," she yells at Dayson.

Shock crosses his face. Kava stops beside me and we gape at Alouette. I've never seen her so upset.

"We could have gotten above it," Dayson argues.

"No!" Alouette snaps. "We should have searched out shelter for the night and waited out this hideous storm!"

The intensity of her anger and the rain pelts my face. *It's my fault.* I let Dayson convince me to keep flying.

"I'm sorry—" Dayson starts.

She waves a hand at him and her eyes blaze with fury. "You can't fix it with words!" Panting, she puts a hand on her side.

Dayson takes a step backward. I choke on the next breath as she whirls around.

"And you!" Her footsteps slap against the wet ground as she puts her finger in my face. "We will get you home. Stop being so…impatient!"

A crash of lighting hits a nearby tree, startling all of us. Tristeh whines and gets to her feet. The cracking of wood echoes around us as the tree falls somewhere in the darkness.

Alouette shouts, "Dayson, find us a place to hide for the night. A hollowed out tree, a cave, a hole in the ground! I don't care!"

He takes flight in an instant.

"I like her," Hollis blurts with a wide smile as Alouette speaks her mind—loudly.

"From now on, we discuss our next steps *together*." Alouette walks away, and I swear I hear her sob over the sound of the pounding rain.

Together. Wouldn't that be nice?

***

Dayson finds us a cave, where we wait out the storm. It takes most of the afternoon and into the night to blow through. Tristeh lights a fire for us to warm up. We lay our overcoats across the rocks protruding from the ground around the campfire so they can dry off.

The girls nestle together beside the fire, and soon their quiet banter turns to rhythmic breaths. My body still buzzes with adrenaline from the nerve-racking plunge to save Alouette. The wound in my arm is starting to sting. When

I slide my hand up my sleeve, I find the rain has begun to wash away the sap.

Hunched over with my knees to my chest, I stare into the mesmerizing orange flames, head swimming with thoughts about what could have happened.

"What is your plan when we reach Balfour?" Dayson whispers.

He swipes away the crumbly rocks and lies back against the hard ground with his hand behind his head. Half of his face is concealed in darkness, and the other half glows in the firelight.

"I think we should tell the elders of Balfour everything. We should ask for sanctuary for you and Alouette." I sigh as the image of Alouette falling to her death torments me. "Then, I can find out who the Ellerian royal is—if they exist at all—and protect them."

"You are unusually optimistic," Dayson says. "Why wouldn't Alouette and I just hide out until we find out if Balfour will accept us? We are risking a lot by trusting your elders to receive us."

The flickering flames glow brighter and brighter until something pops in the small campfire. Small sparks skitter toward the ceiling and sneak toward the mouth of the cave, where they sputter out.

"They aren't known for being accepting, I'll admit." A yawn stretches my jaw and fills my lungs. "But in my experience, honesty brings the best results."

"I've never known anyone like you, Ledger," he says, rolling away into the shadows.

The flames crackle and echo down the throat of the

cavern. When Dayson starts snoring, I resign myself to the heaviness of my eyelids. I miss my home. My family. My life.

***

In the morning, I wake to the echo of a chirping bird and the pain of hunger rumbling in my empty stomach. Something moves in my hand, and I peer over to find Hollis asleep with her hand in mine. I run my thumb along her soft skin.

Whispers drift from the mouth of the cave. I lay Hollis's dainty hand on the ground and join the winged silhouettes outside. Alouette and Dayson abruptly stop talking when I come into view. He drops a hand that was resting on the small of her back.

Her long brown hair is neatly pulled to the side, and her wings are clean and white. She combs through a few of her long wing feathers with her fingers, smoothing them out.

Her tunics are dry, and she seems quite well after the near-death ordeal yesterday.

"You all right?" I ask.

Alouette fixes the last feather and flexes her wings. Tipping her head, she says, "Look," and directs my attention to the valley below. I scan for anything unusual.

"What are you pointing at?"

She leans toward me, pinpoints a hill with a grouping of trees and bushes underneath. "That's where we were yesterday."

My heart sinks. *We did not gain any ground.* We fought a storm for nothing. My face burns with embarrassment.

Dayson sighs and walks inside, black wings swinging with his steps. *I should not have let him convince me to outrun that storm. I thought he knew better than me.*

"I'm sorry, Alouette." I don't want to tell her Dayson strong-armed me into getting above the storm. I don't want to talk bad about him or look like a complete pushover in front of Alouette.

"I know," she says without hesitation. She slides her hands into her trouser pockets. "I feel we could all be a bit more thoughtful and a little less hasty. We're on the same side here."

"I agree." I rub my tired head.

Dayson is being a bit intense and commanding. I thought he was only escorting us off the island, not coming home with us. Although I could never tell him to go back to Ellery.

"Come back, Ledger," Alouette says in her sweet, small voice. "You never change, do you?"

"What do you mean?" I shift from one foot to the other.

"Always daydreaming, flying off to crazyland. I always wondered where you go when you zone out like that."

I laugh to let the pressure off. Footsteps approach as I give her a smile and a shrug.

"When are we getting out of here?" Hollis asks. A bird chirps in response and flies from a nearby tree. Her hair tosses about in the breeze, golden against the sunrise. She slides her hands around my waist in a hug.

A look of revelation raises Alouette's brows.

I blush, unsure what to do with my arms or my face.

I never thought to tell Alouette about Hollis. We spent several weeks in prison together, but Alouette was barely conscious. We never had a real discussion. But I can’t have this conversation now. I swallow the awkward lump in my throat and try to think of something to say that has nothing to do with anything.

My mind is blank.

TRUTH 20

TOLLIVER

"What in the bloody world is going on here?" a voice rips me from a peaceful dream of home and Kava.

I sit upright, pull the curtain back, and find Belamy standing over the washmaid I tied to the leg of the wood table. His hands are on his hips and black wings poised like raised hackles on an angry dog.

"She found me," I explain. "I couldn't have her giving away my position."

"You are terrible at this game." The tension in Belamy's stance eases. He kneels and wakes the washmaid by jiggling her shoulder.

Confused, I ask, "What game?"

Belamy chuckles to himself and unties her hands.

"I'm sorry." I hate having had to tie her up. "She could have run off with a gag over her mouth. That would not have been good."

"Little Beauty, you're okay." Belamy unravels the gag from her mouth. "I'll get you away from the bad man." He winks at me.

"He's wingless," is the first thing gushing from her mouth as soon as she can speak unhindered.

Wingless. That's what she was saying last night. I've never felt more embarrassed for not having wings. I climb from my hiding place.

"He is Balfourian…sort of." Belamy scowls at me. "Anyway, he has asked for my help. Can you keep this between us?" He helps her to her feet. She rubs her mouth where the gag must have been rubbing too tightly, red with wear-lines. I look away, ashamed of what I did to her.

I hope Belamy has enough sway with her to keep her quiet.

Belamy takes her hand and pinches his eyebrows together. "Pretty please?" He bows his head, treating her like royalty.

Her eyelashes flutter and I roll my eyes.

"Oh, Belamy," she says. "I won't say anything. For you." Her top lip curls up in a sneer as she eyes me. "Not for your sake—Snake!"

"Thank you so much, darling Hana," Belamy says, his hand gliding down her reddening cheek. He guides her to the door and out into the light of the washroom. His muffled voice drifts in. He says something like, "I knew your cousin was kindly; I didn't know you were so…" The last word drifts off as they walk away.

Belamy is a smooth-talker. No wonder he knows things.

I take a moment to relieve myself and eat the last of my stash of food.

Belamy saunters back into the storeroom with a smile on his bronze face. "You, sir, have made me a lovely new friend."

I feel the urge to punch him in his overconfident face, but it's just my hatred of appearing evil that provokes me.

"What's the news, Bel?" I can't let him ramble on about his jaunts with women. I may have just tied one up, but I don't treat them the way he does.

"Oh, yes," he says, pulling me away from the door and into the shadows. "Here's the deal. I'm finding out many kids were smuggled off the island. But the name you told me. Tylanu? That was the key. Problem is…your father is…"

"Who is he?" I ask.

He barely opens his mouth in a nervous grin. His eyes give away his fear of telling the truth. "He's an advisor."

An image of the table of advisors flashes through my mind. They all seem to blend together. I feel bad because none of them are significant. I wish I could remember their faces. "Which one?" I cross my arms.

"If I'm wrong, or if he doesn't want anything to do with you," Belamy says. "He might execute me for simply asking about it."

I sit in the heap against the wall and stroke my chin. "So I have to be the one to make first contact, that is for sure. How were you led to an advisor?"

"Well, I talked to one of the midwives. Only two are left out of six, by the way. How sad is that? So many people didn't survive." He shakes his head and tucks his hand under the black leather strap across his chest. "Her son is a guardian. I went to her about him first. Then I ran into her again later that day." He wiggles his eyebrows guiltily because he probably followed her. "I told her a rumor I heard about the murder of second-borns. The expression on her face was telling. She didn't even have to agree. She told me to keep quiet. But I asked her about wingless ones. She nearly cried." He frowns as if it bothers him. "She said yes but wouldn't talk to me out in the open."

Blinking slowly, I wish this story were shorter, so he'd get to the point quicker. Excitement and worry go to war in my mind. I am one small step closer.

"I met with her last night, and she told me about the one who coordinated taking care of second-born and wingless. Guess who she was?"

"I don't know, Bel," I blurt, frustrated with his games.

"No, really guess," he says, face gleaming.

"I don't know anyone on this cursed island, besides you and Dayson!" I snap, a bit too sharp.

Belamy frowns, "Great skies, Tolliver. I'm just trying to help."

I shake my head, disgusted at my outburst. I'm so irritated by his wordy explanation, it feels as though I'm recovering from a gut punch. I breathe through it and force an apology. "Sorry. What were you saying?"

He flexes his black wings, nearly covering the doorway. "It was the informant who knew about the royal in Balfour. She used to smuggle wingless ones off the island. Crazy, isn't it?"

"Isn't she dead?"

"Yes, but she kept a list," Belamy says, smile widening.

I tense, wary of getting too excited. "Did you get the list?"

"No."

Disappointment smacks me in the face.

I want to yell, but he disrupts the rage coursing through my veins when he says, "I was able to read it, though."

I release my fists. "Why didn't you just say that?"

"I found *Tylanu*. It listed your father's name and your mother's name. I have to tell you though..." He looks at me thoughtfully. "Your mother is not alive. She has been dead for years. I was maybe eleven or twelve when she died of the Zara Flu. Many did."

Pain hits me deep in inside. My mother is dead. I will never see her face or know her voice.

"We have to choose our timing well," Belamy continues. "I don't know if Advisor Tiberius will accept you. These are volatile times."

"Is that his name?" I ask. "Which one is he?"

Belamy squints as he remembers, "When you saw him at your trial, he was to the right of Advisor Caedus, the one who did the talking."

I can't even recall what he looked like. I'm annoyed because I didn't notice at any of them, really, besides the overly-vocal man in the middle.

I make my mind up. "Don't approach him. I will do it. If you can get me to his quarters, I will tell him who I am. You don't have to put yourself in any more danger."

Belamy chuckles. "Any more danger? Getting you to an advisor's quarters will be massively dangerous." He smiles and speaks in hushed tones, "I've learned more about my people in these last few days than in the many years I've grown up here. I'm glad to know the truth."

"Thank you, Belamy." I place a hand on his shoulder. "If

you can get me there, I will do the rest."

"Yes, yes. Good thinking." He laughs, rolling the tension from his shoulders.

TOO LATE 21

LEDGER

Soaring over peaks and valleys, the landscape grows increasingly familiar: the purple haze of the mountains, the variety of trees, and the crisp smell of autumn. The trees have almost all changed from the solid green of summer into the brilliant oranges, yellows, and reds of harvest. My favorite season. I've loved this time of year for so long, it's hard to say why. Was it because of the colors, the smells, and the promise of a good crop? Or was it because of Alouette and our secret rendezvous?

Now, atop the dragon, I reach around Kava and graze Hollis's elbow. My heart aches and the wound in my arm hurts; I need to touch her. I feel lost and worried. The wind whips her hair to the side as she turns toward my hand. Reaching with her opposite hand, she slides her fingers between mine. My still-empty stomach warms with the contact.

Kava huffs and leans away from our entwined fingers.

Blue eyes full of joy, Hollis gazes deep into mine from

the front of the dragon. She smiles wide.

Kava interrupts our moment with a gasp, pointing to the horizon. A pale stream of smoke trails through the evening sky. Not a new fire, but a dying one. It disperses in the wind as it rises.

"Is that Balfour?" I say, releasing Hollis's hand.

"Oh, no," Kava says.

No, no, no. They are fine, it's only a bonfire. It's the annual Harvest Festival. Early. Even though it's supposed to happen after Ellery goes by.

Alouette and Dayson see it too. They point animatedly.

"Balfour," Alouette's voice is carried on the wind. Dread fills my gut with a shot of pain.

"Are you sure?" I ask.

She nods and darts ahead of us. Her white wings swish and work the air.

Hollis leans forward, says something to Tristeh, and the wings on either side of us beat faster.

The sun descends behind us. The reddened clouds streaking across the sky feel like a warning. The moments drag on and on as the pillar of smoke nears. We crest the last peak and soar over a swath of woods with colorful leaves and spiky pine trees. *My spiky pine trees.* The smoke reaches to the sky like the deathly hand of a ghost. The wind swats at it, and it disperses erratically. It is the ghost of the Hundred Harvest Tree. I would recognize my clearing from land or sky. The bald patches in the grass are exactly where I left them.

The Tree is the centerpiece of our sacred grounds. We gather beneath the safety of its branches twice a year for a feast and a ceremony, where our first-fathers settled.

We all lean forward, directing the dragon to land near the smoldering stump.

Tristeh's feet land with a thud in the clearing.

"Oh my goodness, oh my goodness," Hollis says.

I shakily unbuckle the latches from my belt. Steadying myself, I stand atop the dragon on our sacred grounds.

Dayson and Alouette touch down in the wide space. Alouette puts a hand to her heart as I climb from the beast. I stalk to the pillar of black smoke. Tears well in my eyes, and I gaze over at Hollis as shouting emerges from all around us.

The voices shout their commands.

"Stop!"

"Get down on the ground!"

I look around in disbelief.

Soldiers come out from the woods. *What happened here?*

Several men grab hold of Alouette. Another few wrestle Dayson to the ground. I fall to my knees in the wet ash as a man's voice yells for me to kneel.

"Come down! Come down from there," a woman shouts at Hollis.

I gasp at the familiarity in her tone. I put my hands on the back of my head in surrender. Tristeh shrieks at the ruckus, and as soon as Kava and Hollis's feet hit the ground, she leaps into the sky.

The woman shouts, "On your knees!"

"Mother?" I face the woman wearing armor and a helmet. Her sword gleams in the evening light.

"Ledger?" She lowers her weapon. "Wait, Hollis? Kava?"

I rise from the ashes and run to her. "Mother!"

"My boy," she whispers. "My Ledger. You are home." She pushes her helmet off her head and it falls to the hard dirt, revealing her face. Her bruised and beaten face.

I gasp and grab hold of her small frame covered in metal. I hug her until it hurts.

***

"What happened here?" Tears streak down my cheeks. "Who did this to you?"

I touch the bruises on her lovely face. Faded purple-brown with green at the edges. She seems smaller than when I left. Her brown eyes meet mine, full of pain and exhaustion.

"I'm okay," she says. "We were attacked."

"Oh no, I'm too late!" I shout at Dayson, "We are too late! The assassin has already come and murdered my people!"

"What?" Dayson says as his captor ties his hands behind him. "No, that's impossible."

I hold my head with shaky hands and fight against the rising anxiety. "How could you let this happen, Dayson?"

Mother touches my arm. "It was not Ellery."

In response to my anger, the soldier yanks Dayson upright and puts a knife to his neck.

"No," I say to the man. "He's with me. You don't have to do that." I shake off the panic and get control of my voice. "Let him go."

"Sorry, Ledger," the man says. I know his firm voice, but his armor is unfamiliar—made before my time. "We can't do that. We must secure the perimeter at all costs. Ellery will be here any day. We cannot take any chances."

He puts his knife away, and Dayson stops struggling against him. The man removes his helmet, revealing his face. Jubal, an elder of Balfour, is tall with a peppery beard and an intense gaze. He holds tight to Dayson. "We must lock him up until we sort this out."

"But—" Hollis starts to argue.

"But he helped us get home," Kava says. Then a cry from across the clearing yanks her attention away.

"Kava," a short round man shouts. His small mouth gapes in shock.

"Father—" Kava's voice wavers. She clears her throat and squares her shoulders. Her father, Healer Clovis, scuttles across the sacred grounds, cloak fluttering behind him, and throws his arms around her. They hug for a brief moment, then he starts checking her over. "I'm fine, Father," she says. "I'm just fine." He blows air from his lungs as tears fall down his round cheeks.

Unconcerned for anyone else, he pulls her toward the village.

"I'm sorry," Kava says. "I must go. Thank you, Ledger."

Jubal flicks a hand at the rest of the troops, and they funnel out of the clearing. Alouette's hands are tied behind and overtop of her feathery wings.

"Wait," I say. "Be careful with her—them."

Jubal lowers his bushy gray brows and says, "Of course." He directs Alouette and Dayson away, escorted by four soldiers. One of them has long red hair jutting out from underneath a helmet. Only one girl has hair like hers: Ryllis. *Balfourian soldiers are women now?*

"What happened here?" I ask.

“What happened to the Hundred Harvest Tree?” Hollis interrupts, taking my left arm in hers. A sharp pain radiates down my arm, but I hide my reaction. She weaves her fingers between mine, completely disregarding the Balfourian boundaries. But I don’t care, I pull her tight and accept the comfort of her touch.

Mother looks around. “Where’s Tolliver? Is he alive?”

“Yes, Tolliver lives. He’s still on Ellery in search of—” I stop short, but she knows who he is.

She finishes my thought: “His family.”

“Where’s Father?” Question after question rails against the inside of my head. *Why are you dressed as a soldier? Why is our sacred tree reduced to ashes?*

Mother winces, loops my other arm, and takes a few steps toward Balfour. “There is much to tell. For a few moments more, please let my heart be happy. My son has returned. Can we leave the talk of pain and sorrow for later?”

Sorrow? Dread drops into my stomach as if I swallowed a peach pit I can’t digest. *Is my Father dead?* Maybe I don’t want to know. She kisses my cheek. For her, I stuff the questions and fear down deep.

Arm in arm with two women I love, I follow our people down the sacred path from the clearing, through the woods, toward Balfour. *Home*.

HUGS OR DEATH 22

TOLLIVER

After the laundry goes quiet and still for the night, I crawl from my hiding place. I wait, listen, and sneak. I peer into the laundry room and breathe deeply with relief. My hair is matted to my head. My skin itches. I'd hate to stand before an advisor, let alone my own father, looking like a homeless beggar.

I tiptoe soundlessly from the storeroom and scan the dark corners. I peel the clothes from my body down to my undergarments and step up to the pool closest to my hiding place. It is especially dark in this underground cave. I consider fetching the torch from the storeroom. When I scoop up some water, I notice it appears dark with dirt or dye. Belamy let me bathe but failed to tell me which pool of water has dye in it and which doesn't.

The next pool is a little clearer with a bit of suds at the corners. I wish I could leap in, but I must be quiet. So I resort to getting in like Ledger would, one toe at a time, barely disturbing the surface as I submerge. It is cold, but I don't care. It feels good.

I sigh at the thought of Ledger. *Has he made it home? Is Kava safe with her father? Will they forgive me for leaving them?*

Scooping some of the leftover bubbles around the edge, I wash my crusty hair. The water smells of lavender and something sweet. I want to wash the worries from my mind. *Will my real father accept me? Will he send me away? I have to blindly trust the man won't cut me down where I stand for telling him I'm his wingless son.* It is a risk I'm willing to take.

Ashamed of who I've been on this island, I wash the sweat and foolishness from my body. I will not act like a monster anymore. I'm not a reckless thug who takes people hostage. I am a good person. If I can trust Belamy to find my father, I can trust my father to hear me out. I must stay *me*, not someone to be feared.

I accidentally splash a little as footsteps echo down the stairs outside the laundry room door. Taking a deep breath, I duck beneath the water. Hopefully, no one notices me. They'll see the laundry room is empty and leave. I clench my eyes shut under the water so the soap doesn't sting them. I wait and wait until my lungs threaten to suck water down my throat. Gently rising to the surface, I wipe my face and gasp at the figure with dark wings standing over me.

"I brought you some clothes." Belamy's voice cuts through the silence. My urge to leap from the water to fight dissolves away.

Belamy tosses me a fresh towel. I inhale the clean dry smell, and Balfour flashes through my mind: the blue skies and the green fields.

Stepping from the waters, I dry myself off. When he doesn't leave, I ask, "Any news?"

"No." He shakes his head and scowls.

"Oh." I tip my head like a curious dog. Why is he still standing here?

"I'd hate to be alone for days on end." He hands me a pile of clothing and leads me to the storeroom. "So I thought…" His voice trails off and I fill in his blanks. He wants to keep me company.

"Thanks." I slip on the fresh clothes, feeling like a new man. From what I can tell in the torchlight, it is a white tunic, black long pants, and soft leather moccasins. There's a hole in the back of the tunic. For wings. I hate that hole. It makes me feel inadequate. It's like a big glaring reminder of what I am not.

Belamy sits on a pile of Hana-approved fabric as he tosses me a small bag. His wings fold tightly on his back. I always wonder how they manage those things. I hate the feeling of envy—throbbing head and hot angry cheeks. Opening the bag, I dig through a lot of fresh food: berries, tubers, nuts with shells, lots of jerky, and a cake of some sort.

"Thanks," I say again, tipping the bag toward him. I stuff the cake entirely in my mouth. Its sweetness energizes me.

"Let me ask you," Belamy says, "How did you get on Ellery to begin with?"

I chew the dry morsels as I answer, "We flew..." A few crumbs fling from my mouth. I smile and gobble it down, not wanting to lose one more delicious crumb. "I could eat ten of those," I say, searching for more.

He laughs at me. "You're wingless, man."

The smile faces from my face as he reminds me of what I'm not. "My brother built a flying…thing. It was sort of a floating lantern, but big enough to carry us. It had a forge with large blankets sewn together to form a large…pocket or bubble. Hot air from the forge made it rise." It's annoying how hard it is to explain.

Belamy says, "Strange."

"Yes, he is."

"Ledger?"

"Yeah. Ledger is an odd one. Always thinking of the most unusual ways to get what he wants," I say, chewing on a piece of jerky.

He smiles and lays back with his hands behind his head.

Feeling more relaxed and well-fed by the moment, I hadn't realized how hungry I was, until the hunger pain subsided. My thoughts and desires come flooding back. I wish I could run the stairs the way I did when Ellery was empty. I wish I could do some sort of work with my hands, like blacksmithing with my father or bringing in the harvest alongside Angus. I ache to do something.

Belamy asks, "What will you do when you find your real family?"

The words *real family* feel like an insult to my Balfourian one. I grind the jerky between my teeth and say, "Introduce myself."

"What do you think they will do when you tell them who you are?"

I shake my head. I have about a hundred scenarios running through my mind at any given moment. "Tell them who I am," I say. "They will probably be confused. I will show them proof. Either they will be happy I'm alive and accept me as their son, or they deny the truth and send me off to be executed."

Belamy's eyebrows shoot up.

"Most of what I've come up with ends in one or the other: hugs or death." I roll up the bag of food and toss it under the table. "It's not really up to me how they respond. I must present myself in the best way possible. I have to at least try."

SO MANY QUESTIONS 23

LEDGER

The bell in Balfour's village square tolls, over and over: a call to meeting. The evening sky casts the village in a red, golden light making it appear as though the Hundred Harvest Tree is still burning. I follow my long shadow dancing in front of me down the path. With my mother on one arm and Hollis on the other, I step from the edge of the woods.

"Look," Hollis says. "Your house!" She jerks on my left arm and chatters on about being home. I want to be excited too, but that awful dread grows in the pit of my stomach like heavy, life-sucking tumor. I can't allow myself to be happy just yet.

My cottage is the first in the outer circle of homes. I reach around Hollis and run my hand along the chest-high wooden fence around our garden as we pass. I want to run in, crawl into my parents' bed, and fall asleep, but I can't—so much needs to be said and done.

"It smells the same," Hollis says. "Like cinnamon and dung. Except for the weird burnt smell. That's strange. I can't believe we can smell the ash of the Hundred Harvest Tree from here."

We pass my father's stone-built blacksmith workshop in the next row.

"Your shop," she says. "Everything is exactly the same, it's almost as if we never left." No smoke emerges from the chimney; the window is dark—*that's not the same.*

My mother pulls me tighter as we leave the stone structure behind and pass three more rows of log homes before we enter the village's center. She tenses and the corners of her mouth droops.

Hollis gasps. There should be fifteen homes all the way around the village square, but three on the southeastern side are burned to the ground as well as several rows beyond. "Oh no! Thelonious's house is gone. Fran and Shurl's, and Angus's too!"

My soul aches. *What happened?* Before I am able to demand answers from my mother, the bell stops, leaving a dull ache in my ears. Doors are propped open all the way around the square, where women and children gather.

"Mother! Heath! Perth!" Hollis's voice reaches the pitch of a twillerbird. She meets my eyes, and I tip my head in their direction. She gives my hand a squeeze, lets go, and races across the square. Her little blond-haired family ambles down the northern path—except for her father and older brother. *That is different too.*

Many men in armor—or what appear to be men—come from the southern path. Another group of men, in regular tunics and trousers, covered in bits of hay come from the harvest fields.

Face after face of people I know appear before me. The last time I saw them, they were raging at me. Angry because I flew to Ellery last year. Upset because I disrupted the norm. I fear their resentment might still be present after all this time when no one says a word as they gather around me. It's eerily silent except for shuffling feet and clinking armor. Many faces show fear, sadness, and confusion.

We approach the platform at the center between the four pillars of the village square. Elder Jubal ascends the three steps, helmet under one arm, the other pushing his shoulder-length gray hair out of his face. "Our children have returned from Ellery with terrible news. The Ellerians are back on the island and planning to attack."

Gasps roll through the crowd, and I jerk from my mother's arms. "They seek only one person, Jubal."

"Regardless, they will attack." Jubal eyes me, attempting to shut me up.

"You don't understand—"

"No, *you* don't understand, Ledger." He places a hand on my shoulder. "We must be prepared."

"But—"

Jubal turns his back and talks over me, announcing to the village, "All over age thirteen must suit up."

Sweat pools under my arms and my thoughts swirl out of reach. I feel like an idiot. *Why doesn't anyone listen to me?*

"It is fortunate you arrived before Ellery. We need you to make armor for our women." Jubal looks down at me from the platform.

"What?" Shock crosses my face, then embarrassment of my reaction replaces it. "Yes, sir."

"The sentries will keep watch. Mothers of Balfour, our numbers are too few to defend against the Sky People. Who else is willing to join the fight?"

"Wait," I interrupt again. He groans, so I speak quietly, "Their numbers are down as well."

"Yes, we know," Jubal says puffing his chest and tipping his chin. He acknowledges several women who volunteer.

"What? How—"

"When the alarm sounds, make sure your families are ready, and you are dressed to fight," he shouts, closing the meeting. Action fills the square. I'm left with more questions, no answers, exhaustion, and a headache.

The light fades from the village in what seems like moments. But the sky still bleeds beyond the western ridge. I allow Jubal to ignore me and walk off. Biting the inside of my cheek, I consider going after him and shouting in his face—something. I hug my thick overcoat tightly around me. I'm embarrassed that I can't stand up to him in front of everyone.

"Ledger!" a booming voice calls over the din. A man with silvery armor runs to me from the southern path. I wait for any sign of who it is. "Ledger, you're here!" He rips his helmet off his head, revealing red curly hair, a burly auburn beard, and the living, breathing face of my cousin.

Angus!

***

"Angus! You're alive?" I screech. I mourned him for weeks, and here he is. Racing down the steps, I dodge a few people between us.

"Ledg—" Angus says with tears gathering. He grabs me in a bear hug and squeezes the sadness out of me. I feel all the stuffed emotions surfacing.

As he sets me down, I ask, "How did you get here?"

Angus wraps an arm around my shoulders. "An angel brought me home." His laugh bellows over the sounds of the busy square. He points me toward the workshop and I beg for more.

"What? Who? How?"

He laughs again, white teeth shining, and brown eyes beaming. His voice soothes me and he wastes no time. "I fought them when we landed on Ellery. A guardian struck me on the head, and I blacked out, the rabid beast!" He curses and rings my neck with his arm. Bending me toward him, he rubs my head with his knuckles.

I don't even care what he does to me, I'm so glad he's alive. He could punch me in the face, and I wouldn't flinch. I grab his beard and yank. He puts a foot in front of mine and trips me. Then he hauls me up, and we scuffle toward my house.

"I woke up in their medical ward," he continues. "Soon as I open my eyes, this pretty little thing tells me to close them. Stay still. Pretend to be dead." He chuckles as if it's a joke and I gape at him, halted in the path. "She even powdered my face to make me look dead! All pale and grotesque."

I want to ask more one-word questions, but my open mouth and bulging eyes ask them all.

"She promised to get me home," Angus says. "And she did. And I think I'm in love—ridiculous love!" His laugh is so loud it rattles my teeth. That or I'm shaking with shock. I don't know which. "Can you believe it, little man?"

"Oh my lands," I finally find words. "Who is she?"

"Her name is Sybella." He sighs like a dope.

I shake my head. "Yeah, but *who* is she? Why did she help you?"

"She and her mother were among the prisoners when the Ellerians were on the ground. Wings tied. Forced into slavery. They are done with Ellery."

"Well, where is she? Can I meet her?" I follow him around the back of the stone building.

"*Shhh.*" Angus steps close to me with his finger to his lips and pulls me into the darkness of the workshop. "Maybe tonight. The elders told them they couldn't stay here." He scowls.

"They?"

"Sybella and her mother."

"Where are they?" I whisper and lean closer.

"I'll take you to them after dusk. Don't need anyone seeing us sneakin' around."

I nod as if I understand. *Is it really that dangerous for Ellerians in our village?* I frown at the thought. It might mean Alouette and Dayson's chances of staying are pretty low.

Grabbing the lantern off the hook on the wall, I light it and fill the room with a warm glow. I want him to stay where I can see him and make sure he is real, alive and well, but Angus hugs me again and leaves for his post. His laugh echoes down the path as he heads back to the southern border, the Brier. I can't wait to tell Hollis. And Tolliver.

Father must be around here somewhere, because the forge is still warm. I light it with ease.

"What are you doing in my workshop?" my little sister, Mila, says, bursting through the door. She is at least two hands taller than when I saw her last, easily taller than Hollis. *How did she grow so much in one year?*

Her hands are on her hips and a twinkle is in her eye. She folds her hands in front of her. "What do you think of the place?"

My brows pinch together as I peer around. It's neat, clean, and orderly. Not one tool is left out. Something which rarely happened when I worked alongside Father.

"I did it." She flashes a crooked grin. "I made this… and that." She points at a couple of odd metal panels on the cooling rack. I'm not really sure what they are.

"Father taught you?" I am proud she is interested in my trade.

"I hated it at first, but I'm pretty good at it."

I smile in agreement, knowing how that feels.

"Oh, I forgot, Mother is asking for you."

My chest aches.

"Is Father dead?" I'm tired of waiting for answers. Afraid of the truth I might find.

The smile melts from her face. She shrugs. "I don't know."

I head straight for the house behind the workshop. Graying logs wrap our small home with red clay between each one. I push the door with my fists. The last time I touched this door, I was running away. I left her—the woman putting bowls around the small table near the fire. The room is full of warmth, and I feel cold and afraid.

I want to ask her about Father. But I hesitate and lose the opportunity as she gives me and my little brother, Killian, our evening meal. He climbs up beside me on the bench. She feeds baby Hazel spoonful after spoonful to keep her shirt from getting messy. I look down at mine, covered in sweat and grime, missing one sleeve.

ANOTHER PUNCH 24

LEDGER

I dream of Father. Cold, pale, unmoving. It appears as if he is asleep. I stand over my parents' bed, heart thudding, eyes stinging with tears. It's as if Mother doesn't see him. She crawls in beside him. Soon her breaths are rhythmic and slow.

Turning away, I hit my head on a wall. My eyes pop open and I find myself in my own bed in the loft of our cottage. The ceiling pitches to a sharp angle next to my bed, and I wake with a lump on my forehead.

A smell sneaks up from the kitchen, my favorite breakfast that Father calls morning stew: coarsely ground corn simmered until soft, eggs, and bacon—all in one bowl. I sat in the bathtub for hours last night and slipped into my very own clothes: a soft linen tunic without a hole in the back, brown trousers, and my favorite green wool vest with bronze buttons up the front. My mother made it for me on my fifteenth birthday. I run my hands along the fuzzy surface and inhale the familiar scents of home.

Feeling achy inside and out, I make my way down the loft ladder. Mother swishes about the kitchen in an auburn dress—quite different than yesterday's armor. She smiles, and exhaustion shows on her face along with healing bruises.

None of the children are awake yet. I seize the moment and whisper, "Where is Father?"

She pours the morning stew into two bowls. I might have heard a sniffle as she flips eggs and bacon in a pan. The question hangs in the air with the bacon smoke as she scrapes them evenly into each bowl. Using her apron to protect her hands from the hot pan, she sets the pan on a towel to cool and sits close to me on the bench facing the fire.

She leans close and kisses my forehead. "He has been taken prisoner."

My stomach leaps into my throat. I choke on a response as tears emerge. I don't know if I'm relieved, or angry, or terrified. Maybe all of it at once.

"I didn't want to have to tell you about it around the children. Or out in the open." She shakes her head. "Or ever." She puts an arm around me and squeezes. I wince at the pain in my arm. "Are you hurt?" She wrinkles the bruised skin on her face.

Steam drifts from our bowls of morning stew, and I can't even care about my favorite breakfast or the teeth punctures in my arm. "I have a few scrapes. Please continue."

"Several weeks ago, a tribe of people came through the mountains. They took us by surprise. We were getting ready for Ellery's return, watching the south. Not the north. They killed many of our men as we defended the children who were roaming freely."

The bad news is like a punch to the gut in a losing fist fight. Normally, we don't make the children hide until Ellery is spotted.

"There is no protocol to defend against anyone except Ellery. They killed, they burned, and they took," she says, flaring her nostrils in disgust. "Our men offered themselves as a sacrifice to leave the rest of us alive. Fergus—your father—was among them. They took them as slaves. He went with them willingly to save us."

A jab to the heart rattles me. I'm relieved to hear my father isn't dead, but so many men are gone. "That is why women are needed for the Protection?" I ask.

"Yes," she says and takes a bite of her breakfast.

A mousy yawn comes from my parents' bed. Little arms stretch and I pause, hoping baby Hazel doesn't get up. There is so much I need to understand.

"Why didn't you tell me Tolliver is Ellerian?" I ask.

She stops chewing, apparently not ready for the question. Swallowing, she looks down. "I couldn't risk you knowing and getting yourself into trouble. Even now, they won't accept any Ellerian in this village."

"Alouette," I breathe her name.

"They will send her away."

Her deep brown eyes are full of love. She's simply telling me the truth as she sees it.

"But if I tell them what she's done for me—"

"No." She goes back to eating. "Angus pleaded the same case for Neelie and Sybella. The elders are adamantly against it—what's left of the elders anyway."

"Who is left?" I ask.

"Jubal is the only original elder still with us."

"That's all?" Another jab to the face. Warnings of panic blare in my mind. "How many people are left in Balfour?" Once the question leaves my lips, I hope she doesn't answer. I can't handle any more bad news.

"A little over half." She wipes her mouth and inhales deeply.

As I peer into my breakfast bowl, tears blur my view. I wanted to get home so badly and go back to the way things used to be. Carefree and peaceful. Back to childhood. Back to the days when I didn't know what in the world was going on. But it's entirely impossible. Everything has changed.

"I have inserted myself as an elder." She raises an eyebrow at me.

"Is that…legal?"

"I don't care. I'm done sitting passively by and letting them make ignorant decisions. When Tolliver returns and tells them who he is, I don't even want to *think* about what they will do."

"So the elders are Jubal, you, and…?"

"Thelonious's brother, Tillman, has replaced him. Chasen, Espen's father, has retaken his position as an elder. Espen didn't survive, so Chasen stepped back in. He has been quite an asset, I must say. I believe Angus is trying to take his Father's position."

"Uncle Roan has been taken too?" I blurt, trying to block another jarring blow.

"No, Ledger," Mother says with a loud sigh and a hint of anger. "He is dead."

No! Another strike lands at the core of my being, and I

feel my body sway backwards. I catch myself before I fall off the bench.

I can't. I can't. I can't think about this anymore. Her story is worse than mine.

I resolve to change the subject and say, "I need to figure something out and I don't know who to trust." I can trust her of all people. This feels like the best place to start. "Ellery is sending an assassin to kill someone in Balfour."

She sits up with a start. "What? Who?"

I start at the beginning. "King Halcyon, his entire family, and his brother's family were all murdered for the throne. Now their government is a mess. Some want a new king, others want to have elders like we do. Someone told them a member of the Ellerian royal family has been living in Balfour for years."

Her mouth hangs open, speechless.

I continue, "So someone is sending an assassin to kill the Ellerian royal. I escaped to get back here in time to find out who it is and make sure nothing happens to them." I touch her arm and say something which has been stirring in my mind since we left. "If their royal is in our village, we could bring peace between Ellery and Balfour. Alouette could stay."

My mother's eyes grow as round as pumpkins. She goes back to eating, chewing her breakfast intensely.

"Do you have any idea who it could be?" I ask.

She swallows her food and responds, "I think this is something to ask your grandmother. She knows everyone and everything about Balfour."

"Grandmother is still alive?" I ask.

"Yes," she says. "Grandmother Huyana has been ill since you left and should not leave her bed now. But she lives."

Feeling like I dodged a fist, I sigh. A surprised smile spreads across my face and tears pool in my eyes. I let them fall for joy's sake. *My grandmother is alive. I will find out who the royal is, and we will make peace with Ellery.*

"What about Grandfather?" I ask.

She shakes her head.

My smile fades and my head throbs. I shouldn't have asked.

I feel battered while finishing my morning stew.

"Do not speak of this to anyone until we talk with her, especially not the elders," Mother says.

DARK HOURS 25

TOLLIVER

"It will be like hiding in the grain sack. But less itchy," Belamy whispers. "I'm just sorry you have to get in it so soon. You'll need to stay still while in the row of laundry bags. Jax will know which one."

Belamy taps the bag with a leaf stamped on the side. Advisor Tiberius's are all tagged with a leaf. He will get two bags delivered tonight. And one will be quite heavy.

"In the morning, while your family is out, Henrick will take you in. He will make several beds and unload clothing as well. Maybe you could help him."

With a curt nod, I say, "Let's do this." Looking around the storeroom, I hope I never have to see it again and yet feel strangely sentimental about leaving. Shaking the conflicting feelings away, I put one foot after the other in the canvas bag, thankful it is twice the size of the grain sack. Belamy tucks a few sheets in around me to make me seem less like a person in a bag.

"If this goes badly, meet me back here and I'll fly you to

the ground as soon as possible," Belamy says with a weak smile. He doesn't seem to have a lot of faith in my plan.

Neither do I. But I have to try.

He cinches the opening closed and yanks me from the ground. He flops me on to his back, underneath his wing. It feels strange and warm through the canvas. He walks with a bounce in his step and stops. I am lowered to the ground, where I must stay until Jax picks me up for delivery.

"Thanks for letting me help out, babe," Belamy says to someone.

A woman's voice responds, followed by a quiet lip-smacking sound. Maybe kissing? I shake my head.

After a long while, someone approaches and taps my bag. I hold my body very still. The person lifts the bag and heaves me onto their back. "Oh bees! You're heavier than an ox."

He walks up the laundry stairs and out into the light. Evening should have fallen already, so maybe it is torchlight in the halls.

I furrow my brow and refuse to respond. But the man keeps talking. "Belamy is out of his mind. This will get us all in trouble. You know that, right?"

He waits for me to say something and when I don't, he continues. "I want to help a friend as much as the next person. But this is—" He grunts and finishes his thought. "Dangerous."

Jax jostles me a little bit on his shoulder, and I feel his wing wrap closer. Maybe he's walking by someone who makes him nervous?

"Here we are." He lowers me to the ground and props

me against a wall. "Put something right here. It looks like a foot." He taps my big toe.

"Jax," I whisper.

"Yeah?"

"Thanks."

"Short ride. Long wait." He bops the top of my head, and his footsteps fade into the distance.

I'm really doing this. Excitement buzzes from head to toe. I'll be waiting all night, but I've been waiting all year for this. I can wait a few dark hours more.

I'm glad I peed before getting in.

26 NOT STRONG ENOUGH

LEDGER

One of the new elders of Balfour sent his youngest son throughout the village this morning to tell us the elders will meet this evening to decide what to do with Alouette and Dayson. I wonder if it is a sign that Mother is accepted as an elder or it's for me to testify for my Ellerian friends.

Either way, we head to Elder Tillman's cottage. A part of me is hollow without my father. He always knows what needs getting done and leads my family with strength and honor. Without him, without Grandfather, without Tolliver, I am the oldest man in my family. The weight of the role is overwhelming.

The air is crisp for early fall. I inhale and follow my mother up Tillman's front steps and through the open door. Dust wafts in with us. In the main room sits a bulky wood table about as thick as my forearm. Tillman is seated on a low stool at the far end in deep conversation with Chasen, father of the dead Elder Espen. I liked Espen. He was the funniest of the five elders of Balfour, always making light of stupidity and laughing loudly. Seems his Father is more serious. How disappointing.

Chasen's white brows are pinched together and he cranes his neck to hear. Tillman speaks louder and Chasen nods.

Tillman is almost as tan as his older brother, Thelonious. His round face is framed by jet black hair cropped short. His muscles bulge from underneath his white tunic, in stark contrast to his smooth brown skin. I look around for his children, who must have already been sent out with his wife.

Mother sits beside Chasen as Jubal walks through the door. "Let's get this over with. We have corn to bring in." He sits opposite my mother and frowns when he sees her.

Another clomping set of footsteps boom up the front stairs and through the door. "I'm here, I'm here," Angus says out of breath.

"What are you doing here?" Jubal asks.

"Elders' meeting." Angus brushes himself off, sits beside Jubal as if he is a close buddy, and pats him on the back. "Let's get started."

"You are not an elder." Jubal crosses his arms.

"We don't have time for debates," Angus says with a wink. "We have corn to bring in and a border patrol to organize."

"He's right," Tillman says. "Only order of business. What do we do with the Ellerians Ledger brought home?"

I scoff because he makes them sound like stray mutts.

Angus eyes me and shakes his head discreetly. I take the hint and sit at the foot of the table across from Tillman, who says, "They can't stay, of course. But I don't like the idea of letting them run back to Ellery with news of our decreased numbers."

"No, they wouldn't do that," I say, ignoring Angus's warning to be quiet. This is why I'm here. To set things straight. Even for Angus and his angel.

"We can't let Ellery have the upper hand this time," Jubal says. He folds his fingers together. "We have to at least appear to have numbers to stand up to them. Possibly even beat them so we can keep our harvest."

"You don't understand," I say. "Alouette is my friend—"

"*You* don't understand, Ledger," Jubal interrupts. "This is war. Nobody cares who you're friends with."

"That's what I'm trying to tell you. Alouette's father was the one who killed Ellery's King and took the throne. They hate her and already tried to execute her. She will not be going back to Ellery. Ever."

I sound pretty convincing.

"It's true," Angus agrees.

The room falls silent as each man around the table thinks about it. Mother says, "I think they should be allowed to stay."

Jubal grunts, "Of course you would."

"I do too," Angus says.

"Also, Ellery is sending an assassin," I blurt. Remembering my mother's warning, I keep the details buried deep.

"Just one?" Jubal asks. "We can handle one guardian."

"Yes, but—"

"We caught all of you landing in Balfour, didn't we?"

"Yes, but—"

"I think we keep the Ellerians locked up until the island passes," Tillman says.

"I agree," Chasen says. His voice is gravelly, and his wrinkly face droops over his eyes.

"Well, we have an agreement," Jubal says, pounds a fist on the table, and stands. "The Ellerians will stay locked up. Adaya, organize food and water for them. Ledger, stay away from them and get to work on the armor. Angus, I'll deal with you later. Let's get back to the harvest before the flying beasts get here. We still have the corn to bring in, as well as raking the hay."

My head buzzes with anger. I feel like a fainting goat unable to move around a threat. I want to scream at him. *They are not beasts! They are people, same as you and me!* Instead, I watch Jubal clomp out the door and toward the ready fields. I shake angst from my bones and force myself to move. I have to tell Alouette. At least they will be safe and well-fed, if my mother has anything to do with it.

***

"They will not be releasing you until Ellery is gone," I explain, fiddling with the hem of my tunic.

Dayson groans.

Alouette takes shallow breaths with a sad scowl.

"Are you okay?" I ask.

"I can't breathe in here," Alouette says, shaking her hands in the air. "It's just…" Tears well as she paces back and forth in a panic.

"I asked the man guarding the door if she could sit out on the steps for a short while, but he refused." Dayson runs a hand through his dark hair.

The guard is Bernhard. He is seated on the front stoop, face to the sun, and nearly sleeping. He was annoyed because he had to get up and let me into the boarded up cottage. I'm surprised they even have anyone guarding lock-up with the lack of men to harvest and fight.

Then it hits me, the last time Alouette was in a cottage like this was when I pulled her from the fire. The Lianmin killed her father and threw her inside to be burned alive. No wonder she is so anxious.

I approach and put a hand on her shoulder. "It's okay, Alouette."

She blinks back tears. She whisks from my reach to the door and back.

"I can convince them to let you stay when this is all over," I encourage. "You can live here in Balfour. Make a life for yourself on the ground." I'm saying it mostly to Alouette. She is the only one who has no more family on Ellery, or anywhere else. At least Dayson has his father.

She puts her shaky hands on her face and whispers, "They will never see me as anything more than the enemy."

My heart sinks and my neck aches.

She drops her hands and says with a hiccupy voice, "Everywhere I go, I am the enemy. Here. Ellery."

She is right. And I feel the same way.

I barely fit in anywhere either. Balfour. Ellery. I feel as though I was born in the wrong place at the wrong time. So, either I have to give up who I am, or everything else around me has to change—because of who I am.

But I'm not strong enough to change everything else. I sigh and feel like giving up.

"We have to escape," Dayson says. "We can't be here when Ellery arrives."

He is completely serious.

A long silence hangs between us as I contemplate any other way, but he is right. Alouette can't be caught between two sides that won't accept her.

"I will help you in any way I can. I definitely owe you that much," I say.

"When?" He leans forward on the bench in front of the hearth. "We must"—he glances at Alouette—"move on. Get as far away from Ellery as possible."

I understand his plan to take Alouette away from Ellery, the need to keep her safe.

"Tonight, I'll return. Distract the guard, or, depending on who it is, he could let you walk out the front door." I smile at Alouette. I want to put my hand on her arm again, calm her down, bring her back to the girl I knew. But I'm afraid that girl died somewhere, before I found her in a burning cottage in Lianmin. I bite my cheek to keep the sadness out.

I head to the door and knock, signaling for Bernhard to open it.

Dayson gazes into the flames of the fireplace. "Did you find out who you need to protect?"

"No," I say. "But I think my grandmother knows who it is. I'm headed there now."

"I'm glad you made it home in time," he says turning to face me. "You're a good person."

My body freezes at his compliment.

He says, "No matter what happens, I'm glad we met."

I look at Alouette, the exotic woman with wings who

swept me off my feet years ago. The goodbye hangs in the air. *I can't. I can't say goodbye right now.* I breathe through the fear of losing her.

"Thanks, Dayson," I say, stopping the corners of my mouth from bowing downward.

As I leave them in the cabin, I fear Alouette will panic all night long. Then an idea hits me. *Yes, yes! I can get them out of here, and it will only cost a few lies.*

FRANTIC WAKE 27

TOLLIVER

The morning dawns excruciatingly slow. I sleep sitting up with my knees in my chest and my head pressed forward on someone else's sheets. I feel bad because drool made its way from my mouth to the clean linens. Light seeps through the tiny holes in the weave of the canvas bag along with distant voices.

My body really wants to stretch, and I resist the urge to yawn. My lower back has a sharp pain which could be relieved with sitting up straighter. But I must stay as still as I can.

Footsteps approach and walk on past. As soon as they are gone, another set and another sprint by. Adrenaline buzzes in my muscles, and I resist the urge to flinch with every voice and movement that passes my hiding place.

A long while after the bustle ends, a quiet pair of feet approaches. Someone touches the top of the canvas bag and drags me around the corner, through a doorway, and quietly shuts a door.

My heart thunders as they approach, and he unties the bag. Light pours in and a face appears. He is a boy of maybe fifteen or sixteen harvests; his pale, squishy face contrasts against his midnight hair and wings. He timidly smiles with a question in his eyes.

"Hello," I say, breaking the silence with pleasantries. "My name is Tolliver." I smile. He steps back from the bag and I stand, handing him the folded sheets with my dried drool.

"I—I'm Henrick," he says, brows pressing together. He is obviously afraid of me. His jumpy reactions make me feel like some sort of wild animal with three eyes. He straightens his gray tunic and looks away as I step from the bag. A second canvas bag sits in a heap beside mine with more clean items for the boy to handle.

"Glad to meet you," I say, committed to helping him feel comfortable with my presence. *Maybe if I offer to help him.* "Where shall we start?"

He stammers for a moment. "You want to help me?" He takes the sheets from my hands. "I, well, we can start in the bedroom."

"Certainly," I say with a gentle smile. No sudden movements, or this kid could run off screaming. I refuse to ruin this.

He kneels and unloads the rest of the bag without taking his eyes off me. I guess I'm a strange sight to see, being wingless. Might be similar to seeing Stephen for the first time, who lost his legs to the green rot.

I breathe the air of my father's home and gaze about. Swords with blades crossed hang above the mantel. A tapestry crest hangs behind them. It must be my family's crest.

I slide my hand in my pocket to make sure my proof is still there. The page from my mother's book she gave me before I left.

I follow Henrick around the lounge chairs and into the bedroom on the left side of the room. Curtains are pulled tight over the shutters, blocking the autumn wind. The room is lit by several lamp stands around the room.

A large bed sits against the far wall, rumpled and slept in. Henrick rolls up the top blanket and sets it aside. He pulls off the sheets next and stuffs them in the bag from where I came.

I step to the opposite side of the bed as he tosses the clean sheets on the bare mattress. Before applying them, his black wings lift him up over the bed. He floats from side to side, pounding out the lumps and dips in the mattress. Many months ago, before the Ellerians returned, I inspected a mattress in a different bedchamber. With a bottom layer of straw and strips of fabric, the top is stuffed with fluff and crushed feather. I never thought of fluffing the one I slept on for most of the year. I shake my head at how genius it is.

Henrick's feet hit the ground and he wafts the first sheet in the air. We wrap the mattress together. He checks each corner to make sure they are folded tightly. My corners are not so neat. He doesn't look at me as he fixes mine. We spread the flat sheet and blanket on top. He folds them squarely and tightly tucks the corners at the foot. I've never seen someone take such care of a bed. He is superb at his job.

"I can get the next one myself," he says with a half-smile. His eyes are kind, and I sense his anxiety. It is obvious I'm making more work for him.

"Okay, no problem. I'm probably hindering your process, anyway." I return the smile as he walks out of the room, finally turning his back to me. He stokes the flames in the fireplace and gathers the next set of sheets. I walk around the entire sitting room searching for something to answer the many questions pounding in my mind: *What kind of man is my father? Did he choose to send me away, or did he have no knowledge of my winglessness?* Frustration wipes the remains of the smile away.

I wander aimlessly as Henrick makes the bed in the room on the right and tucks clothes into the dresser of each room. He seems to be rushing about and then declares, "I am finished." He meets my eyes for a moment, unsure what else to say.

So I complete our pleasantries. "It was nice to meet you."

He gathers the canvas bags full of dirty clothes and darts out the door, shedding a black feather in his frantic wake.

***

Alone in my family's quarters, I sneak through the second bedroom. There isn't much to find since all of the Ellerian people recently came back to Ellery in a hurry. A dress hangs from the side of the dresser. A woman sleeps here. I stand there staring at it, considering how Belamy said my mother was dead. *So who lives here?*

Drawings of people with wings, dragons, and horses are strewn on the small table next to the bed. Not a woman. A girl.

I can't remember which advisor was which. Weeks ago, we stood before them for our trial. The one who spoke the most, Advisor Caedus, was unmistakable. Intense and harsh. I search my mind for any other faces and am ashamed I can't bring up one, let alone my own father. He is a stranger to me. And I am a stranger to him. I should have recognized him or felt some connection. But I didn't. My shoulders droop as my feet carry me about the living space of strangers.

I sit on the lounge chair, untying and retying the laces down the front of my white tunic. It didn't get too wrinkled after being cramped in a laundry bag for hours. I neatly roll up my sleeves to the elbow and lean back against the cushions. I don't put my feet up because I'll need to jump up at any moment and meet the man who might be my father. At the thought, I decide to not get comfortable and rise from the seat.

At one of the many windows, I pull back a curtain and find a closed shutter. The hook turns hard, and I open it to the afternoon sun. This is the northeast side of the castle, and craggy mountains span as far as the eye can see. *We must be getting close to Balfour.*

I stretch my neck against the irritation in my bones. I want to meet my Ellerian family, but I miss my Balfourian one more than ever now. I lock the shutter, pulling the curtain neatly closed.

Wandering around the sitting room, I run my hand along the mantel and stand for a few moments to warm myself by the fire. I know I'm an intruder: uninvited and unwelcome. Maybe I shouldn't surprise him like this. Maybe it will make a bad impression. Maybe I should hide, watch him, and assess who he is first.

The door squeaks and a girl enters—actually a young woman. She swishes into the room with brilliant white wings, golden corn silk hair, and bright blue eyes. Her cheeks are speckled with freckles. She pushes the big door shut and says, “Henrick,” in a sing-songy voice.

She spins, her golden dress twirling and shimmering in the firelight, only to find wingless me.

She freezes, eyes wide with fear.

“Who are you?” she asks.

“I’m Tolliver.”

With a frown, she reacts hastily, grabbing for the doorknob.

“Please wait.” I rush to the door and put my hand on it, keeping her from opening it. “I am here to talk to Tiberius. Is he your father?”

“Let go!” she screams.

I resist the urge to restrain her and cover her mouth. I remember the fear in Hana’s eyes and remind myself I am not an evil man. “Please listen. I am here to talk to Tiberius. Do you live here?”

“Yes, yes, yes! He is my father, and he will be furious to find a…freak in our quarters, holding me prisoner.”

At her panicky words, I release the door. As she turns the knob, I say as fast as I can, “I am Tiberius’s son. I was taken away after I was born for being—” The door slams in my face as I finish my sentence. “Wingless.”

Her footsteps race down the hall, followed by her screams as she calls for a guardian. Balling my fists in frustration, I can’t stay here, or I’ll be found and executed.

I must run.

Pulling open the heavy wooden door, I scan the empty hall and run toward what I hope is another empty hall.

28 WAITING MY WHOLE LIFE

LEDGER

It isn't until midday meal when Angus visits me at the smithy shop that I have a chance to ask him if he can take over guarding lock-up tonight. He agrees, loudly, slaps me on the back, and scoots off to some business I don't care about. I feel odd wanting to hug him every time I see him. Alive. Healthy. Smiling.

"How's my favorite man?" Hollis's voice startles me, and I drop the mallet in my hand, barely missing my toes. She giggles and says, "Oh, dear! Don't break off your pinkie toe."

I smile as she peers out the door. For what? I don't know. Then she enters with a wild look in her eyes, making me nervous.

"What's the matter?" I'm worried she is about to attack me with her bony little fists.

"Nothing, I just miss you," she says in a nasally whine, slinking toward me.

"Stop it, Hollis," I say. "You're being strange."

She drops her hands and stands up normal. “I miss you, Ledger.”

When I think she is dropping the act, she darts toward me and shoves her tiny hands in my armpit—tickling me. I resist laughing. I hate being tickled. But her eyes are so vibrant and her frame bouncing around, showering me with attention and touch, she shatters my resistance.

Her little fingers find a spot on my neck that makes me hunch over and gasp for air. I let out a snicker and when it starts, I can’t stop. She pushes me across the room with her little jabs and hysterical laugh. When I can’t take anymore, I grab her in a tight hug, trapping her arms between us. I lift her off her feet and turn her round and round in the small workshop until one of her legs bumps the anvil and another tool goes crashing to the ground.

We pause, guilt on both our faces. Then we burst out laughing together. Her fingers wiggle toward my neck again and I squeeze harder. “Hollis, stop!” I say through a belly laugh.

She snickers as I squeeze the air out of her, “All right, all right.”

I release her slowly, and then her hand moves swiftly at my neck. As I squeeze again, I stop them short. “Hollis!”

She raises her eyebrows at me.

“I need to get to my grandmother’s cottage,” I say, setting her down slowly.

“Well, then why did you summon me?” She smiles wide, biting her lower lip. A weird feeling fills my gut. I can’t remember why I called for her. When she’s near me, I can’t think straight.

When I release her onto the ground, she straightens her pale blue dress. I miss the rebellious black leather pants she used to wear when we were on Ellery—wildly different from what she is supposed to wear in Balfour. There are a lot of things I miss about being on Ellery. One of them is being myself. The other is being myself *with her*. She seems to be able to be herself wherever she is, whoever she is around. I admire that about her.

She straightens my tunic, and I jerk away like a startled lamb. She giggles. "Did you want me to go with you to your grandmother's?"

"Yes," I say, desperately needing to speak to Grandmother about the Ellerian royal and irritated that I'm expected to do smithing work all day—without a break. "I'm headed there when I finish my work."

"Is your work ever done?" Hollis teases.

"Not really." I smile. Donning a leather belt, I slip a small blade I found in the overstock bin into the sheath on one side. My father made the knife. I dismiss his name from my mind and think ahead—clean up and hurry to Grandmother's before nightfall.

"I still can't find Tristeh," she complains while moving tools around on the workbench. "I keep hiking the North Mountain to see if I can find her…but nothing."

I think she is organizing, but she stacks them up and pushes them over with one finger. I reach around her and put the tools back where they belong. I have a system.

"I'm sorry you can't find Tristeh." I am not sure if I want to ever see another dragon again. I feel safer without the unpredictable variable around. But for Hollis's sake, I pretend to care. "Do you call her?"

Hollis wanders to the forge and grabs the coal rake. "I call her and call her from the mountain pass."

I step to her side, ready to take the tool from her hand. She parts the red coals as the flame disperses. I'm impressed she knows what to do.

Placing a hand on her back, I say, "You know she can hear you. She's just being stubborn."

Setting the hot tool aside, slides her arms around my waist. "Where do you think she keeps going?"

I return her embrace and consider what a large hungry beast would be doing away from its handler. "Probably hunting for food, or meeting new friends, or laying eggs."

She gasps. "Wouldn't that be wondrous?"

Hollis laughs and leans into my embrace as Mila sticks her head in the door and yells, "Oh, are you kissing in here?"

Before I can say a word, Hollis blurts, "Yes! So if you don't want to be sickened, you better leave!"

Mila closes her mouth and darts out the door into the fading evening light.

***

As Hollis and I walk around the last row of homes toward my grandmother's house, the light bounces off her flaxen hair. She is chattering about Tristeh. I feel bad for not listening. I like the sound of her voice but can't focus on all the words. I can always rely on her to fill my silent sadness with her joy.

The sun is setting beyond the ash of our dead Tree. Despair threatens to drown my intentions. There is so much to be sad about, but I don't have time to face it right now. I push it away the same way I pushed little Killian away this morning. I felt bad for doing it. I'm sure a five-year-old would be confused and scared without a father too.

Shuffling and hushed voices come from inside my grandmother's cabin as we climb the front porch steps. I knock and announce myself, "Grandmother, it's Ledger."

"Come," a faint voice says.

I steel myself and push the old wood door into the old musty cabin. My grandmother is nestled in her bed, beneath several quilts. She is sitting up in an ivory nightdress with her back against a thick pile of pillows. Her straight white hair lies neatly on her shoulders.

I'm surprised her cheeks are rosy and eyes are bright with life—better than before I left. Something in me needs to see each and every person I know who survived the attack on Balfour. It is reassuring to hug them and tell them I'm glad they are alive. Mother was right, a little over half of our people are still here.

"Come, Edgy," Grandmother calls as I close the door behind Hollis.

"Hey, little old lady," Hollis says.

I'm embarrassed at her words.

Grandmother exchanges absurd pleasantries with her. "Dear Hollis. You look as untamed as ever."

Hollis smiles like it's a compliment as I offer her the single chair next to the bed. She sits primly, smoothing out her powder blue overdress and white underdress as she crosses her legs. She strokes Grandmother's old wrinkly hand as I gather my thoughts.

"I need to ask you some questions about the old days," I begin. "Are you up for that?"

"Of course I'm up for it. I'm not dead yet," she says, sounding out of breath. Hollis giggles. Grandmother smiles, pushing her sagging cheeks back from her yellow teeth, and gives an airy laugh. I feel even more uncomfortable after she says the word *dead*. It scares me to even think of it and she just blurts it out.

Under the blanket, Grandmother slides her legs to the side and pats the bed. "Sit here." She puts her hand back in Hollis's as I sit beside her. "Well, ask me."

I am taken aback by her directness, and remember it's Grandmother. She will listen to me. She's never shut down our conversations like everyone else does, like the elders of Balfour. At a sound on the roof or in the loft, I pause before divulging my secrets. But it must have been the wind.

I say, "While on Ellery, we heard a rumor. Someone said there was a person living in Balfour who is Ellerian royalty." I cut right to it and hope she knows something. Anything. "Do you know if—"

"It's true," she interrupts.

My jaw drops and eyebrows raise.

She leans forward and whispers, "I am an Ellerian princess."

Hollis gasps and my face flushes. *Is she kidding? Is she crazy?* I should have asked my mother how well her mind is.

"Sunshine, I've been waiting my whole life to tell someone that." She lays back on the pillows and exhales so long, I fear it's her last one. I wait for her to take another. When it comes, it is deep and full of relief.

“You?” Hollis asks before I can even take a breath. “How can this be?”

The front door creaks loudly and my mother comes through with an arm load of vegetables. “Oh good, you made it.” Mother smiles. “Help me with these.”

Hollis leaps up and catches a handful of carrots before they hit the ground. I hope we can return to this conversation. Moving quickly, I help Mother with a basket of eggs and a mess of greens.

Mother thanks me and tells me to get back to Grandmother.

“Does Mother know?” I whisper, hoping we can continue.

“Oh, yes. Adaya knows all my secrets.”

Hollis takes her seat. “Tell us.”

“Yes, yes. The story we tell around the Hundred Harvest Tree begins with a flat out lie and a few half-truths, but the rest is true. I agreed to tell it that way so our people had a reason to fight and remain separate.”

The history of Balfour told around the sacred Tree is based on a lie? My brows lower as I sift the lies from the truth on my own. But if it is built on lies, how can any of it be true?

She continues, “I am the youngest granddaughter of King Rayven. I wasn’t lost in the woods. I was left behind.”

“Oh my stars,” Hollis says.

I want to shush her, but I don’t want to waste the time.

“I was left behind because I am wingless. I remember my grandfather. He loved me. I was his favorite.” Her gaze grows distant and she smiles at the pleasant memories. “I made him laugh. He had the greatest laugh.”

“Mother, tell him why,” my mother interrupts.

"I'm getting there, Adaya," she says sternly. "This is my story, and I'll use however many words I want."

Mother shakes her head and goes back to shucking peas. Hollis giggles and puts both her hands in Grandmother's, as if bracing herself.

"Anyway, Ellery discarded wingless children. They claimed it was too dangerous to live in the sky without wings. That's how they justified it. They threw them out like criminals—tiny, helpless babies. Then, when a wingless was born to the royal family, well, they didn't know what to do with me.

"I remember a fight between my parents. Mother feared someone would kill me. Father argued, saying they should have obeyed the laws and got rid of me when I was born." She purses her lips, pressing through old wounds. "When I was about four, during one of the feasts, my mother left me with a family in Balfour. The lady who I came to know as my new mother hid me in a dug-out cellar every year. Each year, Ellery battled us for supposedly abducting me."

I sit back on the bed feeling dizzy with the new information.

Hollis says, "What in the name of sanity—" She shakes her head as Grandmother continues.

"So I fought them in my own way. I helped smuggle wingless children off Ellery for years. My dear friend, Gracelyn, would meet me out by the lake, and I'd receive a bundle."

"You?" I ask. "You're the one who brought Tolliver here?"

"Well, that was the year I started needing help and I sent

someone else." She peers around me and raises her eyebrows at my mother.

"I brought Tolliver home. He was my first success." She looks down at her hands cracking open the green shells and dropping peas in a bowl in her lap. "I had to keep him."

"How many wingless Ellerians did you bring into Balfour?" I ask.

"More dead than alive, I'm sad to say," Grandmother replies.

Anger balls itself in my gut and I want to unravel it, but it grows thicker with each word.

"It's like wingless ones were banished before they had a chance to live," Hollis says.

"You're exactly right." Grandmother gives one solid nod, sticking out her chin. "Wingless are considered lower than the lowest class on that island, all because of the way we were born."

Another thud comes from the loft and something moves from the corner of my vision. I leap from the bed and yank the blade from my belt to protect Grandmother.

"Oh, Ledger, you don't have to do that," Grandmother says, patting my weapon-wielding arm.

"You are the lost Ellerian princess?" an unfamiliar voice whispers from above. A woman steps to the edge of the loft. Her eyes are round with surprise. Brown and white-tipped wings spread wide, ready for flight.

"Who in the wild world are you?" Hollis blurts.

"Hollis," Grandmother reprimands. "She is my guest."

"Sorry," she says, confusion and shame burning in her cheeks.

Unable to understand all of this at the same time, I turn back to Grandmother. "Ellery is searching for you." Panic spins the ball of anger out of control. "They are sending an assassin to kill you!"

Grandmother shrugs. "Sounds about right." Her eyes twinkle with defiance. Hollis gives me the same look sometimes.

"What should we do?" My mind reels, and the blade glints in my hand.

"First, put the knife away," she says.

I shake the tension from my shoulders.

Grandmother continues, "Second, now that I know they are coming, all we can be is ready." She smirks at Hollis. "It's about time, too."

LET ME GO 29

LEDGER

"Who is she?" I gape at the woman who spreads her tan and white wings and flies from the loft to the other side of Grandmother's bed. She is hefty and muscular for a woman. Her body is draped with a long, sweeping gray dress with an apron tied at her waist like the washmaid who walked us to the bathing rooms on Ellery, except for the missing headpiece.

She pushes her short brown hair behind her ears and says, "I am Sybella."

Her brown eyes have an intensity that makes me look away. The name comes rattling back to my memory. *Angus's angel's name is Sybella.*

Another woman lands beside her, barely making a sound besides the ruffling of feathers. She is an older woman with short, spiky silver hair in the same dress, with the same tan wings with white tips.

"This is my mother, Neelie." Sybella touches the woman's shoulder.

"Hello, Ledger. We've heard so much about you." Neelie peers at me, then Hollis.

"I'm Hollis." She scoots to the edge of her seat.

"The elders refused to let them stay in Balfour," Grandmother explains. "I'm harboring them until Ellery breezes on by, or the elders have a change of heart. Whichever comes first."

I ask, "You are the ones who helped Angus escape?"

Sybella's intense gaze softens at his name. One cheek pushes upward in a half smile. "Yes."

"And are you the one who smuggled Tolliver from Ellery?" My eyes connect with the older woman.

"No, no. Morgania was the one who did that. We assisted her on Ellery. We are nurses as well." The corners of Neelie's mouth droop. "But when she passed away, we knew we had to leave. Her death was not an accident."

"The informant? Is that who you mean? The one who said a royal lives in Balfour."

"She thought it would help keep her safe to tell the advisors of the living royal and withheld the name—your Ellerian name, Paloma." She gazes at Grandmother.

Her Ellerian name is Paloma? White hair frames her face. She probably would have had white wings, like Alouette.

"Revealing that information got her killed," Sybella says and closes the distance to Grandmother's bedside. "You are the lost Ellerian princess?" she asks again. "Do you realize what this means?"

Grandmother tips her head toward Sybella, eyebrows raised. "It could mean a whole lot of things, darling. Some of which I'm not willing to put myself in the middle of."

Sybella puts a hand to her chest and kneels before my bedridden grandmother. Neelie lowers her head.

"Oh, don't do that." Grandmother waves her hand and Sybella rises.

It slowly seeps into my mind what all of this means. "You can bring peace between Balfour and Ellery," I say.

She laughs but Sybella agrees, "Yes, you can change the laws. Our people can have a choice to live in the sky or on the ground."

Shaking my head, I consider how they sound like prisoners to that island.

I stand up tall. "And you can put an end to discarding the wingless."

Grandmother smiles and I take it as an agreement.

Hollis stands up and takes my hand. "And you can help me get my dragon back."

***

Angus smiles at me in the darkness. I approach from the shadows and walk up the front steps without so much as a creaking board. He slides away the wood barring the door. It was easy for me to sneak out of Grandmother's cottage. I'm sleeping there voluntarily to keep her safe because she refused to allow me to place a guard at her door. She doesn't want anyone to know who she is. So I will be the guard for now.

Inside, the lock-up cabin is dark aside from the soft orange glow of the fireplace.

"Time to go," I whisper.

A sharp gasp comes from Alouette. "Oh, Ledger. You scared me."

"Sorry." I tiptoe to the back room where Alouette is sitting up on the bed. "Where's Dayson?"

She points to the loft. I'm relieved she isn't panicking anymore.

"I'll fetch him," Alouette says stretching.

I don't want to be the one to wake him. He can be pretty intense. It would be like waking a hungry dragon.

She rubs her eyes and glides past me. As her wings flap air across my skin, my curly brown locks float out of my face. She wakes him quietly, gently. She did better than I would have.

Both of them step from the edge of the loft and join me on the first floor. The small amount of light bounces off his face. One side of his black hair is sticking out at a weird angle, and a wrinkle mars his cheek.

"It's now or never," I say heading for the door. Alouette catches up with me quickly.

She stops me. "Thank you, Ledger." Putting both her hands in mine, she looks me full in the face. "I wouldn't be alive if it weren't for you. I will never understand why you traveled all that way for me. But you did. And I will always be grateful for you."

Shuffling from one foot to the other, I glance out the door. I don't want to talk about this right now. We need to get out of here, and I need to get back in bed before anyone sees anything. With no idea what to say, I stand there silent for a few awkward moments.

She snickers with a sad smile. “The best way to send you to crazyland is to say something meaningful?”

I give a fake laugh as my cheeks warm. “I don’t want you to go,” I admit.

“I know.” She smiles. “I wish I could stay—we could stay. If only the rest of Balfour was as loyal and as kind as you.”

She turns to Dayson, who’s pressing his hair flat. He yawns. She releases my hands as I get my wits about me. They pull their cloaks on, buttoning them in the front.

“Oh, by the way. I found the royal,” I say, shifting the conversation from something sad and desperate to something happy. “The last living royal of Ellery is my grandmother.”

Dayson raises his eyebrows.

“She will make a great queen.” I realize I’m wasting time to get a few more minutes with Alouette.

“Is she still alive?” he asks.

“Yes. I wish you could meet her. You’d like her.”

He takes a breath to say something, when Angus pops his head in the door, “Are we going to read sonnets and kiss in the firelight, or are we going to get a move on?”

Alouette smiles at him and follows him out the door.

“I’m glad you found her, Ledger,” Dayson says as he offers to let me go through the door next. “I wish you well.”

I am grateful for his friendship. He didn’t have to help us get this far and risk being executed by my village. I owe him—a lot.

We sneak around the back of the cottage, where I take the lead. Passing three more rows of homes, we duck from shadow to shadow. Dayson’s gray wings blend into the night. I'm not sure how well hidden Alouette's brilliant white wings are from sight, but I press on anyway. We reach the edge of the north woods without incident. Sneaking a few paces into the dark cover of the canopy, we stop to say our last goodbyes.

I don't want to cry about her leaving, but it feels so final when she says, "Goodbye, Ledger."

All those times she would float off to her island in the sky, I at least had the reassurance I'd see her again next year. "Please come back once Ellery has gone by," I plead. "Promise me."

Alouette shakes her head. "You know what it's like for me here."

"But what if we can make peace with Ellery?" I ask.

"What if you can't?"

"What if…" I lose my train of thought when she hugs me. Despair has been chasing me for so long. It catches up with me, barging right in. Tears claw their way out, and sadness chokes the breath from my lungs.

"Let me go, Ledger."

It's hard to let something go that I've wanted for so long. Her hair brushes my chin and I sink my face into it. Shaking my head, I can't let go.

"I love you, dear friend," she says into my chest.

What does that even mean? To say I love you and goodbye.

She pushes away from me and I release my hold. The ache in my heart overwhelms me.

"Take care of her, Dayson."

"I will." Dayson shakes my forearm, the Ellerian sign of

respect, and pats me on the shoulder. "Goodbye."

"Thank you for getting me off Ellery," I say with a quivering voice. "And getting me home safe." I wish I could be more like him: powerful and determined.

He nods and releases me.

They head into the darkness together. Gray wings. White wings. Walking side by side. I quietly follow them through the trees until they reach a small clearing. Simultaneously, they leap into the air. Wings beating. Getting smaller and smaller until they disappear into the night.

30 DELIRIOUS

TOLLIVER

At every turn, more winged people flood into the hallway. I tuck into a doorway and wait for them to approach. At the last moment, I turn the knob to hide in whatever room I find.

A cold draft hits me in the face. The voices recede in the hall and I twist the knob again, pulling it gently closed. More shouts fill the hall as someone says the word Balfourian. This dark place is the only option. I tiptoe toward the outside wall where slivers of light peek between thick curtains. Tripping over a small table on my way to the light, I gasp. My toe throbs as I recover my pace. Behind the curtain, I find several closed doors with carved crests in them that feature a bird with a leafy branch in its beak.

I'm in the royal chambers! Beyond these doors is a wide balcony with no way down. I would be trapped.

Something shuffles outside the door, and I dart into the next room. My eyes adjust to the dimness. The light creeps in around more curtains on a large bed in the center of the room. The white curtains hang all around its frame with neatly made blankets atop. This is where we laid Hollis with her broken leg, in the king's chambers. I remember the determination on Kava's face as she set Hollis's leg. I also didn't miss the tear that streaked down Kava's cheek after she yanked the broken bone back into place. Ledger and I carried Hollis into this room, where she spent weeks recovering. She left it a mess, I'm sure of it.

It doesn't matter. I must hide. Under the bed is a wide expanse; anyone could see me under there. Then the door in the sitting room squeaks open and light floods in. I scramble around the bed and slide under the mattress toward the headboard. I hid from Angus like this and he never found me.

Maybe they won't notice the pillows a few inches higher, the way Angus didn't. The mattress is very light, and with my head facing the headboard, I can breathe.

"Search these rooms," a guardian yells. "Bring torches. Light one over there."

Footsteps and voices fill the royal quarters. I hold very still. Someone places a hand on the bed, maybe to check underneath.

"No one is here," a man says.

"She said he was wingless."

"We should check the Balfourians' rooms," a lower voice says.

They scuffle out and shut the door with a boom. I have to get back to the laundry room, but now I am being hunted.

My gut twists as I realize I must wait here until nightfall. Waiting and patience don't come easy. I tally how many times I've had to fake patience: cramped in the laundry bag, stuck in the storeroom, locked on level three, trapped in the prison cell, and an entire year on Ellery waiting for this day. And I blew it.

I need to make my way to the laundry, where Belamy can get me off Ellery—immediately.

***

It's been quite a long time since I've heard any sort of movement from the hall or seen any light between the curtains. Well past whatever curfew they have, I take the chance that they aren't patrolling their own halls through the night waiting for me to emerge. I pull the door open and scan the hallway. No one is around. I sneak to the end and peer around the corner into the high-ceilinged royal hall. I went the wrong way and need to go back, past the king's chambers and to the north hall to get to the laundry. I keep scuffing in the leather shoes, so I kneel and remove them to keep my steps as silent as possible. I tuck them in the back of my waistband.

My bare feet pad across the cold floor, carrying me down the inner hall. Silently, I pass door after door of the upper class of Ellery and the royal chambers. A torch lights the end, and I guide myself toward it with stealth.

No one stirs. I peek around the bend into the north hall and find it empty as well. I stay close to the wall and keep my head down until I reach the door leading downward into the laundry. In the darkness of the stairwell, the familiar smell of suds and lavender waft in my face.

I dart past the pools of water and swing into my storeroom,

glad to be hidden and safe. A fading lantern sits in the middle of the floor. I frown. *What is that doing here?*

"Toll?" a voice beckons from the back corner. He moans and rolls toward the small bit of light.

"Belamy? What are you—" I stop short. His dark face is covered in blood. He is holding the right side of his torso. Blood seeps from a gaping wound.

I run to him and snatch a few cloths from the table on the way. I pry his hands away from his side and press folds of fabric into it. I do as I remember seeing Kava do on more than one occasion. Press on the wound. Wrap it tightly. Stop the bleeding. With plenty to wrap it, I hand him a piece to press against the gash on his forehead.

"Where do I find fresh water down here?" I ask.

He takes a moment to answer. I think he is trying not to cry. "On the far wall is a pump," he says.

I take off through the laundry room. The pump overhangs a trough leading to a pool of soapy water. Clear liquid comes out as I pump it up and down. I fill a metal bucket from nearby and lug it to the storeroom.

I dip a cloth in the water and wipe Belamy's forehead. Grabbing the light, I hold it over the wound. The slice is only the width of my knuckle, but it sure is gushing a lot of blood.

"Press hard to get it to stop bleeding. Head wounds are the worst." I repeat Kava's words that rattle around in my head. I sit next to him on the mound.

"Thanks Tolliver," he says, choking on the pain. "Did you talk to your father?"

I'm ashamed that I lost the opportunity. "No, I didn't. This girl came in and found me."

"Your sister," he says.

"Why didn't you tell me about her! I wasn't prepared. I wasn't expecting—her." I bring her face to my mind. Pale, blonde. I never considered how much I don't look like my Balfourian family. She definitely looks like me. I put a hand to my forehead where a headache pulsates.

"Oh, I didn't realize I hadn't." He scowls and it's obvious his brow hurts. Then he laughs at his pain with a goofy grin.

"You should have at least told me she might come around before my father. I scared her off and had to hide." I throw up my hands, feeling guilty for snapping at a bleeding man who's done nothing but help me.

"Sorry, man, sorry."

I shake my head. He doesn't need to apologize. This is my fault, not his. "What happened to you, Belamy?"

"I was guarding three-eight and they burst in looking for the Balfourians– well, you." He takes a deep breath and lets it out slowly, pressing harder on his torso. "If I wasn't caught off guard, I could have lied my way out of it. But me and Char got into it. I never liked that man anyway. He jabbed me in the gut and I punched him in the face. Then he clipped me with the butt of his sword." He points at his forehead.

"How deep do you think the cut is in your gut?"

"It's only a slice through the skin, not a stab." He presses again, and tears form in his eyes. He is lying.

I consider what we could do. "We need to get out of here. This is one of those scenarios where we both end up dead, and I'd rather escape before that."

He gasps at the pain as he leans forward. I put a hand on his chest, keeping him from getting up.

"But we need to get you some stitches." I wish Kava were here. She'd be able to stitch him back together in no time, and then we'd be on our way before sunup.

Belamy says, "I could use a drink."

Peering into the bucket full of blood and rags, I flare my nostrils at it. Remembering the bottle in my hiding place, I stick my head under the table and feel around for the cylinder. As soon as I get my hands on it, I jiggle it. *Nearly empty.* So I dart off to fill it under the pump.

Belamy guzzles nearly the whole thing. "Whew!" He hands it back and pants for a moment.

I lift the bloody cloth from his forehead. It has stopped bleeding. I touch it, and it oozes a little blood.

He groans in pain.

"Sorry." I place a clean cloth over it and he holds it in place. "Where can we find thread? And a needle? You have seamstresses on this island. Do they have a room off the laundry where they keep stuff?"

"No, they are on twelve."

"Twelve?" I yell. My voice echoes out of the storeroom and around the laundry. I clamp my mouth shut, regretting my outburst. "I can't get to twelve. Can you walk?"

"It was hard getting down here. I nearly fell down the stairs."

"Do you think if we wait for morning, Hana will be able to help us?" I ask.

His eyes light up. "Yes, yes, we could ask her." He smiles and lays his head back. His words start to slur. "We can ask the girl with the round cheeks. She's so pretty…"

He drifts off and I touch his arm.

"Don't get delirious on me."

His reaction is delayed. "I'm not. I'm just…tired."

I switch out the folded bandage on his torso and tuck another tightly beneath the wrap. I swallow the regret that wants to leap its way out of my stomach. This is all my fault. "Okay," I say. "Let's wait till morning, and then you can fly me off this island."

31

SO WAS ELLERY

LEDGER

Sweat trickles down my temples and through the scruff on my chin. Heat rolls from the blacksmithing furnace as Mila pumps the bellows. The large, triangular bellows are almost as big as she is. She isn't as small as Hollis, but it takes a lot of effort for her to pump them. Mila is quite strong for a girl. I said she probably couldn't work the bellows for the amount of time needed to finish today's projects. She stuck out her chin and proceeded to prove me wrong. She is sitting on the low stool, dusty blue skirts gathered out of the way, and presses the handles of the bellows together over and over. Her curly brown hair is disheveled and hanging in her face. It would have been easier for her with Father's small bellows, but I borrowed it for my flying contraption, and is still on Ellery. Somewhere.

The coals glow red as I insert the bottom edge of the breastplate I'm reshaping. I spread the word yesterday that it is quicker to resize a breastplate than create a whole new one. So people have been showing up all morning to drop off armor for their mother, or sister, and in one case a daughter.

"Wah Caaaaaaw!" A voice screams. I leap into the air and drop the tongs with a clang.

"Hollis!" Mila scolds. "He could have burned me with something!"

It takes a moment to regain my thoughts as Hollis hauls several pieces of metal through the door. "I made sure he wasn't doing anything dangerous. Calm down." She lays them on the table along the wall and dances over to me. She bows and picks up the tongs. "Your tools, Your Highness."

Mila laughs and says, "Oh please. Ledger is the farthest thing from royalty you can get."

The offense hits me in the forehead at the same time as a revelation. If my grandmother is Ellerian royalty, that means—

Hollis blurts, "I beg to disagree, Ledger is—" I cover her mouth, stopping the secrets from tumbling out. No one can know about Grandmother being Ellerian royalty.

I release her, and she grumbles. "Yuck! Ledger, keep your filthy hands off my face. They taste like rancid cow sweat."

"I was trying to keep you from saying certain things out loud." I press my lips tightly together and wipe my hands on my leather apron.

"Oh, yes. Sorry." Slowly, Hollis's understands what I'm saying.

"What? Say what?" Mila asks. When neither of us look at her or answer, she whines, "Come on!"

Through the door comes Angus with several breastplates and a sword. "Hey, hey, hey. What's going on in here?"

"Ledger has a secret he won't tell me," Mila says.

"Oh, that he's in love with Hollis?" Angus winks. My heart tremors out of control and Hollis smiles wide. She grips her yellow skirts and curtsies.

"Everyone knows that." Mila crosses her arms.

"Hey!" I frown.

Hollis laughs, and Kava comes through the door, filling the room nearly to capacity. Or at least to *annoying capacity.*

"What are we laughing about?" Kava hefts her medical bag onto the workbench.

"Ledger is in love with Hollis." Mila sticks her tongue out at me.

"That's old news," Kava says flaring her nostrils like something stinks. "I'm here to check your wolf bite. Roll up your sleeve."

I pull and roll my sleeve until it's all bunched at my shoulder. She peels off the bandages and checks my upper arm.

"Good. The swelling is going down." She pokes one of the puncture wounds and says, "This one is forming a scab. They should be all scabbed up by next week."

As she slathers it with fresh ointment, I say, "Ellery should be here any day now. How are we going to get Tolliver down here? Did he tell you his plan, Kava?"

"Good question." Angus grabs a poking tool and messes with my perfectly lit forge.

"He told me nothing," Kava growls, and her brows press low in anger. She presses a bit too hard on my wound and I wince at the pain.

"Nothing at all?" Angus asks.

Hollis glances at Angus. "Did he tell *you* anything?" She starts handling a few daggers I sharpened yesterday. I run a hand through my oily hair, annoyed that everyone is touching my stuff.

Angus chuckles. "Think about it, lil' missy. I was pushing up daisies for all he knew. I haven't seen Tolliver since my last dragon flight. Oh, and you never did tell me how you got off that floating castle."

"You should ask Kava," I say with a smirk, as Kava finishes wrapping my arm with clean bandages.

Angus turns to Kava. She starts adjusting her brown dress, fiddling with the ties on her sleeve.

"You should ask Kava how many times she threw up." I smile and step away from her, pulling my sleeve back into place.

Hollis giggles.

"First of all!" Kava snaps. "Climbing down a privy is beyond revolting."

"But what about all the other times?" Hollis teases.

We all laugh together, even Angus who has no idea why.

"Second of all…" Tears well in Kava's eyes as she shouts, "I'm pregnant!"

I freeze. Hollis shrieks. Angus and Mila jolt. We wait for her to speak again.

I don't know what to say. *Is she happy? Is she mad?* I descend into more questions as Hollis flaunts her feelings about it.

"That's wonderful! You're the first one of us! I seriously thought I could beat you to it, but hey—"

"Stop it, Hollis. Just stop it!" Kava cries. "I can't do this without Tolliver." She yanks her bag from the workbench and stomps to the door.

Angus catches her and says, "Hey, hey, hey." His voice is low and soothing. "It's okay. Tolliver will be back any day now." Her tears flow as Angus folds her into his chest. He pets her long brown hair as if he's taming a wild mustang.

Hollis approaches and strokes her shoulder. "He will be back safe and sound. And you will have stressed for nothing."

She recovers from her fit as Angus releases her. I feel as if I'm supposed to say something. Nothing comes to mind. I'm better at changing the subject.

Hollis and Mila hug Kava one after the other and walk out the door chattering about babies and cute things.

I can't even think about Tolliver not making it back safe. Not with my father missing, with Alouette gone forever, and with so many other people I know dead or missing. It all makes me want to scream and throw things. Instead, I grab the tongs and pull the heated metal out of the fire.

Angus breaks the smothering silence. "I don't exactly know what to do about Ellery. But I know once Tolliver comes back and Ellery is long gone, I am going to find our men." Angus slides the many projects to the side of the worktable and heaves himself on top, legs dangling off the edge.

With his hands on the knees of his brown trousers, he details a plan to rescue the men of Balfour. "Toll and I will gather anyone who wants to go. We will head east, probably before the Harvest Festival. We will track those savages down and save Fergus, Berthold, my father, Cullen, Brecken, and whoever else they took. Maybe we can sneak up on them in the night to release them."

He includes his own father in the list. Before I can stop myself, I ask, "Is your father alive?"

His intense glare makes me nervous. "We never found his body, and only one man said he saw him fall. Which could mean he is still alive. Maybe wounded."

His intensity is hope.

I nod, pushing up my bottom lip. "Okay, I'm in."

Angus smiles with sad eyes. "You don't have to do that, Ledger."

"You came with me. Why can't I come with you?"

"I don't know. But take some time to think about it. It will be dangerous."

"So was Ellery."

"It will be a long trek."

"So was Ellery."

"You could get killed."

I raise my eyebrows at him, hoping I don't have to repeat myself again. I feel a bit ashamed because I didn't think of rescuing my own father. "I'm going with, Angus. You can't get rid of me."

INJUSTICE 32

TOLLIVER

"*I love you more than the sun; I love you more than the moon.*" The song drifts into my dreams and pries me back to reality. I awake in the storeroom, hidden under the table. Belamy is asleep in the corner, out of sight of the door. The lantern is extinguished, but the washmaids light the laundry area brightly.

I crawl from my bed to Belamy. He is lying awkwardly on his black wings. They are splayed to one side, and his face is half hidden in cloth with his mouth wide open.

"Belamy," I whisper, placing a hand on his shoulder. "Bel, wake up." I jostle him and his mouth clamps shut.

Good, he's still alive.

He groans, and I shush him. "Belamy, quiet." He rolls onto his back and puts a hand on his head.

He smacks his lips together as if they are dry with sleep. The bandages on his gut are soaked through.

"You need to get Hana," I say.

I heft him up, grabbing his dark hands in my pale ones.

He winces at the pain of standing upright. *Definitely worse than he says.*

He stumbles from the storeroom and whispers, "Hana," several times. A feminine gasp and concerned whispering drift through the door. Belamy replies quietly. She shuffles off and Belamy returns. He pushes the fabrics aside and hops up on the table. Tucking his wings tightly against his back, he leans against the stone wall. "Wake me when she returns," he says.

He dozes off for a long while. I stretch and pop my achy joints while I wait. Worry and suspicion drown my senses. *How long does it take to fly to twelve, get thread and a needle, and get back down here?*

Moments later, More than one set of feet stomp through the laundry. Intense, heavy feet. Hana says, "In there."

Instead of her round face, a guardian with an angry expression enters the storeroom. He glances briefly at Belamy, then dives into the air like a hawk after its prey. His wings carry him above me and his hands come down hard. I swing at him, batting him away. Belamy comes to and shouts, "Char! No!"

Belamy rises to my aid and growls as he keels over from the pain in his gut.

Char is barely distracted by Belamy's actions as he shoves me into the corner of the storeroom. He leaps on my back and holds me down as he ties my hands behind me. My head overhangs a pile of cloth and I notice the rotten outline of a snake—the dead animal Hana disposed of.

***

The morning light stings my eyes as two hulking guardians drag me up the laundry stairwell. I glance over my shoulder. Belamy is being hauled up the stairs by Char. His face is etched with pain, and the other guardian doesn't take it easy on him. His bandaged torso is covered in dried blood.

Before we reach the tall, closed doors of the throne room, they stand me on my own two feet. The last time I stood before these closed doors, I was pulling them open and walking to my young bride. She stood at the end of a path of flower petals, in the middle of the room, beside tall candlesticks lighting her face. She glowed. A vision of beauty. Her brown hair framed her face with delicate pink lips, and a flowing white dress hugged her slender frame. I remember she was fiddling with the violets in her hands. She was nervous. I made her nervous.

The doors swing open, and the guardians push me forward. The many wings and faces in the throne room yank me from the memory as they watch us approach the table of advisors.

Which advisor could my father be? I inspect each of their faces from left to right. An elderly gentleman sits on the end, disinterested and tired. That can't be him.

Beside him is a dark-skinned man with black wings. His dark beard is sprinkled with gray, making him shimmer in the light.

Next is an intense man with a black and white striped beard. Like a skunk. The look in his eyes promises murder. His muscles bulge beneath his black tunic. I tense and form fists behind me.

In the middle, Caedus laughs and says, "What is this?"

I ignore his rude smirk. The man next to him, I recognize him from somewhere. *Is he my father?* Sandy hair, gray-blue eyes, a strong, angular jaw. I want to run my hand along my face. *Do I have a jaw like his?*

The man next to him is slender, worried, and young. Maybe middle aged? By the pinched brows, he seems to be new to the table.

On the end is the small man who wanted me executed. I scowl at him. *He* had better not be my father.

Belamy is dragged to my side and is held up by Char. I want to punch the guardian in his smug face as he says, "Belamy assisted in this Balfourian's escape."

I want to defend him, but anything I say will confirm it's true.

"Where are the rest of them?" Advisor Caedus asks.

The guardians around me have blank faces. Char pushes his black hair out of his face, covering the guilty look in his eyes. "They are missing. When I searched their quarters, I found only Belamy."

Caedus turns to Belamy. "What do you have to say about this, Guardian Belamy?"

I grind my teeth together. *Trust Belamy. Trust Belamy,* I tell myself.

He takes a ragged breath. "They don't deserve to be treated like prisoners. All they wanted was to go home."

"That was not your responsibility," Caedus's voice booms and I steel myself. "You will take their place in prison for the treason you've carried out."

"Aye," the murderous man casts his vote.

"Thank you, Talon," Caedus says.

"Aye," the tired old man on the far left of the table agrees.

Advisor Caedus scans from left to right and eyes the young man who chimes in with his vote at the last possible moment, "Aye."

Caedus grabs his staff, slams it on the ground, and waves his hand. Belamy groans as Char and another guardian lift him into the air. They fly out of the tall throne room doors in a heap of wings and bloody rags. My gut rumbles with frustration. *I should have defended him. I should have said something.*

"The Balfourian is sentenced to death for trespassing beyond the designated quarters," Advisor Caedus declares.

Two of them agree, but before the third can speak, the dark one says in an old, shaky voice, "I think it's in our best interest to hold this one for collateral. Balfour may keep our royal from us, and what will we have?" He peers down the table. "We'll have nothing."

"Dear Samul, you are brilliant," Advisor Caedus says. His curly, peppery hair bounces on the top of his head.

"Get rid of him," Talon says. "He's made enough trouble, breaking into Advisor Tiberius's chambers. What's next? Yours? Mine?" He glowers at Caedus with low brows, lips pursed angrily.

"Nothing was taken. And I do not hold it against him," the man with slate-blue eyes says, connecting with mine. *Advisor Tiberius.*

I cannot confess who I am, not here. I do not want to risk my father's safety. But maybe I could buy myself some time? "I wasn't breaking in. I was searching for something."

The men around the table gape at me, as if just now

realizing I am a living being.

"What were you looking for?" Caedus asks.

"I found nothing in his chambers," I make sure to say first. "I was looking for evidence of who sent an assassin to Balfour to kill your so-called royal."

The room suddenly erupts with shouting. Men disagree with me. Some are flabbergasted as if it was new information, as if they'd not heard the rumors. The table of advisors shout at one another. I feel as though I dropped a torch on a massive stack of dry wood, ready to ignite at the tiniest spark. Blame is shouted around the table. The old man on the end is out of his seat pointing a finger at Talon. I would have pointed at him too. His dark brows lower even more as he rises from his chair, shouting back at the old man.

A loud sound cracks in the middle of it all. Advisor Caedus slams his staff on the floor. It takes a few more moments for the voices and rage to dwindle. Then he says, "How dare you make such an accusation, splitting our alliances with your lies."

I frown. With a loud voice I look him full in the face and say, "It's true. My brother and our friends escaped the island to stop it."

"Only one man could do something so audacious," Caedus says in a preachy tone. "Advisor Tiberius would kill our only chance of getting the rightful heir to the Ellerian throne." The voices explode again.

Tiberius leaps from his stool, knocking it to the ground. His white wings spread defensively. I can't hear him, but his mouth is forming the word no, over and over.

My blood rages through my body, shaking my limbs and

pounding through my head. *It can't be him. My father cannot be a murderer.*

"I want a republic, but not that way," Tiberius yells as the voices die down. He gently rights his stool, but his wings are still poised aggressively. Anger is etched on his face. "I want justice and collaboration. Not tyranny and absolute rulership." He opens his mouth to say more.

"Exactly!" Caedus interrupts. "You'll do anything to make sure no one is king. Even kill for it!"

"No!" Tiberius yells. "No, absolutely not!"

But the men around the table are all standing, many with angry eyes and mouths agape in shock. They believe Caedus.

"I think we should lock him up until we reach Balfour," Talon's voice booms over the others.

Many in the room agree: guardians, advisors, and people of the court. Advisor Caedus takes his staff and marks the finality to the debate. "I declare we lock up Advisor Tiberius, and anyone who supports him should be confined to a cell."

"Aye," the same four men declare one after the other.

The blood drains from my face. I caused my father to get locked up. Several guardians come around either side of the table, take Tiberius by the arms, and escort him to the door. His face is crimson and eyes blazing against the injustice.

"What of the Balfourian?" the young man on the right side asks.

Caedus waves his hand. "Just lock him up. We will deal with him when we arrive."

33 BREAKING THE RULES

LEDGER

When I arrive at Grandmother's cottage to guard her for the night, I find Angus standing with Sybella in front of the fire. His cleanly shaved cheeks are flushed as he leans down to kiss her hand. "I bid you goodnight, my dearest one," he says and presses his lips to her fingers.

I stifle a laugh.

Sybella blushes and her eyes are round with joy and surprise, like she's never been spoken to that way. I'm just as shocked to hear Angus romancing a girl—let alone a girl with wings. Then I think of how I adored Alouette for all those years and understand.

With a hand pressed to her heart, she says, "Goodnight," in an airy voice.

Angus is the most unkempt person I know and wouldn't dress neatly even under threat of death. But his tunic is tied neatly at the nape of his neck and his hands are almost clean. Angus spins and heads for the door. With an unabashed smile, he tips his head toward me. "Goodnight, old pal."

The door clicks shut, and I secure the lock. Sybella walks away dreamily as I lock the back door and make sure all the windows are sealed tight. Gathering her gray skirts in her hands, she flutters to the loft.

The cottage falls silent.

Grandmother doesn't say anything for a long time, until she sighs loudly. I need to check the loft window, but instead I ask, "Are you okay?"

Her wrinkled cheeks push up briefly, then droop again. "It's difficult to lose a husband of fifty seven years."

In her nightdress, she is wrapped in a knitted shawl of swirling gray and white. I sit on the chair at her bedside. "Can I ask what happened to Grandfather?"

She lowers her voice, as if too much volume would make her cry. "They came in two waves through the mountains. They had red warpaint down their cheeks. The men of Balfour fought on our sacred grounds. Just when they thought we had them pushed back to the mountains, another battalion of them came through the pass and overwhelmed our numbers. Grandfather joined the second battle. I told him not to. I told him he was too old and slow." She shakes her head. "But he wanted to defend his home."

She closes her eyes, and tears spill out. I wonder if I should leave her be.

"Jubal said he fought valiantly. He stood strong for so long." Opening her eyes, she says, "But I don't know if he was appeasing me with lies, or if it was true. It's too painful to ask anyone. So I hold onto a picture of him cutting down the enemy with endurance and strength."

Touching her arm, I give a gentle smile. Murmuring

comes from the loft and I remember the window. "Sybella and Neelie, are you still awake?"

"Yes," Neelie says.

"Can you make sure your window is locked?"

"It is."

Thanking them, I kiss Grandmother's wrinkly forehead, and then snuff out all the candles and lanterns lighting the big room. I pull my tunic over my head and collapse on the mat along the wall near the fireplace.

Awake for a long while, I hope I won't have to encounter an assassin and whatever skills they possess. I hope my being here is enough to ward anyone off. But Ellery still hasn't arrived, and no one has made an attempt at my Grandmother's life since I've been back. It feels like I'm guarding her to relieve my own paranoia.

My dreams swirl in and out of darkness, including men with bloody tears.

When a floor board squeaks, I am startled awake. My heartbeat is racing long before my mind comes to consciousness. The room is pitch black. I wait for another sound. Did I dream it?

I should have stoked the fire to keep some light in here.

My pulse pounds in my ears. I hold my breath to slow its rhythm.

A barely audible swish of feathers pierces the silence.

I pull a dagger from beneath my pillow.

"Who's there?" My voice cuts into the night.

A faint silhouette of wings and a male figure move in the dark. The assassin!

I dart from my mat and leap on the intruder's back so his

wings are unable to lift him. Feathers hit me in the face.

Dagger in hand, I slash at him. The blade hits an arm or something. He cries out and flips me over his head. I land flat on my back one pace away from Grandmother's bed.

I scramble from the ground and grab at his legs, stopping his forward motion. I stab my dagger into his thigh and he cries out in pain. "Ledger!"

Hearing my name disorients me.

Grandmother lights a candle on her nightstand, revealing the face of Dayson.

A gasp escapes my throat.

Blood spills down his leg. Flustered, I'm unsure whether I should help him or attack again. He drops his pearl-handled knife.

The two Ellerian women in the loft come running to the edge and peer down at us.

"What are you doing?" I demand. "Why are you sneaking in here?"

He gasps at the pain and falls back against the dresser near the door. The blade sliced through the skin, and maybe some muscle, and juts out the other side.

"I'm sorry, Ledger." He pulls the dagger from his thigh, moaning as it emerges. Dark blood runs down his black leather pants.

"Why?"

"I had to. I didn't have a choice." He reaches for the doorknob. "I had to." He dives out the door and his gray wings carry him from the steps into the sky.

I can't stop the rush of anger pounding in my head. *It was him this whole time. He was the one I was trying to outrun.*

I've never felt more betrayed, even when I found out Tolliver wasn't my blood brother.

I grit my teeth and resist the truth about him.

Furious at myself for trusting Dayson, I pound my fists on the floorboards and cry, "Why him?" It feels like a knife to the heart.

"Dayson, son of Caedus." Neelie's voice drifts down from the loft, soft and monotone. "Caedus is the one who ordered Morgania to be killed."

Grandmother lies back in her bed, angry and tired—but alive and well.

"Advisor Caedus is his father?" I growl. His father murdered the informant and sent Dayson to become a murderer. I feel the knife turn in my heart.

***

I slam around the cottage a bit too loudly this morning, and Mother scolds me as though I'm five years old again. I deserve it, I guess. So I leave early and violently hammer out breastplates to relieve the anger caked onto my whole body, as if I've been dipped into raging wax, over and over.

I have no choice but to harden.

Dayson betrayed me last night. I trusted him, brought him into my village. I told the elders he was safe to have around. I even helped him escape lock-up. *I am such a naïve fool.*

Jubal commanded me to finish smithing during the day and walk sentry duty on the north side of the village through the night. I told him Dayson attacked Grandmother. When

Grandmother shook her head at me from across the room, I couldn't even tell him it is because she is an Ellerian royal. Telling half-truths makes my head hurt.

Jubal wouldn't allow me to guard her cottage, and placed a *real* guard at her door in case Dayson comes back.

Ellery will be here any day now and I'm grounded. I might as well be imprisoned in my own workshop.

I accidentally pound the bottom edge of a breastplate too thin. I growl and toss it on the workbench. *What happened to Alouette? How badly is Dayson wounded after I stabbed him? Gah! Why am I worrying about him?* He betrayed *me*.

A whisper drifts through the door, "Ledger."

I clamp my lips shut, not wanting to talk to anyone right now. I turn around to find Hollis with her billowing yellow skirts gathered in her hands as she tiptoes into the workshop. "You okay?" she asks.

I hold back a sharp retort. Instead, I inhale through my nose and nod. She approaches slowly. Anger coats my heart again at the thought she might be afraid of me.

She reaches out and puts her cold fingers on my arm. "I'm not supposed to be here." Her little white teeth appear beneath a sad smile. "I had to tell you I'm forbidden to see you."

My eyebrows twitch low. I'm confused. *She came to see me…to tell me she can't see me. Only Hollis.*

She says. "I love you, Ledger. I needed to make sure you're okay. When this blows over, things will be okay. *We* will be okay. Okay?"

The anger melts off my skin as she repeatedly says okay. I set the tools on the bench.

"Okay?" she asks again.

"Fine," I grumble, refusing to let her melt my heart. I want to stay mad. I overcompensate with a big frown, and my eyes respond by welling with tears. I try to suck them back in, hoping she doesn't see.

"Oh, Ledger," she coos. "You're not okay." She slides her arms around me, and I accept her hug. After a few moments I sigh, and she takes it as proof that her hug worked. She pulls me toward the ladder on the wall. I hang my heavy leather apron beside the forge and climb to the roof for a break from smithing and Balfourian life.

We sit with our backs against the knee-high wall facing the North Mountain. She leans on my shoulder and slides her frigid fingers between mine.

"I've been climbing to that summit and yelling for Tristeh every day." She points to the western edge.

It's where I used to meet Alouette each year when Ellery returned. I don't tell Hollis because I'm not sure what level of anger it would cause. I can't handle any more conflict.

"I'll find her. I know I will."

"I don't know which feels worse," I say. "Not being listened to by the elders, or being betrayed by Dayson, or stabbing him in the leg."

"It's all pretty bad." Hollis touches a finger to each of the brass buttons all the way up my green wool vest.

"I'm sorry about your father," I say. He too was taken prisoner with my father and many men of Balfour.

She says, "I am sad, but I can't cry. Is that wrong?"

"No." I pat her on the leg. "There's no time to cry. It's time to survive and fight for what we believe is right."

A sound cuts through the air. Three long blasts. It means Ellery has arrived and is within view of our southwestern borders. My body clenches with anger again. There will be fighting and killing, all because I can't get anyone to listen.

Hollis and I stand, scanning the horizon. Between the Briar to the south and the setting sun drifts a tiny mass of land far off in the distance.

"We could make peace with Ellery," I say. I clear my throat as tears threaten to fall. "No one else has to die." I think about Dayson out there somewhere bleeding to death.

I squint, but the guardians aren't descending yet. *Maybe Tolliver has intervened. Maybe he's gotten the Ellerian advisors to strike a peace treaty first.*

"I've got to go," Hollis says. She yanks me to her and kisses me hard on the mouth, then races down the ladder and off toward her home. Blood pulses through my head with mixed feelings of desire and foreboding. The last time she kissed me, bad things happened. Maybe if I stop breaking the rules, things will turn out the way they should.

But I have to do *something*, or nothing will turn out right.

34
THROWN AWAY

TOLLIVER

The dank smell of the prison hits my nose before we arrive at the entrance. I hold my breath against the stagnant stench of sweat, dirt, and desperation. The guardian pushes me down the first hallway, turning right down the hall of cells. Panic wraps its slithering fingers around my throat as I ache for air. Exhaling slowly, I walk past door after metal-barred door. They are all occupied, but not as full as they were when I was last down here.

I've failed, coming full circle back to the darkness of the dungeon. I inhale the smell of failure and let it choke me.

The seventh door hangs open, ready for me.

The tenth door, up one and across the hall, is being locked by a guardian with pale white wings. They glow in the torchlight of the hallway.

Advisor Tiberius's voice fills the air. I catch a glimpse of him arguing with the guardian. He pounds a fist on the iron bars. "I am innocent, Char. Advisor Caedus is taking control of Ellery and persecuting me to get there." Char doesn't acknowledge him and walks away. "He is planning something, something terrible. You must stop him!"

My escort pushes me into a cell on the left and slams the door behind me. At least I'm not in the cell at the far end of the hall with the solid metal door and one tiny window. At the back of my cell is a man seated on the floor, with his arms resting on his knees.

"Estephano," I say with recognition. "I'm sorry I got you thrown in here.

He leans his head against the stone wall, presses his dark hair behind his ear, and says, "I got myself thrown in here."

Tiberius's voice is laced with anger as it echoes down the hall. "I didn't even know an assassin was dispatched to Balfour. Who would do that?"

A man replies from another cell, maybe across from him, "I don't know. But something's wrong."

"I'm sorry you're stuck in here too, Advisor Cabot," he says.

A second advisor is imprisoned?

"Yes, several more were snatched up," Cabot says.

Feet shuffle as guardians shove another prisoner into a cell across the hall.

Eventually, the doors are all locked, the guardians back upstairs, and the torches flicker in the quiet hallway. I sit in the doorway facing the direction of Tiberius's cell, though I can't see him. My feet are propped against the door frame, cold and bare.

"Advisor Tiberius?" I call, unsure whether I can say everything I want to say to him. "I'm sorry."

There is an extensive awkward silence.

"You are not to blame for Caedus's knavery." He says finally. "He has something planned. I don't know what it is, but it can't be good."

Cabot's voice drifts down the hall. "He must have sent the assassin and waited for the information to come out so he could blame you. Or he never sent anyone. Who knows."

"Is it true?" Tiberius asks.

"I don't know," Cabot replies.

"I was asking the Balfourian."

He doesn't even know my name.

Should I introduce myself? As Tolliver? As Tylanu?

Nothing has gone right trusting these people. It always comes back to bite me. I shake my head against the distrust.

"My name is Tolliver."

"Tolliver," the man repeats. "Is it true an assassin on their way to Balfour?"

"I don't know if the information is true. But it was true enough for my brother to escape to stop him."

"Well, I hope he succeeded."

My heart soars. *He is a good man.*

"Me too," I say. I think of Ledger. He is the last person who could stop a trained killer. I hope someone will help him.

I want to tell him who I am, but I can't see him from my doorway. I want to tell him face to face. I want to watch his reaction, to see the look in his eyes—guilt or regret—about why I was thrown away.

35

DONE HIDING

LEDGER

I awake to the sound of the shofar. My head is heavy with sleep as I climb down the loft ladder. Mother is dressed and is lifting her newly resized breastplate over her head. I rush to help her place it correctly over her shoulders and tie it together at her sides. Most men don't like front and back armor pieces, but she specifically asked for it. I am proud that she likes things her way.

"I should be coming with you," I say, my voice cracking at my first words of the morning. "Sentry duty is such a waste."

She pulls her long, brown, graying hair from beneath the breastplate. "I might have to cut all this hair off, if this continues."

I frown. "It won't continue. Well, it shouldn't. If we could get Grandmother to declare who she is, we could end this."

She lifts my chin. "She is a stubborn woman. Kind of like a young man I know. I can't make either of you do anything.

The choice is yours alone." Her smile makes me feel better.

I wish I were more like my father. He would brazenly head into battle. I wish he were here to at least imitate, so I could find safety in his strength.

Then I realize what she just said. "You won't stop me from coming to the battlefield?"

"I am doing my part to keep this village thriving. You must do yours. No one else can do what you can. No one else knows what you know." She wraps her belt around the base of her breastplate. "If you don't, who will?"

"No one listens to me. I don't have influence like you, or Father, or even Tolliver. How do I get them all to listen?"

"You don't need all of them to listen. You just need one."

The sounds of the village fill the air. A shofar blast, horses neighing, and the undeniable clank of armor. She grabs her helmet off the table, beside four bowls of steaming morning stew for me, Mila, and the two little ones. Always the mother, even while being a warrior and an elder.

She kisses my cheek and heads into battle.

Mila is the Shield this year, the one who secures the house and keeps the children safe. She will hide in the cellar.

But I cannot hide anymore.

I am done hiding.

***

As soon as Mila, Killian, and Hazel are beneath the floorboards, I race from my cottage dressed in the armor my father made me. It is inflexible, but safe. Heavy and full of memories.

The village is silent. The children are all hidden, and most everyone over the age of thirteen is out on the battlefield. I shove back the fear, but thoughts of blood and death surface.

My sword slams against my thigh as I jog the last bend to Grandmother's house. I pound up the steps, past Ryllis guarding her door. I crash through the front door, and several voices gasp.

"Grandmother," I say boldly. She is not in her neatly made bed. I scan the cottage. She is seated at the table next to two winged women. Neelie and Sybella. "Oh, you're out of bed!"

"I'm not an invalid. I can walk, you know." Her voice is sharp with reprimand.

"I'm sorry, Grandmother. The last few times I've been here, you were…"

"Tired," she completes my thought with her own.

"Grandmother, I think it's time to tell everyone who you are." I am panting from the run, and don't form my words very well.

She laughs. "Are you here to tell me what I'm supposed to do, Ledger?"

I take a deep breath, calming my insides. Bossing her around won't work. So I change my tone. Taking off my belt and sword, I stand it beside the door and join them at the table. "It's an injustice that no one knows you are the missing Ellerian princess. Balfour has been battling your people for years with no knowledge of who you are. Now Ellery is looking for you. They want to make you their queen."

I pause. I don't ask any questions on purpose. I don't want her to say no.

“They do not want to make me their queen. You saw it for yourself. They want to execute me so they will be free to do whatever they want.” She sips her tea and looks at the ladies across from her. “Their monarchy has never worked.” Straight white hair neatly frames her face. Her brown eyes are sad. Still wearing rumpled and worn nightdress, she takes another sip.

“She’s right,” Neelie says. The old woman meets my eyes. “They will just kill her. It’s pointless.”

“What if she declares herself, becomes queen for a short time, and changes it to a republic?”

Grandmother’s laugh is less the silly one I’m used to, and more of a scoff. “I wouldn’t even make it that far. Who’s going to protect me? You?” She points at me. “These two?” She thumbs the Ellerian women at the table. “I have no way of ensuring we even get far enough to negotiate anything.”

“You’ll never know if you don’t try.”

Then we hear it. Three blasts. *They descend.* I’m missing it.

“I have to go,” I say. “I have to at least do something. People will die on both sides today if I do nothing.”

Stomping to the door, I grab my belt and wrap it around the bottom of my breastplate. My finger brushes the spot where my father left his smithing-mark. I push away the terror blocking the door and turn to my grandmother. “The Huyana I knew would say it like it is, no matter what anyone thought. That’s what you always taught me to do. I’m sorry you lost Grandfather, but it shouldn’t stop you from being you.”

She looks down, as if I shot her in the heart. She squeezes

a kerchief in her lap. It's the one Grandfather used to wear around his neck while working in his garden.

I feel bad for causing her pain. I wait for her to say something, but she doesn't. So I leave, pulling the door closed behind me, trying not to slam it. I imagine punching the guard at her door, but it's a girl. And Ryllis doesn't deserve to be punished for my frustrations. She watches me kick up the dirt on the path.

I can't even get my own grandmother to listen to me. I needed one person. I needed *her* to listen. She could change everything. I push myself to walk.

"You're going the wrong way, Ledger," a voice calls from behind me. "You're supposed to be on sentry duty."

Stopping in my tracks, I scream at Hollis, "I will not be on sentry duty no matter what anyone says!"

Startled by my reaction, the smile slips from her face. "I'm sorry, I was just teasing."

I'm erupting with emotion, and it burned her. Air fills my lungs and I shake my head. "I'm sorry. I can't get anyone to hear me. And I'm sick of everyone telling me what to do!" I can't keep the screech out of my voice.

I stomp away. I shouldn't be near her when I feel like this. I'm just blowing up at her.

She isn't frightened away from the anger bursting from my mouth as she hurries to catch up.

"Who won't listen?"

"Grandmother!" I shout. *Stop yelling at her, idiot!* I tell myself.

I bring down the tone my voice. "She could stop this war. She could make peace between Balfour and Ellery."

With the handle of my sword in my hand I slam the sheath against my leg. It stings almost as much as Grandmother's stubbornness.

"I'm sorry she won't listen," Hollis says. "She was usually the one who *did* listen to you."

"That's what I thought too," I whine. My tone irks me and I shake it off. No sense acting like a child if I don't get the benefits of being a child: living carefree, without responsibilities. I guess that's my problem. I've wanted to go home and back to the way things were, so I've been acting like a child. Letting people walk away, not listen, or dismiss me. I am done with that.

"Aren't you supposed to be doing something right now?" I notice she is wearing armor, men's trousers, and a sword.

"Don't you worry about me, Ledger, dear." She laughs and gives me a mischievous grin. "I'm on my way." She hits me in the middle of my breastplate and races off to the north.

"Now *you're* going the wrong way," I call, but she is already gone.

WITH OR WITHOUT 36

TOLLIVER

I called around the prison for Belamy, but he never answered. The last time someone didn't make it down here alongside me, he died.

"He would have been taken to the medical ward first," Tiberius says.

I nod even though he can't see me.

I ask, "Is it normal for people to be treated badly on this floating island?" As soon as the words escape my mouth, I realize they are harsh and judgmental. I ball up my fist and grind it into the stone floor, scraping my knuckles.

I hear a distant chuckle, maybe Cabot. "Didn't used to be that way, but I fear you are right, son."

"So much needs to be righted," Tiberius says. He seems loud, close to his door. "Limits on where we can live, the ground or the sky. The justice system has been a mess for years. Our advisors are split down the middle. Caedus doesn't know it's more than just Cabot and me. Many more wish to vote on our laws and change the way life has been.

So much death. So much loss."

I should tell him I am someone he's lost. Does he know the wingless are murdered or cast away? Maybe I should ease my way there. "Why are there limits to family sizes?" I ask.

"The real reason or the lie?" he asks. "Well, not really a lie. But we can only fit so many people on Ellery. We've built upward as far as we can. Believe it or not, we brought more stone on the island. When we did that, we sank several hundred feet in the sky."

I'm surprised it can even be affected. Ellery has always been the same height from the ground as far as I can remember.

He continues, "The real reason is control. If the royal family limits us, we remain at their mercy."

I slide my hand against the dusty stone floor and take a chance to trust. "What about the wingless?"

"Another form of control," Tiberius says. "Wingless have been born on Ellery for generations, then the king decided it was safer to purge the gene pool. So many were lost, adults and children. But that was before I was born. Not many know the truth about what happened back then." He raises his voice, "You're welcome, prisoners of Ellery! You will hear the truth before I die."

I am taken aback by his passion. *Can he be trusted with who I am? Should I trust this whole prison with my information?*

"Ever since those days," he continues, "When children were born—they called them deformed. They would be cast into the ocean. A quick death, they said."

I risk saying the words aloud. "I am one of those wingless children."

Silence follows.

"What?" Tiberius's voice is sincere with shock.

I gather the dust of the floor into a pile as I tell the truth. "I am a wingless Ellerian. I was smuggled off Ellery as a baby." I swat the pile away.

"You were smuggled off? How? By who?"

"Ellery's midwives started taking the wingless to Balfour."

"My stars," he whispers.

The light from the prison hall seems to dim.

I must tell him. "I came here to find my family."

"As you should."

I press my hand into the dust and leave a perfect outline of my hand. "You, Advisor Tiberius, are my father."

Keys jingle down the hall, and I wish I could punch the words from the air. Tiberius doesn't answer as a small woman sneaks past my cell. White wings, blonde hair…

"Kailani!" Tiberius gasps.

"Father, I've got to get you out of here. We are at Balfour. Caedus and the others are on the ground. Dayson is missing. I've heard terrible things about what he plans to do to you. So I hid until I could get to you."

"Kailani, this is so dangerous." The keys jingle again and clink into a lock. Voices drift from the head of the hallway. "Hurry, Kai, get in here."

The lock gives way, and the door grates open and drags closed. As footsteps enter, and another set of keys are brandished, she is hidden away in his cell and quiet.

A guardian appears in front of my door. “Time to go, Balfourian.”

Rising from the dust, I tense my arms and situate my feet beneath me.

He unlocks the door, reaches for me, and I punch him in the face. Fist throbbing, I dart past him down the hall toward my father’s cell. The guardian recovers and races after me. He yells to another guardian at the end of the hall.

I reach Tiberius’s cell and grab the bars. Kailani hides behind him with fear in her eyes.

I say, “With or without wings. I am here. I am your son, Tylanu.”

His chin juts up at the familiar name, eyes wide with shock.

The guardian grabs my arms and wrenches them behind me. With the help of a second guardian, they haul me out of the prison hall.

REACH JUST ONE 37

LEDGER

Staying away from the main road from Balfour to avoid being stopped, I scamper through field after ready field. Only half the fields have been harvested so far, and it's easy to stay concealed in them as I race toward the battlefield.

At the Briar, I search along its prickly edge for the next opening. The Briar is a natural fortress protecting our southern border. Paths wind through the thicket from one end to the other with openings here and there, large enough for a full-sized man, but small enough to block those with wings from entering. Our men retreat here when they know they've lost to Ellery. Again. I'm frustrated about always being on the losing side.

Holding my sword secure against my metal breastplate, I find a gap in the Briar with a path leading inside. Turning right, away from the main corridors filled with voices and footsteps, I look for an exit out the other side. My sleeve snags on a leafless vine. I yank and keep walking, hoping no one sees me. With the anxiety pumping through my veins, I no longer feel the pain of the wound in my arm.

Around the next bend in the maze of bramble, I find an opening to the south. I peer out from the far-right flank. The many men and women of Balfour stand in formation overlooking the open, rolling hills beneath the drifting island of Ellery. It looms to the southwest, and the morning sun casts a shadow toward us like a giant threatening to stomp us out.

Row upon row of Ellerian guardians face us. At the front are three Ellerian men. They are in heated conversation with Jubal and Chasen.

I can't find my mother. Everyone is wearing helmets.

Popping out of the Briar, I join the ranks. *What they are saying?* Shoving my helmet on my head, I sneak to the back row of Balfourians. Hopefully, no one will recognize me. I square my shoulders with my head held high and walk a little more Tolliver-like.

I press toward the front, row by row, and catch Caedus saying, "We've heard a rumor that a member of our Ellerian royal family is living among you. I just want to know if it is true. I wish to extend him the hand of hospitality and welcome him home."

I gasp at Caedus's lies. *He sent Dayson to assassinate the royal!*

Maybe Grandmother is right. She would be murdered if she came out here. I let out the breath I was holding. *I can't let him spread these lies.*

"We do not know who you speak of," Chasen replies.

"I know who you speak of," I yell, shocked when the words come flying out of my mouth. All the men glare at me. Those beside me seem to step away, making me stand out even more.

I pull the helmet from my head. "But you sent an assassin to kill her."

"Assuredly, it was not me," Advisor Caedus bellows. He turns to his men with a laugh and they stand completely still. General Talon, with his black and gray striped beard, is the largest among them. Every muscle in his body is taut.

"You sent your *son* to kill her." Feeling intimidated, I step forward one pace anyway. "Dayson is your son, isn't he?"

Several guardians look at him in surprise.

"He is my son, but I did not—"

"Lies!" I scream. My voice cracks, but I refuse to let him finish that lying sentence. "You want to be king, so you sent Dayson to kill her so she could not take the throne. Well, I stopped him!"

"Where is he?" Caedus takes a step in my direction. Talon and the company of guardians behind him take a loud step forward as well.

My body buzzes with fear. They could kill me at any second, with a flick of his finger.

"Ledger, be silent!" Jubal shouts.

"No! I will not shut up any longer. Balfourians need to hear the truth, just as much as Ellerians need to hear the truth." I point to Caedus's men. Their wings are poised ready for action, but their faces are glazed with shock. *If I can reach just one.*

"Where is my son?" Caedus demands again. He casts an intentional glance at Ellery suspended in the sky behind him.

"He's gone," I say. "I stabbed him and he's probably dead in the dirt somewhere."

His blue eyes glare with hatred. "That's too bad," he says with a wicked grin. "I have someone you might want."

We all gaze up at the edge of Ellery, where several winged men stand on either side of a wingless man with sandy hair—Tolliver.

"But since my son is dead…" Caedus turns to Ellery and lifts a hand straight up in the air.

THE FALL 38

TOLLIVER

I fight and rage against the guardians carrying me up the dark stairs from the prison. I kick the taller one, cracking his head against the wall. He groans through a string of curses. I twist one arm free and swing at the other one, connecting with his gut. He doubles over, releasing my other arm. I scramble through a stairwell splattered with blood and feathers. They grab at my ankles, tripping me at the top of the stairs. My face slaps against the cold stone landing.

"Get him up," the tall one says. He dabs his bleeding nose with the back of his hand. The other releases my ankle and drags me off the ground. He strips the torn sleeve off his arm and yanks my hands together in front of me. Wrapping the fabric around my wrists, he snickers at me.

"Stop fighting, wingless." He says it like an insult. It doesn't sting. "Or I'll throw you off even if he *doesn't* give the signal."

I jolt upright. *Throw me off?*

"Yeah, that's right. It's execution day." The tall one

laughs and leads the way through the grand hall. The other pushes me forward, toward the sun and the surface of Ellery.

The afternoon sun shines harshly on the stairs descending off the side of the island. Terror hits me in waves as I consider a quick plan to get away. The guardian grips the back of my shirt. I could swing around with my bound hands and run back up the steps. I could fight my way out of this. But as soon as I turn, he yanks me forward and kicks the back of my knees. I sail forward several paces, catching my balance two steps from the edge of Ellery.

"Want one last look at your wingless people?" one says.

"They can't save you, even if they wanted to," the other says. They both laugh together.

Down below, the men of Balfour are like the size of ants, gathered on the south side of the briers, the way we do for the Clash between Balfour and Ellery. Strangely, no one is fighting. The winged people are positioned on the ground. A man with gray wings stands at the front. Caedus.

The wind rages against my ears and flaps against my dirty tunic. Facing death, my heart rattles wildly. Long breaths bring it under control as I look straight down. *This can't be how it ends.*

I squint at movement directly below. A person. No, two people standing below, gazing up at me. The one with gray wings puts his hands out. He signals something to me. Is that Dayson?

A girl with white wings gapes at me with her hands on her hips. Long dark hair…Alouette?

Is he trying to say he will catch me? The way he caught Alouette? My gut wrenches and I lean back from the edge.

Ledger must have sent them to catch me.

Above me, in the blue sky, wispy white clouds gently roll by.

I'm going to fall.

I'm going to fail.

These men will push me off, the way they tried to execute Alouette. Dayson will attempt to catch me, but Alouette is much smaller than I. *How will he—?*

I peer over the edge again and Dayson speaks with his hands, explaining something to her.

Are they both going to catch me?

Oh, no, no, no.

I inhale through my nose and out through my mouth several times. I think of Kava. Her brown eyes. Her tender smile.

I must survive this for her.

I must trust Dayson and Alouette.

I must trust Ledger.

I must.

For her.

How can they possibly catch me? If these two men shove me off, I'll flip and twirl erratically. I need to control my fall.

Between the facing armies, the man with the gray wings—Caedus—lifts one hand in the air. *The signal.*

Before the two men can put their hands on me, I leap from the surface of Ellery, stretching my body out into a daring belly flop.

A strangled groan escapes my lips. My stomach slams into my throat as I choke back a gag. The air whips in my face and loudly past my ears. My first instinct is to close my eyes. Instead, I watch Dayson and Alouette leap from the ground.

As I descend alongside the massive rock on the underside of Ellery, thoughts flash through my mind. I'll never see Kava again. Never touch her face. Never say goodnight to my mother. Never work in the smithy shop again. Never learn another tool from my father. Never talk to my Ellerian father. And never meet Kailani with a smile.

I war against the rising despair and anger, tears dry as soon as they escape.

No! I will survive. I will get home. With my hands still tied, I lean into the fall, extending my arms over my head to keep from flipping over.

Halfway down, beneath the inverted mountain of Ellery, they reach me and twist into a dive alongside me.

Alouette's face is full of terror as she loops an arm under mine. Dayson doesn't even acknowledge me or meet my eyes as he grabs my other arm.

"One, two, three," Dayson shouts over the wind and they scoop all three of us from the dive at the same time. My insides lurch again, and dizziness hits me in the forehead. They pull up in time to soar across the treetops and toward the Briar. Toward my people. *All of my people.*

Shouting erupts from both sides of the battlefield. Rage and joy thrash in the air at the same time.

Caedus's contorted face follows us, and I know this has disrupted his plans.

Dayson and Alouette take me to the Balfourian people dressed in battle armor.

He releases my arm first and limps a few paces away,

visibly tired, almost gray in the face. A bloody bandage is wrapped around this thigh. He is wounded.

Alouette holds on to me for a moment longer, steadying me. A nearby Balfourian soldier wrenches her away from me. I scowl, confused. I thought Ledger sent them to catch me.

Before Dayson can be apprehended, he leaps into the air. Gray wings lift him over our heads.

"Thank you," I shout above the chaos. Dayson barely acknowledges me and flies toward the middle of the battlefield.

Alouette's wrists are tied around her wings, and the Balfourian pushes her down to kneel.

"What are you doing?" I ask. "She just saved my life."

"I'm simply following orders," a woman's voice emerges from beneath the helmet. I am startled by the sound, but before I can ask who she is, another voice draws my attention.

An armored woman runs from the left flank. "Tolliver," the woman says and lifts her helmet off her head.

Mother slices through my binds and wraps her arms around me, squeezing the breath from my lungs. I lift her small frame from the ground.

"Why are you out here?" I set her back on her feet.

"There's no time for that," she says. "I'm so glad you are alive."

INTO THE FIGHT 39

LEDGER

Dayson's voice booms from the sky, "It's over!" He lands in the middle of the battlefield and walks a few more paces to his father. "We do not need to gain the crown this way."

I wish I could run to Tolliver, but he is all the way on the other side of the Balfourian formation. He hugs Mother. My chest aches. *Will he be the same Tolliver I left on Ellery?*

Caedus yells at Dayson for all of us to hear. "You are weak! You couldn't even do one simple thing."

"That one simple thing is murder. No one else needs to die."

"This is what kings do. They *kill* to get where they are." He laughs as he angrily closes the distance between them. "You would have made a lousy king. It doesn't matter, though. I wasn't planning on dying anytime soon, so you'd never be king anyway."

Dayson's face pales with shock. A muscle twitches in his jaw as he pulls the sword from his side. Caedus matches his movements. Swords glint in the morning sun. The sound of their blades crashing together echoes across the wide space. All eyes are on them as they hack at each other. Caedus is red-faced and taking ground. Dayson, with clenched teeth and tears in his eyes, limps forward and back. I remember the gash in his leg, which I caused.

He will never survive.

I cannot let Caedus win this.

My hand drifts to my sword. Dayson blocks a blow, and Caedus is one step ahead, whirls around and slices his son across the back.

My feet are scrambling before I can think about what I am rushing into. *Don't think. Just fly.* I draw my sword and run into the fight.

Dayson is drained of energy. His movements are slow and laborious as the older man pushes him back toward the Balfourian front line. With two hands on his sword, Dayson brings it down at Caedus, who steps to the side and jabs his sword into his son's gut.

"Noooooo!" I yell, diving into the action.

Caedus draws back to slice again. I hit his sword with mine. He is surprised, and I swing at him, driving him several steps back. Dayson drops to the ground, blood seeping through his tunic.

Caedus looks at me with rage and satisfaction in his eyes. "Charge!"

Ellerian voices cut through the air, and both sides dive at each other with weapons raised. Jubal is first to Caedus's raised sword and pushes him back from me.

I drop at Dayson's side and press my hand to his wound, turning my fingers red.

He slumps into the dead grass, dropping his sword. "I'm sorry," he says. "I'm sorry."

I shake my head and scan the area for Alouette. A guardian darts over top of us, and there is no time to find her. I need to get Dayson out of here.

I duck a blow from another guardian and peer up into the face of Angus. He swats the sword from the guardian's hands and dives at him. All the men and women have such intensity on their faces.

Not only did I *not stop* this, I started it. For Dayson. The one who betrayed me. Swallowing the bile stinging my throat, I get to my feet and shove my hands under Dayson's arms.

I must get him out of here.

Shadows flit across the ground, and I catch a glimpse of more guardians coming from Ellery, old and young. Dread rattles my teeth together. I can't keep pretending to be brave when I am not.

It takes all my strength to drag Dayson toward the Briar. Across the field, the new guardians aren't fighting the wingless. They are fighting Caedus's men.

WE ARE ONE 40

TOLLIVER

Sword in hand, I swing at a guardian darting past my head, just out of reach. I've always thought it was cheating that they can defy the pull of the ground and escape a fight. Anger energizes my arms as I block a jab.

More men flit from the island's surface, and I recognize who it is: Advisor Tiberius and the others who were trapped in lockup. He leads the charge and blocks Caedus's men in from the south.

The guardian over my head lands, and I overpower him easily then shove him aside. Darting ahead, I fight my way toward the man with gray wings—toward Caedus.

I catch the glint of a sword and duck to the ground. The winged man's sword clangs on another and I glance up to find Belamy. His gut is bound tight with gauze, with a black leather breastplate cinching it all together, and he wields a sword with skill. Belamy pushes the man back and says, "Stop hacking at me, Zander! I don't want to have to kill you." The man takes to flight, leaving me with Belamy.

"Hey there, brute," Belamy says with a brilliant smile.

"That's *wingless brute* to you," I say.

"Looks as though you need a hand." He reaches down and lifts me up. Before I ask him how he's doing, a shrill noise cuts through the air, stopping everyone mid-fight.

Three heartbeats.

Another shriek stings my ears, and fire blasts from the sky.

A red dragon swoops around the battlefield, heading straight for the middle of the Clash.

Atop the red dragon, white wings with brown tips are poised wide open behind an older woman with stark white hair.

Balfourians and Ellerians alike scurry away from the center of the battlefield as the dragon descends to the cold hard ground. Belamy gasps and pushes me behind him, as if he could protect me from it. I swat his giant black wings out of my view and stand beside him, gaping at the sight.

My grandmother's face smiles wide from atop the dragon. *Wings?* I wonder. *Since when does she have wings?*

Caedus's wings and wild gray hair blow back. He is stunned by her arrival. The dragon lands in front of him and steps forward, lowering its nose close to his face.

I am several paces behind him, where I stand gaping at my grandmother, wings poised aggressively, eyes focused and stern.

"I am Paloma, daughter of Cecil, granddaughter of Raven, King of Ellery."

I gasp. "My grandmother is the royal?"

Belamy mutters, "That's *your* grandmother?"

Her amber-gold dress flows down either side of the dragon, flapping in the breeze. Her short white hair is stirred by the wind. She doesn't move to fix it. Her face is unwavering, royal in every way.

Adrenaline races through me. The battle has been halted. Everyone is watching her. I am suspicious of the stillness. I must protect her no matter what happens, I lift my sword and adjust my grip. Belamy holds his sword out, ready for a fight alongside me.

"Impostor!" Caedus shouts. "You're not—"

"I don't need *you* to tell me who I am," Grandmother cuts him off. "For your sake, I have proof of my royalty. Send an unarmed scribe so you can confirm my identity for the dim-witted unbelievers among you."

The wind whips through the silent battlefield. Caedus whispers to a man beside him.

From behind me, a man's voice commands attention. "I have brought a scribe." Tiberius takes flight, with smaller man at his side. "He has brought the records along with him, in anticipation of meeting you." He bows his head reverently.

Smart, I think.

Grandmother stays seated, wings rustling in the wind, but holding strong. "Your scribe may approach," she says to Tiberius. To Caedus she says, "You cannot be trusted at this time, Advisor Caedus. You are lucky I did not command this dragon to crush you."

A small voice says something and Tristeh takes a step forward, putting her spiky nose to his chest. Caedus steps back as if he's taken a heavy blow.

I know that voice. The dragon-girl herself is here

somewhere. Hollis. I almost killed this red beast on Ellery when we were surviving on our own. She fed it a lot of our food supply. When I discovered she was harboring it, she wouldn't let me kill it and released it instead. I chuckle to myself, grateful of her concern for the animal.

A winged man has taken flight over my head and suspended himself above the dragon. Tristeh turns her head toward him. He is visibly afraid, and his nervousness makes his flight erratic.

Grandmother hands him something small. He flies to the back of their lines. He lands out of sight. I consider asking Belamy if he would lift me to see. Voices rise from the back of Ellery's forces.

Tiberius rises into the sky. "You have the royal ring of King Raven himself!" His gaping mouth turns up in a smile. "The histories say he gave it to his granddaughter the day she was lost on the ground. You are the lost princess." He bows mid-air, showing reverence. Approaching the dragon, Tiberius hands Grandmother the ring and declares, "All hail Queen Paloma!"

He lands beside Caedus as everyone with wings kneels before her, and I join them in the dirt. They shout into the air, "Long live the queen, long live the queen, long live the queen."

My voice blends with theirs, and all of Balfour is on bended knee as well. They too have honored the new Queen of Ellery. Her voice fills the battlefield once again as we rise.

"People of Ellery and Balfour, I declare peace between our lands. You do not remember, but we are one people, winged and wingless. We all are Ellerian."

Several people gasp as she continues, "Our families divided long ago because of our differences."

The impact of her words quakes from person to person.

Belamy blurts, "What? More bloody secrets!" He shakes his head with tight lips.

"There will be no more fighting; no more death because of differences." Grandmother's voice echoes across the battlefield.

Shock covers the faces of each one across the hills and grasses.

"With and without wings. We are one," she says.

Grandmother continues, "If anyone has a problem with my rulership, speak so we may deal with you right now." She pauses for a long moment, and no one moves all across the valley, not even Caedus. "Well then, let us come together in peace. I invite you to the Balfourian Harvest Feast in two days' time."

Her eyes blaze in Caedus's direction. "Caedus, you are guilty of attempted murder and will remain in lock-up until I can deal with your dark ways."

The fact that she used the Balfourian term of "lock-up" instead of the Ellerian word, "prison," makes me smile.

The crisp scent of fall wafts in my face, and I realize change has come to Balfour.

Sweeping her eyes across the battlefield, Grandmother says, "Return to your homes. Balfour, go care for your children and prepare the feast. Ellery, to the sky. Advisors, meet me in the throne room immediately upon your arrival. We shall bring order on Ellery first, then we shall convene with advisors and elders together to discuss how to move forward."

A word is whispered and Tristeh's wings press the air, carrying her into the sky, but Grandmother is not alone on the dragon. Two other people are seated behind her.

My grandmother did not suddenly sprout wings!

An Ellerian woman with brown hair sits at the back with her brown wings with white tips spread wide. Between them, Hollis grips Grandmother around the waist and commands the dragon, "Fly, Tristeh!"

The woman folds down her wings as all three of them lean forward on the crimson dragon and soar into the sky.

On the ground, everyone hesitates for a moment—obviously marveling at the sight of her.

Belamy shatters the moment, saying, "See you in a couple days, apparently." He puts out a hand, and we shake forearms as true friends and countrymen.

As soon as the dragon reaches Ellery, everyone with wings takes to the sky and follows their queen to the island in the clouds.

Except for Dayson.

I follow our people toward the Briar. Ledger is pressing his hands on Dayson's wound. Blood is caked between his fingers. He must have wiped away tears, leaving a streak of Dayson's blood down his cheek.

Kneeling beside him, I meet Ledger's sad eyes. I touch two fingers on the side of Dayson's neck the way I've seen Kava do to check if someone is alive.

No heartbeat.

I gently shake my head at Ledger. Pulling his hands away, he stands and gazes from one side of the open field to the other.

"Release her," he shouts, pointing a blood soaked hand at Alouette.

Ruben unties the ropes from Alouette's wrists and she rips herself from his grip. Her face is distorted with horror: bared teeth and angry eyes. Alouette runs toward us, side-stepping Balfourians, making room for her enormous white wings and billowing black cloak.

"She should not see him like this," Ledger says in a panic. He scrambles a few steps toward her.

Yanking my dusty shirt over my head, I lay it over top of his face and wound.

"I'm sorry," Ledger says, blocking her way to the dead body.

She shakes her head vehemently and falls against him. He doesn't put his arms around her but stands there with his bloody hands at his side.

He guides her to Dayson.

"I think he knew he wouldn't survive this," she says staring at his frame on the ground. "The last thing he said to me was, 'I'm sorry I couldn't be a better man for you.'" She releases a silent sob.

Kneeling beside Dayson, she pulls the tunic from his face. "Goodbye, love." She touches his cheek for a quiet moment and puts her hand in his.

Several soldiers arrive with a stretcher. They lift Dayson onto it.

"What are you going to do now?" Ledger asks. "Go back to Ellery?"

Alouette peers up at him and shakes her head. "I can't

go back there." She releases Dayson's hand as the men carry his body away.

"Come to Balfour. Let us care for you."

She rises from the dust. "You really are the bond that holds us all together, Ledger. That's what Dayson said about you." She squares her shoulders and walks toward the Briar, toward Balfour.

Before following her, Ledger looks at the sky, chin quivering, and says to me, "I have a lot to tell you."

"Yeah," I chuckle, making light of a dark moment. "That you're Ellerian too?"

He sighs. Then someone slams into me from behind. I nearly topple onto Ledger, but arms grasp me, spinning me around. I clench my fists, ready to knock them out as I face my cousin.

Angus is alive!

Bliss shatters my sadness and I dive at him, grabbing him in a bear hug. I squeeze him so hard he gasps.

"Toll, you're killin' me!"

The sound of his voice makes me wail aloud. I pull away from him and gaze at his dirty, sweaty face. I'm filled with such joy; I kiss his dirty freckly cheek.

He squawks and yells, "Gah! Save it for Kava!"

41

HARVEST FEAST

LEDGER

The leafy path from Balfour to the Hundred Harvest Tree consists of mostly yellow leaves this year, not much orange because our sacred Tree was burned to the ground. We will never experience its blazing orange leaves again.

When the procession from Balfour to the Tree ends, all of Ellery is already there. Men, women, and children from the sky and the ground, dressed in their best, are crowded in this wide space. Mother made me wear a brown plaid wool jacket over my neatly pressed, collared tunic. I can't wait to take it off once the formalities are done.

The elders of Balfour and the advisors of Ellery met yesterday and this morning while the feast was being prepared. Now they are seated at the center of the clearing, around the grave of our sacred Tree that has been scraped flat and covered with a wooden platform.

Jubal climbs the six steps to the top, neatly dressed in black trousers, white tunic and black overcoat. A hush comes over the crowd as he speaks. "Our Harvest Festival usually begins with a wedding, but we do not have any new marriages to celebrate this year except the marriage of our people: Balfour and Ellery." He opens his arms and announces, "The Queen of Ellery, the advisors of Ellery, and the elders of Balfour have deliberated about how to proceed, and we have come to a delightful conclusion, at least for this year." He clears his throat. He doesn't seem happy about what he is about to say, by the subtle downturn of his mouth and twitch of his brow.

Grandmother is seated to the left of him with a quilt across her lap. Her eyes are clearer than they've been since I returned home.

"All of Ellery is invited to live here in Balfour," Jubal says. "We have many available homes and will also build during autumn before the snow falls. You are welcome here; we open our village to you."

Advisor Tiberius ascends the platform with Jubal and declares, "On behalf of the queen and the people of Ellery, I accept your invitation. We knew we could not survive the winter without the help of Balfour. Thank you."

Jubal shakes arms with him.

Cheers go up all around our sacred grounds.

As the voices dissipate, Grandmother rises from her chair. Neelie assists her, catching her quilt before it hits the ground. "Today, we unite our people and our governments," Grandmother says. "And soon, families will be reunited with children or grandchildren they lost." She reaches for my mother's hand, and they stand up straighter together. "It will take some time to organize our new way of living, and our new way of governing, so have patience with us"—she gestures to the advisors and elders—"and with each other."

I drift in and out of awareness as the festivities of the Harvest Festival carry on. All around the clearing where I first met Alouette, the winged girl from a floating island, my people and hers lounge and eat together. A bubbly laugh draws my attention. Becarah sits in the grass with several women, passing a tray of fruits.

Tables were brought to accommodate some of the older people who can't sit on the ground. It is strange to see wings in this place. They are beautiful white, gray, black, and even variegated feathers. I want to walk around and touch each color. I want to collect a feather from each and build my own. I hesitate, remembering what happened the last time I built my own wings, and laugh at myself.

"What's so funny?" Hollis and her family are seated close to mine. The men of our homes are missing, and it was easier for our mothers to work together to care for their children. "Ledger?" She swats my arm.

"Oh, I was thinking about how amazing this is." I sigh.

Alouette laughs and says, "He always gets a weird look on his face when he's daydreaming and drifts off to crazyland."

Hollis and Alouette laugh together. My cheeks warm at their teasing. I couldn't have asked for a better day. All of my friends are together. Everyone I love is on these grounds around the clearing. Then, I realize it's not true. *My father is not here.* He gave his life for my family. I take another bite of meat, pushing sadness aside like a rotten vegetable I won't let touch the rest of my food.

Alouette reaches for a handful of berries, and one of her

wings swats Hollis on the arm. They laugh about it, and it draws me back to the present.

Hollis smooths the front of her clean blue dress. It's new, apparently. I didn't notice. She told me on the way to the feast. She also gave me a twenty minute explanation of how her mother gave Alouette a dress to wear and how they fitted it around her wings. They did well. Alouette is lovely in the emerald Balfourian overdress.

Hollis rises from her lounging position and tugs at my arms. "Ledger, I want to ask you something."

I stand with her.

She gets on one knee before me, with a fist to her chest, and other hand extended to me. "Will you marry me?"

My eyes bulge and my mouth hangs open for a long moment. Too long.

Her twin brothers giggle with Mila. Tolliver peers up from his meal alongside Kava. Angus bursts out laughing.

Is she kidding? This is the man's responsibility, doing a marriage proposal. My responsibility.

I know our parents already made the agreement, and the proposal is just a formality, but…

Her face goes from cheerful and hopeful, to offended and frustrated in an instant, brows lowering like rafts over a waterfall falling to their death.

Oh my lands, she is serious!

"Yes," I say quickly. "Yes!"

Her cheeks push back into the brightest smile. I lean into her and mumble, "I'm supposed to do the asking."

"If we waited for you to make up your mind as to how and when, we'd be old and rickety by then!" Hollis chuckles.

I gather her small frame into my arms right in front of all of Balfour and Ellery. I lean in for our first permitted kiss and press my lips to hers. I lift her in the air and twirl her round and round. She giggles and tilts her face to the sky.

We spend the afternoon telling everyone we will be married on Delineation Day. It is the spring festival where we read the history of Balfour. It gets me thinking. I shed the itchy green jacket and plop it in the grass near my mother.

I find Grandmother seated at a table with several elders and advisors. "You should see the tapestry, Jubal. It is beautiful. I was about four years old. And you know what I noticed? Adaya looks exactly like my mother."

Her bright eyes connect with mine.

"Grandmother, what story will be told on Delineation Day?"

She smiles and says, "The truth, my dear. The truth."

A loud shriek peals through the air. A shimmering green dragon, chased by Hollis's red dragon, dances across the sky.

WHOLE FAMILY 42

TOLLIVER

"This is Mila, Killian, and baby Hazel." I lift Hazel in my arms, bundled tightly in a blanket with a knitted hood over her head.

I am proud of my Balfourian family and hope Tiberius and Kailani will like them as well. Kailani smiles and touches Hazel's small hand. The glow of the harvest bonfire reflects in her happy eyes. She is nearly fourteen, and Kava says she has my eyes: steely, grayish blue. She is quite a bold force and independent, maybe because she grew up without a mother. I marvel at her wispy white wings. They sway with the breeze and twitch with excitement as she puts her finger in the grip of baby Hazel's tiny hand.

With a frown, Tiberius says, "I never even laid eyes on you when you were born." He looks away, ashamed. "I was told you were immediately…disposed of."

Kailani offers to hold baby Hazel. Her eyes light up when I place the baby in her arms. Grabby little fingers pull on the neckline of Kailani's cape.

"I'm so sorry, Tolliver," Tiberius continues. "I've never felt right since that day, like there's been a void in my soul ever since. I understood the laws with my intellect, but never understood them with my heart. Your mother never recovered from losing you. She feared having another wingless child would break her. But she was already broken. She died giving birth to Kailani and never got to see either of her beautiful children."

I shake the sorrow from my body. *I am done with sadness.* I found my father. And a sister. My whole family.

Yesterday, the elders accepted my marriage to Kava, even though we were on the island. Mother was quite proud that we held to our traditions and carried out our own little ceremony.

I turn my attention to my family, Balfourian and Ellerian. "I have something to tell all of you." Some are sprawled out on blankets around the grassy area. Some are standing, staring at me expectantly.

I offer my hand to Kava. She rises, straightening her long soft burgundy overdress, and slides an arm around me. Her skirts flap against me in the cool breeze, and I place a warm hand on the small of her back.

Ledger and Angus are deep in a discussion, seated at the back of the group. "Ledger. Angus. I have an announcement." They turn to me, along with all the faces I know and love. The light of the bonfire makes their faces glow—winged and wingless.

"You want to tell them?" I ask Kava.

"Oh, stop being dramatic, Tolliver," she says with a chuckle.

"Kava is with child," I announce. She puts a hand to her stomach but isn't showing yet. I place my hand over hers.

Cheers wrap around me and give me hope in the next step of my life. *Fatherhood.* I am terrified and overjoyed at the same time.

Loosening the collar of my shirt and unbuttoning my coat, I lean back on my elbows to relax in the grass.

"I am proud that you are my son," Tiberius says. "You will make a great father, I have no doubt." He defies his formal nature and leans back on his elbows alongside me.

I am surprised he is willing to get down in the dirt with me in his dress clothes and gaze at the purple and pink streaked sky, especially with his wings tucked awkwardly behind him.

"You have gained a son and a grandchild all at one time," I say.

His warm chuckle relieves the last bit of tension and worry in the back of my mind.

The evening hushes into soft tones and whispered conversations around the bonfire. Hollis and Alouette discuss babies with Kava. I join Ledger at the stacks of sky lanterns he made to honor the dead. There are hundreds.

"Six hundred and fifty-eight," Ledger says. "I wanted to make eight hundred, but ran out of time and papyrus." Families drift through the line, claiming a lantern for the one they lost this year. Eventually all of Balfour is ready.

Jubal then takes a position in front of Ledger and the stacks of lanterns. "People of Balfour and Ellery," Jubal bellows above the chatter. Eventually everyone quiets as he explains, "Each Harvest Festival, we light a sky lantern for anyone we lost this year."

Ledger whispers something to him and Jubal scowls. They bicker under their breaths for a moment, until Ledger steps up.

"I have made enough sky lanterns for the people of Ellery too," Ledger says. "If you have lost someone this year, I invite you to come and get a lantern. Let's celebrate their lives *together* this year."

My brother gives directions about getting in line and how to light them. His voice is clear and loud and doesn't waver. His face is different: happy and confident. *He would make a great king.* Technically he is Ellerian royalty, the grandson of the queen. I am proud of who he has become. I wish I had something to do with it. But it's all Ledger.

He saunters to my side, and together we hand out lanterns to the winged men and women who've lost someone this year. Estephano, one of the guardians from three-eight, tucks a strand of hair behind his ear and accepts a lantern with a smile. Even Char walks through the line and thanks Ledger. He briefly throws a sideways glance at Belamy beside me and walks away. When the line depletes, Ledger says, "I'll be right back."

He carries a lantern to the spot on the grass where our families sit with a lantern honoring Grandfather. Ledger approaches Alouette. The evening sun hits her tilted face, and a glimmering tear streaks down her cheek as he hands her the lantern. "For your father," he says.

Her lips form the words *thank you*. But no sound comes out.

At the back, Angus stands with his arms crossed and

no lantern nearby. He should have one for his father. I grab a lantern from the last few in the stack and approach him. His mouth is pursed in an angry pout, beneath his sprouting beard.

"For Uncle Roan," I say.

"No, Tolliver!" he refuses.

"Let's honor him."

"He is *not* dead," he growls. "I can't stand here and pretend as if everything is fine. As soon as this charade is over, I'm going to find him." He uncrosses his arms and stomps away.

I start to go after him, when a small hand touches my arm.

"Let him go," Mother says. "Whether Roan is alive or dead, Angus has his own process of grief."

I agree. We won't be releasing a lantern for Fergus.

All across the sacred grounds, families pass taper candles from one to the other, lighting their sky lanterns. Their faces glow with sadness and reverence.

Ledger steps to the center of our people with a papyrus lantern for his grandfather. Our grandfather. "We honor those we've lost and celebrate the union of our people!"

Holding the lantern out in front of him, he opens his hands, and it lifts slowly in the air. Everyone imitates his actions, letting hundreds upon hundreds of lanterns float into the night sky. They are yellow and white squares against the midnight blue. They mix together, Balfourian and Ellerian.

The gentle breeze pushes them higher as they drift east over our village, toward where the many men of Balfour have been stolen. My heart tugs toward them.

I scan all the faces gazing skyward. Only one is not. Angus is on the edge of the woods; his angry eyes connect with mine.

I nod at him. *I will go with you.*

Angus eyes someone near me. It's Ledger.

Ledger watches him intently then turns his gaze toward me. He pushes one cheek up, but his sad eyes betray him. He whispers, "We must bring the fathers of Balfour home."

THANK YOU

Thank you for reading *Wingless* by Heather Trim. Independent authors rely heavily upon reviews and word-of-mouth to reach new readers. If you have a moment to spare, please leave a review on your preferred site. Honest reviews, short or long, are greatly appreciated.

Leave a review on Amazon:

Leave a review on Goodreads:

ACKNOWLEDGMENTS

Thank you, my Love in the sky. You are the reason I write. To find You and hang out a while. I thought I needed wings to reach You, but you are always near. Together we watch this movie in my mind where You show me winged people and floating islands. I'm the blessed one that gets to write them down to share it with the world.

I'm so grateful to my amazingly understanding hubby, Kevin, and fantastic five kids: Daisy, Daphne, Gabriel, Amaryllis, and Violet. It's so encouraging to have such dedicated fans right in my own home.

Thank you to my Big Fam for always believing in me and pestering me for a sneak peek at the next manuscript. Mom and Dad, you're the reason I like fascinating people—because you two are the most interesting pair.

Cheers to a job well done by my rockin' Beta Readers: Lisa Coetzee, Eileen Dudley, Laurel Pinson, Shannon Johnson, Becca Hickman, Leah Rollins, Jessica Domelle, Becki Czerwonka, Suzette Lambert, Lauren Shields, and Bill Gilmore. I love how each one of you sees a different hole and helps me fill it. You get the Golden Shovel Award!

Thanks, AWC Critique Group (Linda, Scott, Karen, and Ted) for challenging my science, story, and grammar. My male POV's are grateful, and hopefully there will be less *fabric* in the next book!

I'm so grateful for my support systems. My always

fabulous Book Launch Team! Thank you for supporting me and always being willing to share the love. The Paulding County Writers' Guild! You are the back-up I always needed.

Jessica Nelson, my fabulous editor, thank you for helping get this story squeaky clean. Your eye for detail is your superpower. Thank you for using your powers for good. Someday my participles and antecedents won't dangle. But probably not, that's why I have you!

I love interesting stories, fascinating people, unique worlds, and writing the words to define all of those amazing things. What a delight to live my dreams.

ABOUT THE AUTHOR

Heather Trim, an award-winning author, conference speaker, and cookie eater, inspires with her unique perspective of spirituality and the world. She lives in Georgia with her husband, Kevin, and five lively children. Heather enjoys bullet journaling, movies, and reading too many young adult novels. She can be found on Facebook, Instagram, Twitter, and her website: www.heatheraine.com.

Sign up for Heather's Newsletter:
http://eepurl.com/cLd0D1

Connect with Heather:
Facebook: facebook.com/heatherainetrim
Instagram: instagram.com/heatheraine5
Twitter: twitter.com/heatheraine
Goodreads: goodreads.com/heatheraine
Amazon: amazon.com/author/heathertrim

www.ingramcontent.com/pod-product-compliance
Lightning Source LLC
Chambersburg PA
CBHW060537310726
48982CB00009B/1284/J

* 9 7 8 1 7 3 2 9 0 9 0 2 1 *